The Geraldi Trail

A Western Story

G·K
Hall
&Co.

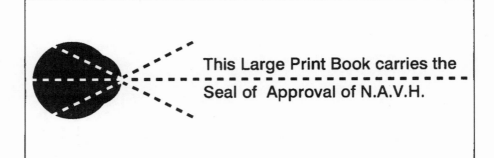

This Large Print Book carries the
Seal of Approval of N.A.V.H.

MAX BRAND™

The Geraldi Trail

A Western Story

G.K. Hall & Co. • Thorndike, Maine

Published in 2000 by arrangement with Golden West Literary Agency.

G.K. Hall Large Print Western Series.

The text of this edition is unabridged.
Other aspects of the book may vary from the original edition.

Set in 16 pt. Plantin by Al Chase.

Printed in the United States on permanent paper.

Library of Congress Cataloging-in-Publication Data

Brand, Max, 1892–1944.
    The Geraldi trail : a western story / Max Brand.
      p.   cm.
    ISBN 0-7838-0314-1 (lg. print : hc : alk. paper)
    1. Large type books. I. Title.
PS3511.A87 G47 2000
813'.52—dc21   00-024240

Editor's Note

Frederick Faust wrote a total of ten stories about James Geraldi, all of which appeared in various issues of Street & Smith's *Western Story Magazine* under the byline Max Brand. Two of the Geraldi stories were published as serials in a number of installments. "Three on the Trail" appeared as a six-part serial in *Western Story Magazine* (5/12/28–6/16/28) and was the first of the two serials to appear in book form as THE KILLERS (Macaulay, 1931) by George Owen Baxter. "The Geraldi Trail" appeared as a four-part serial in *Western Story Magazine* (6/11/32–7/2/32), but its first book appearance was complicated by the fact that Dodd, Mead & Company, which was publishing Faust books at the time under the byline Max Brand, did not want to publish a Max Brand novel featuring a character that had already appeared previously in a George Owen Baxter novel issued by a competitor. Therefore, the character's name was changed from James Geraldi to Jesse Jackson, and the book published by Dodd, Mead in 1932 was accordingly titled THE JACKSON

TRAIL. There were also significant textual differences between the serial "The Geraldi Trail" and the book THE JACKSON TRAIL. In preparing THE GERALDI TRAIL for its first book publication as the author wrote it and as an integral part of the James Geraldi saga, a concordance has been achieved in combining these varying texts to provide the story in its authentic form. Once the James Geraldi stories have all appeared in Five Star Westerns, they will at last have been published for the first time in book form in definitive texts so they can be read as parts of a continuing saga — which was ultimately the author's intention in writing them.

Chapter One

THE HOUSE
IN THE POPLARS

All through the lava flows and the blow sands of the desert, the hunt had ranged, and then up through the foothills, through the heights of Jackson Pass, and still beyond the pass and into the open, flowing country on the other side of the range, the green side, where the rain clouds were ever and again tangling about the summits and sending down showers that fed the grass. Through it all Larry Burns had kept the hunting pack at a distance.

It was a pack in more than name, for they were using dogs to get Larry Burns, and behind those dogs rode a dozen picked men. Among these men was a fellow with hair so pale that it was almost white, with eyebrows that were, literally, silver, and a mouth pinched hard together as if he were continually fixing his mind upon some hard problem.

The vision of that face, that narrow-shouldered fellow with the dusty gray skin, and the implacable eyes had never left the mind of Larry Burns. When he first heard the dogs howling, he knew that he was done. He knew, for

7

all his fine riding, his clever wits, and his knowledge of the country, still he was doomed, and that knowledge worked like an acid in the heart of Burns. A fine pack of hounds, trained to the work, and Marshal Tex Arnold at the head of them made a combination that he could not elude. Still he persisted.

He had ridden more than two hundred miles, and he had managed this by changing horses twice. The new horses he had not asked for. He simply had taken them as he found them. For what is horse stealing to a man convicted of murder and wearing upon his wrists the little steel bracelets that seem light as silk but are as strong as the grip of the devil?

When he changed horses, the posse which followed must have changed, also. For still they came on, and now, as he entered the open country beyond the pass, he could hear the booming and the chime of the dogs, a music that crowded the throat of the cut and came faintly out to the open.

Larry Burns licked his lips and tasted from them the salt of sweat and the dry burning of alkali. He was very thirsty. He had not tasted water for more than half a day, and the horrible fatigue that worked in his body from head to foot was matched by the water famine that ran in his veins and centered in the hollow of his throat. But he licked his lips, turned his head, and grinned at the sound of the dogs. He had made up his mind that he would die fighting.

He knew all about the death cell. It was the one thing he feared — not death itself, not the foolish simplicity of the hanging, not even the knotting of the rope about his neck, or those terrible moments of pause when he would be asked to speak his last words, if there were any to utter.

He had made up his mind what those words should be: "I lived my own way. I've had a good time. About this gent, Carson, I tell you again that I never killed him. But that don't matter. You've got me squeezed for it, and I might as well die for a job that I didn't do, as for one that I did. My pipe is filled to the lip, and I'm ready to smoke it, if you hold the match. That's all I have to say. I never played no favorites, and I never asked for no partners but one. And he's turned straight . . . the fool! As for the rest of you, you can all go to the devil. I've lived my life. I've liked the taste of it. That's all I have to say. Turn me off, and be damned to you!"

That was the death speech that he would make. He had framed and reframed it, and he could not find a word that he wanted to change. It was the truth, from first to last, because, really, he had not killed Carson. All of the rest was true, also — particularly that he had no partner except one.

Ah, if that one had stayed with him, he never would have come to grief. If the magic hands of that helper had been working beside him, he could have laughed at all the power of the law, he was sure. Even now, he had aimed through the

9

pass and toward the house of that partner, as a drowning man aims for the bit of floating wreckage. As he went on, he pondered in his mind the reception he would get.

To that old partner, he had not been entirely true. He had cheated his friend. When the years have passed, however, we are likely to forget the bitter and remember the sweet, and Larry Burns fervently prayed that it might be so now.

He eased himself a little forward in the saddle. The ache of his legs above the knees, along the inner muscles of the thighs, was a thing not to be uttered in words. It could only be expressed by groans and curses. The back of his neck ached as though someone had been beating it with a club. He thought that aching might come from the nodding of his head. A dozen times in the last twelve hours he had found himself nodding. Sometimes he felt that his head would jerk off, or that the stroke of his chin would fracture a rib. His chin was bruised with the pounding. It was sore to his touch. So he eased himself forward in the saddle. It was not really ease that he found. It was only a change of pain. At that change he grinned and felt, with his smile, no familiar furrowing of his cheeks. They had been sleek, fat cheeks, when he had left the jail. But they were drawn hard now. He could guess that he had lost — say twenty pounds during these two days of punishment.

If he had been that much lighter from the start, who could say that the posse ever would have managed to hang to his heels so closely? Aye, if only he had kept himself in training in the jail. In spite of the restricted space, he could have done setting-up exercises. He could have walked a pace and made a turn and walked again. He could have done this for about an hour a day and so kept from his body the filthy sleek of prison fat.

So thought Larry Burns now and thrust out his big, square jaw and glared ahead of him, but dared not look behind again. For he could hear the noise of the dogs breaking out from the mouth of the pass, and he knew by the way that the sound flowed down the slope behind him that the riders were gaining. He gave his own horse the spur. But there was little response. The mustang began to trot, but the trot was a stagger. The weight of his rider had killed him. Burns cursed that weight.

Many a time he had boasted of his inches. Many a time he had been able to stand straight and look down on others. He had had his own way through a crowd. There were very few who had cared to face him. So he had loved the big-ness of his body and had been proud of it, but now he cursed it, because it was just that which was anchoring him, while the posse swept up from behind.

He listened to the sound, and he tried to calcu-late the distance they were behind and the rate at which they would overtake him. It might be in half an hour. After all, their horses were tired,

11

too. It was not for nothing that he had ridden himself to the dropping point and worn out his third horse in two days.

They would talk about this — the newspapers. They would make a great thing — not of him for the heroism of his flight — but of the marshal for the terrible resolution of his pursuit. That's what they would find to praise. The marshal.

Once more, the soul of the fugitive rose in a mighty dread and a mighty hatred for that pale, thin face, the color of dust. He felt that he would be willing to die, that he would gladly die, if only he could remove the honor of his death from the head of the marshal. If only he could manage to thwart that famous manhunter, it would fill his cup.

Now, as the trail wound and lifted to the wave of a green hill, he saw before him his chance. It was a small house, painted white, with a red roof, and it was not large, not imposing. Behind it was a little barn — that was not there when he last saw the layout — and behind the barn there was the tangle of corral fencing. That tangle had grown, too. The place was enlarging, prospering. One did not enlarge corrals without a reason.

He thought of that prosperity as he saw the white of the house winking through the silver shimmer of the poplar trees that surrounded it. Prosperity, to Larry Burns, always had meant the wealth that succeeds a good haul, but it meant something else in this case. It meant that the owner of that ranch had worked his feet into the soil, just like a tree, and that he was drawing nutriment and strength out of the ground.

Yeah, he was right, thought Larry Burns. *We all give him the laugh, but he was right. That's the nacheral way. That's the right way.*

His jaw fell. He gaped vaguely at the house and at his own thought. He was too weary to stick for long to his own idea. His brain ached almost as much as his body ached. But somewhere in the back of his mind, he registered that thought. He had been wrong. One could raise money, fast enough, at the point of a gun. But money was not happiness. Happiness grew only on cultivated soil — with hard work — like wheat. He nodded at the thought, and then shook his head over it. He wished, vaguely, that he could have reached this conclusion when he had been a boy, but, when he was a boy, he had not been hunted for his life. Then, too, he had not had the great exemplar of that house on the hillside, the twinkling of the poplar trees, the fat-sided barn, and the bright curve of the creek that ran down the valley bottom.

Ah, what a sleek valley it was. The fat of it shone green and smiling upon the troubled mind of the outlaw. He almost felt — in honesty — that, if he had looked with a clear eye at that spot in the old days and if he could have made it his, he would have given up the wrong path.

He pressed on. The mustang was very tired now, but it seemed to guess that the white house and the poplars were the final goal, so it freshened its pace and even lifted its lumpish head a little. It had seemed a miracle to the rider that the mustang could keep up its head at all on such a long, scrawny neck, during the interminable and nodding leagues of their journey. So they pressed on toward the house among the poplars until the trail turned into a road, and from the road Larry Burns could see the house in more intimate detail. He drew up his mustang at once, with a grunt of dismay.

Chapter Two

THE GERALDI FINGERS

It was a lonely part of the world. Neighbors were few and far between. Larry Burns had counted upon being able to see his friend alone. But he was wrong, it appeared, for yonder were a dozen horses hitched to the rack near the house, and at a second hitching rack there were buggies, also, as well as the tough buckboard that could be driven almost anywhere that a horse can walk. There was some sort of a celebration going on in that house. What could it be? Men did not gather like this, except for a birth, a wedding, or a death.

"Jimmy's gone and died on me," said Larry Burns.

He almost forgotten his own terrible weariness, his more terrible fear, in the thought that his friend might have died. For that was like imagining the life gone out of a thunderbolt. What a brilliant stroke was gone from this world, if Jimmy was no more.

Larry Burns wagged his head again at the thought, meanwhile pushing the mustang on. He thought, as he rode, of what that other man had been, and of the lightness of that body, light as a leopard and as terribly swift and strong as one. He thought of the thin, handsome face, the flash of the dark eyes, and, above all, he remembered the smile that was forever appearing and disappearing about the corners of the mouth of the man. He remembered the hands last of all, the hands of a magician, the hands that worked, as it were, with independent brains and found their way into secrets of their own accord. Aye, if he were gone, the world would never see such another after him.

But now the booming voices of the pack came in a swelling wave down the slope behind Burns, and he drove home his spurs and made the mustang sway into a tired, rickety lope. Something had to be tried. And that house was his only resort. He drove the mustang straight into the poplars, dismounted, threw the reins, and stumbled on toward the ranch house. He was so blind with fatigue that he did not go toward a door. He simply ran on with his arms thrown out before him, toward the nearest side of the house.

Then he saw, with his bloodshot eyes, a swirl of men and women in a front room of the house. No, it was not a funeral. He could tell that by the sound of the laughter. It was something else. A birth? Well, perhaps, but *men* did not gather to give congratulations for a birth. The womenfolk might be foolish and gay because of such an event, but not the men. Yet, the men were there, also, striding about with pleased and silly looks.

Now it came about that Larry Burns, as he ran

forward, passed a second window, and there he saw a thing that smote him, suddenly, beneath the fifth rib and to the heart. It was a girl in white, in flowing white, with a white veil over her head and a face of such loveliness that it was luminous to the thought of Larry Burns. He could remember now. He had heard of her. He had heard her described to him in painful, absurd detail by friends who strove in vain to paint the unpaintable.

She was no Venus. She was no queen of beauty. She was simply a pretty girl — and something more. Aye, much more, for she had been true to that strange fellow who stood there before her, that lean and flickering sword blade of a man, that handsome, smiling, subtle fellow who had the grace of a cat and the wit of a cat, also, compared with all others. For there was the object of the quest of Burns — there was Geraldi himself.

All the meaning of this gathering came suddenly home to the fugitive, and he saw that he had arrived upon the wedding day of his friend. For that matter, could he even call himself, now, the friend of Geraldi who had put away his old ways and his old companions and become strictly a follower of the law? Had he not, long before this, given Geraldi sufficient cause to disown him? So pondered Burns, miserably, as he wearily strode up to the open window.

That window was open, with the full sun striking upon it, but a shower of climbing vines, that rose from the ground and descended again like a fountain of fine green spray, allowed Burns to stand there as an unseen witness.

He had two things in his mind. One, frightfully acute and burning in his consciousness, was the cry of the pack that began to boom upon his ears like the sound of waves roaring and beating in a cave. The other thing was what was passing in the room before him. He stared, most of all, not into the bright face of the girl, but at Geraldi and at Geraldi's smile. She put her hands upon the shoulders of her lover.

"Now, Mary," he said, "you're going to be serious about something. Let me know what it is and get it over, quick, will you? It always scares me when you look at me with pity, as you're doing now."

Her own smile came and went. "You know what it is, Jimmy," she said. "This is your last chance to think the thing over and change your mind."

"My chance to change my mind?" he said.

"Yes," she answered. "It's not too late for that, either. You know what's before you."

"*You* are before me," said Geraldi in a voice that stirred even the heart of the man who waited and watched outside of the window.

"I'm before you," the girl said gravely. "But other things are before you, too. A lot of dull, monotonous work is before you . . . and you've always been as free as a hawk. A lot of stupid

18

days are before you, too, and you've always hunted for pleasure a good deal more keenly than a prospector hunts for gold. There'll come a time when this little farm will seem smaller to you than the palm of your hand, and you'll want to leave it. But when you want to leave, you'll find yourself tied by a lot of invisible ropes which will be harder to shake off than any of the handcuffs you're so capable of loosening. You'll be tied to me. Even if you've stopped caring about me, you'll be tied by the thought that I'm a duty to you. And perhaps there'll be children, and you're too big a fellow to hurt small things, even those of any other man. You see, Jimmy, you've been running up hill and down dale, and taking whole mountains ranges in your stride, and now you're thinking of popping over the fence into a corral . . . an easy fence to jump over, going in, but you'll never be able to jump over it, to go out. You'd have to tear it down, and wreck everything, and break my heart."

"Listen to me," broke in Geraldi.

"I'm making a speech," she said, smiling now, "and I want to run on to the end of it. Then you can speak. I lay awake last night and composed this. I mean every word of it. It would break my heart to lose you, later on. But if I lost you now, my heart wouldn't break . . . quite. I could manage to stand it. The reasons would be pretty clear, you know. And I'm going out of the room for a moment, and leave you here to think the thing over. Give the pros and cons a balancing.

19

Make up your mind about what you wish to do. You've got all of your former life on the one side, the wildness, the happiness . . . and the freedom. Then, on the other hand, there's I. And I'm going to be a dull woman, many and many a time. You stay here behind me, Jimmy. I'm going through that door. I'm going to wait in that next room and harden my heart. You stay here. In five minutes, I'm coming back for your answer. But during those five minutes, I want you to stay here and think."

She turned away from Geraldi, and she went with one smile for him over her shoulder through the door and into the farther room. As the door closed behind her, a great rumble of laughter came from the people who had gathered in the front of the house. It seemed like a stage stroke of mockery — the mob amused by a tragic moment.

Geraldi started toward the door through which the girl had gone, then he turned toward the window with a solemn, thoughtful face. At that moment he saw, framed in the tender, showering green of the vines, the face of Larry Burns.

He sprang back. It was not a step, but a leap. Then, with that gliding and cat-like gait which Burns knew so well from of old, Jimmy Geraldi came to the window.

"What the devil is this?" he asked.

"It's Larry Burns," said the criminal. He held up his manacled hands. "It's Larry Burns today, and a dead man tomorrow, Jimmy. I come here to say good bye to you." With his shackled wrists he made a gesture toward the sound of the pack that was pouring steadily nearer and seemed at any instant about to burst through the screen of the poplars.

"I've rode two hundred miles in two days, and I'm beat," said the husky voice of Larry Burns. "I know that I about crooked you once in those days long ago, Jimmy. But now I'm beat. They're gonna get me."

"You killed Carson. I hope they hang you as high as the moon. I don't care what you did to me. I can forget that. But you killed poor Carson. I hope they hang you up and let you rot!" He smiled as he spoke, and his smile iced the very soul of Burns.

Burns said: "Will you listen, Jimmy?"

"Aye," said Geraldi, sneering. He seemed to be subtly withdrawing from the other, as though there were a contagion in the breath of the criminal.

"I never killed Carson," said Burns. "Look! I tell you straight. I never killed Carson. I bumped off others. I don't cry none. I got it coming. Only, I never done that to Carson."

"Who did?" asked Geraldi.

"Blaze done it. You know that Blaze could do it as well as me. Blaze done it and. . . ."

"Where's your horse?" asked Geraldi.

"There in the poplars."

Then Geraldi reached down and took the

21

manacles of the other in his slender fingers. While he held them, he stared down into the face of Burns. There was no great friendship in his look, but there was a profound understanding of the lines of weariness and exhaustion that he saw there — the red of the eyes and the grin of fatigue about the lips. He cast one look over his shoulder toward the life that was around him, the life from which he was stepping, he could not tell for how long. Then, setting his teeth, he touched the handcuffs, and they fell, as if by magic, from the wrists of the other. Geraldi leaped down through the window to the ground, merely saying: "Head for the barn. Lie up there. Then go to Mary, after dark, and she'll see that you have everything that you need. Tell her that I sent you. I'll get your horse and try to pull the hounds off the trail."

Chapter Three

THE GREAT SPRUCE

When Geraldi ran through the poplars, he found the roar of the hunt rising in his face like steam, and, there, among the slender trees, he found the mustang as the other had left it, head fallen, knees bowed and trembling. It was a done horse, a sagged and beaten horse, and, as Geraldi ran his wise eye over the animal, he shook his head and the corner of his mouth lifted a trifle. Yet, he did not hesitate. Having committed himself to his course, he would not draw back. He swept up the reins, and, without touching the stirrups, he leaped lightly into the saddle.

Even at that shock of a weight far less than the burden that it had been carrying, the mustang staggered and did not find its balance again for a moment. Geraldi, setting his teeth, waited patiently for that instant, and then he took the mustang out through the poplar wood. He did not spur, and he did not strike with a whip, but he seemed to gather the horse, just as he gathered the reins in his hand, as though down the taut reins there were flowing an electric current of increased power that passed into the animal itself and renerved and loosened thews and the sinews.

He headed not out into the open, where the going would have been much easier and faster, but straight up through the trees, following the windings of the grove. As he rode, with the mustang coming to some faint life again beneath the saddle, he heard the hunt strike the lower end of the poplars, and at once the din of voices was blanketed and softened by the trees.

The mustang shuddered. It had been running away from that sound long enough to know that there must be peril in it. It shuddered and raised its head a little. So Geraldi brought it to a feeble trot. Now they came out from the screen of the trees and into a meadow where twenty of his own horses were grazing. He groaned as he looked at them. They were his pride, his master work, the breeding of those horses. There was not one dash of Thoroughbred blood in them. They were mustang pure and simple, but they were hand-picked mustangs, and that good and ancient blood of the Barbs and Arabs that had been brought by the *conquistadores* into Mexico now was showing itself. Many weeds would crop up in that garden, but he vowed to himself that he would persist in the labor until he had managed to get together a true strain, which would remain flawless forever.

What horses they would be! Here, before him, was a fair promise, here, wandering over the grass of the meadow land. They were not large.

Not a one of them stood more than an inch or so above fifteen hands. But they were made of hammered iron, and they worked on springs and cogs, not muscles. Tireless, active, wise, they looked as fierce as beasts of prey, rather than servants of man. Geraldi had not tried to tame them. He let them run wild. When the time came to try and test them, he knew that he could manage that task — when the time came. In the meantime, he felt that it might strip some of the native bloom from the wild flowering of their strength, their courage, and their greatness of heart, if he were to handle and fondle and subdue them from the start. He wanted them to grow up on this range as grim and keen and gay as the wild lads of the West who grow in the saddle and learn the smell of gunpowder before they know the smell of flowers.

So, as Geraldi broke from the shelter of the wood and crossed this pasture land, he looked at his own horses with a sort of fierce envy. He could pick any one of the lot, throw a saddle on its back, and then laugh at all of the best efforts of the posse that was hunting poor Larry Burns. But he could not do that. The whole point of his maneuver was to lead the hunt astray by riding on the horse of Burns, and so work them to a distance.

What would they do to him, then, if they caught him? Well, it would be a tight fix and very uncomfortable. His own reputation was far from a sound one, and, of course, he would be accused of complicity in the escape of a condemned criminal, a man beyond and outside of the law.

So he pushed the mustang on. He had to get across the clear and open meadow and into the woods beyond before the hunt broke out from the poplars, or else, at one sight of him, every man of them would realize that the bulky figure of Burns was no longer before them.

He hurried the horse on, but, as he neared the shadow of the woods beyond, with the noise of the dogs thickening always behind him, he looked longingly back toward the house.

It was almost time for Mary, the five minutes up, to come back into the room. Surely, she would come with her head high and in smiling confidence. When she saw that the room was empty, what would she think? Would she stare around, incredulous? And then, as the blow sank home, what would come over the girl? To think that he could run away like a whipped cur, instead of taking advantage of her generosity to stand up like a man and announce that his mind was altered . . . ?

It would be almost the death of Mary, and might it not, in the end, be the death of her love for him? Sweat streamed on the face of Geraldi at the thought. Well, he would have to round off this business of the posse and of Larry Burns as quickly as possible. But his heart misgave him. The thing had happened too pat, on his wedding day, like a trick devised long ago and carefully rehearsed and planned by fate. So he was snatched away from Mary once more. Although he told himself that the intervening time must not be long, still he was in doubt and in great trouble.

He was well inside the fringe of the woods, when, looking back, he had a dim glimpse of the dogs breaking out through the poplars. They were very tired dogs, but still they ran gallantly. After them came the riders on horses that staggered with fatigue. But they came on. Suddenly the heads of the hounds were lifted from the ground. A new and higher note, a terribly exulting note, rang in their crying, their tails lifted with their heads. All in a sweep, they broke forward at a freshened pace. At the same moment the riders behind them began to shout to one another and to point ahead. Then, with a yell, they put whip and spur to their mounts.

There was no mystery about this change in the eye of Geraldi. He simply knew that the dogs had caught sight of their quarry, as he hurried away through the trees, and for that reason they lifted their heads. Geraldi had had one chance in ten of riding that horse away from the pursuit. Now he had one chance in a thousand, and he knew it. He knew, furthermore, that among the dapplings of the shadows in the woods, the posse, when they sighted him, would not be so readily able to distinguish between his bulk and the former occupant of this saddle. They were likely to open fire at once, and they would certainly shoot not for the horse alone, but for the man, and to kill. They had ridden far enough. Their weariness must be almost like the agonizing fatigue of Larry Burns.

He realized these things, as he pushed the mustang on. On his right, there was a rolling sweep of trees, high, dense brush in patches, and on his left there was a creekbed with precipitous banks. In any one of those patches of brush he might have hidden both horse and man with the greatest ease. But he did not dare to take that chance, of course, now that he had dogs at his heels.

Something about the yelling of the dogs maddened Geraldi. He jerked about in the saddle once and glared behind him, his fingers working nervously at the handle of the rifle that protruded from the long saddle holster, running down under his knee. He was of half a mind, in that savage burst of temper, to wrench out the weapon and open fire through the trees.

What if he only knocked over some of the leading dogs? No, he dared not. He dared not adventure the smallest thing that might appear to be a crime. For a single vestige of a crime might ruin his chances of happiness with Mary. He was riding and fighting, not for Larry Burns, really, but for his own chance for an honest life. The old life was not beckoning to him, in spite of what the girl had said. There was only fear that he might fall back into a semblance of it.

He knew, as he listened to the roar of the dogs

and the crackling of the shrubbery as the horses crashed through it, that they were gaining fast. Yet he could not get the mustang above its present shambling dog-trot. He felt, if he urged it beyond that gait, the beast might crumble to the ground like a stack of cards.

He veered a little toward the creek. In the wild tangle of thorns and shrubbery that grew along its precipitous banks, it seemed that there might and must be some means of escape. That was a labyrinth. But it was no mask against the trailing hounds. Not even the semblance of a real trail problem could be created for them in such a place.

As he went on — his eye dim with puzzlement and with thought — twisting a little from time to time in the saddle, he came to the place where a great spruce had fallen some years before, making a natural bridge across the creek, sagging a good deal in the middle now, but still holding its place, powerfully, from bank to bank. When he saw it, Geraldi caught his breath. Then he knew, in an instant, that he must succumb to the thought that had just come to him. It intrigued and maddened him with fear and with delight.

What if he could ride the mustang across that sagging tree trunk? He dared not walk and lead the animal. The scent of his boots on the ground might be enough to falsify the trail. Besides, there would be no time to dismount and urge the weary beast along by pulling at the reins. So, instead, he drove the horse straight up to the lofty butt of the tree, at a place where the truncated roots offered something of a natural stairway to the top. The mustang merely paused, put down its head, and braced all four legs.

Chapter Four

THE CROSSING

It was as though the horse realized in that instant what was in the mind of the rider. Geraldi, sighting down the length of the tree trunk, saw at once that the tree was neither so large nor so secure as he had remembered it. The trunk had been used by various animals to cross the chasm. The bark had gradually been worn slick or rubbed in places to the inner wood. Lying in continual shadow, slippery with the moss that was growing upon it here and there, that trunk afforded a surface hardly more secure than a rock covered with a film of oil. Even Geraldi shuddered at the sight of it.

A moment later, however, he had fairly lifted the horse up the ascending roots to the top of the big trunk. One could not have told how he had managed the thing, but again it was certainly not with whip or with spur. It was that grip on the reins and that voice, never raised, quiet and insistent, that seemed to carry with it both a reassurance and a command.

Balanced on top of the rounded surface, the horse pricked its ears at the terrible way that lay

31

before it. Then it flattened them in a resolute denial from which even Geraldi could not have persuaded it had it not been that, at this moment, the hounds, straining forward at full speed, came nearer through the woods. A fresh burst of their yelling gave the mustang the needed impetus. It went forward suddenly, with small, dancing steps. Its knees shook, not with weakness now, but with the desperate desire to maintain a more delicately sure balance. It dropped its head, not so much in fatigue as in the desire to sniff out each footstep that it should take.

So they passed from the verge of the ground and out onto the sagging strip that suspended them above the cañon. And the mustang went on, with ever shortening steps. When the hounds roared through the woods close behind, the horse shook from head to hoof, but still it went on. Geraldi, nicely poising his weight in the saddle, tried to sit firm enough to keep the horse encouraged, but lightly enough so that, if the slip should come, he could hurl himself to either side out of the saddle and so attempt to gain a hold upon the trunk of the tree in falling. That chance, he knew, would be desperately small. The simplest lurch to the side would ruin him. Measuring the distance of the fall beneath him, he knew that such a drop would kill both horse and man instantly.

A sense of fatality came over him. It seemed to him, perhaps foolishly enough, that the tree had been knocked down and had fallen here under the weight of the wind, only to provide this trap for him, and that the years, the mold, and the wet had accumulated to make that trap yet more and more perfect.

It seemed to Geraldi that he had passed this place before, and that always, in so passing it, he had felt a breath of disaster on his face, as he felt it now, coming damp and cool down the ravine. The wet smell of the ground and of the rotting leaves was to him like the smell of the grave.

So they came out to the very center of that natural bridge, and, as they reached the place, a hound, that had raced well in advance of the rest, sprang up to the top of the trunk and came howling at the heels of the horse.

The mustang shivered, and then stopped. Geraldi, turning delicately in the saddle, shifting his weight not a scruple from the exact center, took his life in his hands to draw a revolver and fire. The bullet split the skull of the big, brindled beast, and it fell like a lump to the ground well beneath.

Geraldi turned back to face forward, but, as he did so, he felt a hoof of the mustang slip beneath him. Only by a hair's breadth of chance was that horse able to hold its balance upon three legs alone. Yet, hold its balance it did, and then stepped forward, and saw safety wonderfully closer and closer, so it hurried and sprang at last onto the honest, kind, safe ground beyond the ravine.

Geraldi did not so much as turn to look at the peril that he had passed, but he pressed on into the screening of the brush, for, behind him, he heard the mounted hunt come pouring, and he heard the yell of their voices, and the rage, and the amazement.

The brush was still stirring behind the mustang, and, into this stir of branches, a dozen rifle bullets came crackling at once. But Geraldi did not flee onward. He felt the mustang drooping and sagging like a rag beneath him, and he drew the poor beast into the shelter of a great tree stump on the very verge of the ravine. There, dismounting, he himself sat down upon a projecting root and, looking at his hands, found them quivering a little — a very little. He bit his lip at the sight. He was getting soft and weak, he vowed in his heart. In the old days, peril — as great as this, fully — had not troubled his nerves at all after the ordeal. Yes, he was getting soft.

He heard them on the other side of the ravine, whistling to the dogs that went scrambling out upon the dangerous trunk of the tree only to crouch down, trembling, when they came to the center of it. The trail clearly crossed here, but it seemed as though death were crossing, also. And, close as he was, Geraldi could hear the conversation clearly.

"I thought that he'd come up Geraldi's way to get a change of hosses," said a hard, clear voice.

Geraldi suddenly stood up, as he heard the answer in a deeper, a gruffer tone: "Geraldi wouldn't deal with murdering swine like that Burns."

Geraldi in person ventured to peek around the edge of the stump, and he spotted the last speaker at once.

It was Marshal Tex Arnold, erect, slender, iron-hard as ever. It seemed to Geraldi's sinking heart that he would rather have had a whole army upon his trail than this single man. His presence there explained how a whole posse had been held together during this tremendous ride in the pursuit of Larry Burns.

"He used to be a friend of Burns," said the first speaker.

"He used to be an acquaintance of his," corrected Marshal Arnold. "He never was a friend. Geraldi never cut as low as Burns in picking out his friends."

"He had some queer ones," persisted the other.

The marshal said, with a tone of finality: "Geraldi was a great man in his line, Tom. Don't you slang him now. Let him be, will you? I would've given ten years of life to have been the catcher of that Geraldi when he was flying his fastest and his highest. But I never had that luck. I didn't deserve that luck, I suppose." He then added, with an angry oath: "What beats me now is how this fellow Burns managed to get his nerve together to ride that tree?"

"You corner a rat, and the rat will bite," answered Tom.

"Not that way," said the marshal. "You can corner a rat, and it'll turn and fight . . . but it won't take wings and start flying. Larry Burns might have turned around and started shooting it out with us. But he never would have ridden across that tree. That takes nerve of a good deal higher order."

"Maybe it does," Tom said. "But he went and done it. That's all."

"He never did it," insisted the marshal, with an odd stubbornness.

"Naw. Maybe he didn't," Tom agreed dryly. "Maybe there was an angel come down to help the horse up steady, and that was how they got across."

"Tom," said the marshal, "you're a fellow with as good a nerve as I know, nearly, and as much at home in a saddle."

"Aw, come on!"

"I mean it," said Arnold. "But you wouldn't try to ride a horse across that tree, I guess."

"Me?" exclaimed Tom. "Nobody but a nut would try to do that. There's a limit, I guess, that a gent has to work inside of."

"There you are," the marshal answered. "And there's a limit inside of which Larry Burns would work. Don't say no to me. I'm sure that it's outside of his limit."

"Facts is facts," Tom replied. "There's the prints of the shoes on top of the tree trunk, and that's all I can say about it," said Tom.

Still the marshal clung to his point of view.

"Maybe it sounds funny to you," he said. "But I stick where I stuck before. There's something mighty queer about it all. And I'm gonna get at the bottom of it. That's all." He added: "There's no man of us that can ride across that tree. I wouldn't let 'em, in the first place, come that close to suicide. But there's one thing that we can do. We can get back down the creek to where the sides shelve. We've lost Larry Burns for today, but we'll catch him tomorrow. We've got the hounds, and we've got the horses, and there ain't any reason why we couldn't catch him . . . only, luck seems to be playing on his side. Luck and something else. I don't yet know what the other thing is."

Geraldi had heard enough. Furthermore, he had breathed the staggering mustang a little. So now he started slowly away from behind the tree, leading the mustang behind him, and taking good care that he kept the tree's bulk between him and the eyes of the posse men. He went without haste. For he knew how far down the creek they would have to journey before they found ground that could be crossed with safety. Yet his mind was not at ease. To lead the trailers away from Larry Burns — a man who would be helpless with fatigue for twenty-four hours, at least — he would have to keep to the horse that he had received from the outlaw. That being the case, the only instrument he had to help him in his own ruse was that exhausted mustang. He would have been far safer on foot — far and away. But he could not venture on that. He had to have the horse with him to lay the trail for the dogs, and, while that trail was being laid, he was each moment in constant peril of his life. But he clung to his purpose. He must give the horse rest, find some way to strengthen it, and out-match the wits of the marshal.

In his own house, Mary was waiting. No, she no longer was waiting. She was taking home to her heart the frightful realization that he had left her and exchanged his love for her for the old life which he had loved, also.

Chapter Five

GROGAN'S MUSTANG

Some men, in the great crisis when life and death stand beside them at the same moment, are sour and sullen. Others lock their jaws with a fierce resolution, and others rage wildly; but Geraldi smiled. His eye brightened. His head lifted. The danger that he breathed was more to him than the air in his nostrils.

So, marching steadily on, he came to a small runlet of water, and into it he brought the mustang, knee-deep in the stream. Then he sloshed the water up over the body of the horse, a little at a time, so that there might be no danger of a chill striking the animal weak.

It was not a chill that hurt the mustang, however. It was the utter exhaustion of the long march that had soaked into its bones, so that its knees were shaking as it climbed up the farther bank of the stream. It was a beaten horse, and a badly beaten horse. But ridden it must be. So Geraldi took to the saddle again.

The instant Geraldi's weight sank down, the horse quaked beneath him. It was murder — sheer murder. The poor brute would die beneath him. The very heart of Geraldi ached at the thought. It was this sense of death under the saddle that made him desperate. If he could change horses in view of the pursuit, but at such a distance that even the eye of Tex Arnold could not make out whether he were Larry Burns or not — then certainly the riders would continue to pour along his trail. But to change horses meant to make himself a thief, and a thief in the vilest sense that the West can give to the word. A horse thief!

They had accused him of many a crime in the old days, rightly and wrongly. But never of anything like this. However, the thing which he had undertaken, he must push through. The life of Larry Burns hung on it. With good fortune, he might get out into the fields of Ben Grogan and pick up one of Grogan's mustangs.

So he turned deliberately out of the shelter of the woods and rode north toward the Grogan range. As he left the trees, he heard for the first time in many minutes the music of the hounds beginning mournfully far behind him.

To ride at a walk was exquisite torture, but only at a walk could the beaten animal proceed. Even so, it stumbled, and, with each stumble, it jerked its head up painfully and sank a little in the quarters.

A quarter of a mile away, he saw the first of the Grogan fences run, the three strands of barbed wire glimmering in the afternoon sun. A pale mist was rising over the hollow, and the sun glowed upon it and made it silver. He never had looked on a scene of more peace, but all that it meant to him now was the distance to be covered — while the song of the pack sounded larger and larger in his ears.

He reached the first fence, the first gate. He dismounted, opened it, led the mustang through, closed the gate, and mounted again. It was a small field — a mere two hundred acres. Yonder, in the farthest corner, was a knot of horses under a group of trees. They had fed full in the first part of the day; they had not yet begun to stir out after the heat ended.

Now, from the woods behind him, he heard the hunt breaking. He turned in the saddle and smiled again as he saw the dogs come from the shadows and the first riders issue forth, with the erect form of Tex Arnold in the lead.

He turned his back upon them. To a degree, nothing but fate could help him now. If that were a wild crew of mustangs, yonder in the corner of the field, and, if they scattered as he came up, he was lost. It was true that a rope was coiled at the saddlebow of Burns, but in the use of a rope Geraldi never had become expert. Those delicate hands of his had mastered arts of far greater nicety, but the arts of labor were not in his field. His clumsy cast would only be able to take a horse near at hand and not too wary.

He eyed the group cautiously, eagerly, as he approached. Two or three lifted their heads with a start when he was still at a distance. As he came nearer, these started away. But there were other and apparently older animals that gave him no heed until he was close up.

His surety strengthened now. He had the rope coiled and ready for the cast, and he picked for his target a big-boned pinto that had the look of a horse which could canter on forever. That was his target when, as he came up, the whole group suddenly opened like a fan and dissolved before him, snorting.

He made his cast, but he knew, as he made it, that he had failed — the distance was too great, at least for one as inexpert as himself. So he saw the flying noose merely strike across the chest of the pinto and whip harmlessly away. He had lost.

No! For as he saw the others sweep away at full gallop, running as though to meet the music of the dogs and the distant riders, the pinto stopped short and stood with its head high, its ears flattened, his legs braced. It had the look of a horse on which the noose has settled. Suddenly Geraldi understood. The mere flick of the lariat across its hide had been enough for a horse well-schooled in all the ways a rope can burn, if pulled against. There it stood, and there it remained, while Geraldi leaped down from the saddle and made his new mustang secure.

Then, like lightning, he changed saddles and, as he cinched up the girth, he measured the distance between him and the posse. They were still sufficiently obscure to the eye. Even one who knew could only pick out the marshal by his style rather than by actual features.

They were coming fast, however, as he jumped into the saddle on his new horse and, looking askance at the weary mustang he had abandoned, he spared an instant to guess whether its sagging knees meant that it would suffer and live or suffer and die. It was a good brute, and a faithful one, and he trusted the tough broncho blood to bring it through.

That glance was all he could spare. The next moment he was straightening the new horse away in a line for the lower gate of the field — the posse was already inside of the other fence line. They had not stopped to find the gate. Three grips of a wire-cutter were sufficient to open a path for them. If there were damage done, the powers behind the law could pay Ben Grogan for it later on.

As Geraldi put the horse to a gallop and rejoiced in the strong striding of the mustang, which promised much, he heard a thin, screeching voice from the tree beneath which the horses had been gathered. He looked up and, through the branches, he saw the freckled face of little Dick Grogan, the only son of the rancher. Dick Grogan, with his hands cupped to give his voice the carrying power, was yelling: "Horse thief! Horse thief! Geraldi, get off of my horse! Horse thief! Thief! Thief!"

There were lists, long lists of various grim deeds which Geraldi had done, but none like that which he almost performed now. For the voice went through him like a volley of bullets, as he realized that this was the end of his law-abiding life. The voice of that lad in the trees would hurl him out of the ranks of honest citizens and make him once more the hunted outlaw. It would throw him from all hope of marrying the woman he loved. It would cover him with utter ruin. So, in the first savage reaction, he wheeled in his saddle and whipped out a revolver to fire.

The eyes and the mouth of the lad opened wide. He made no attempt to dodge, and there was no need, for Geraldi, with a groan, had put up the weapon again and turned to the jockeying of his horse.

His brain whirled. His wits had come to the end of their uses, it seemed. He saw no opening in life before him, but only blank misery ahead. All this for the murderer and ruffian, Larry Burns! He, Geraldi, had been hunted in his time, as hard as ever Larry Burns was chased, but when had he thrown the burden upon a friend? A friend? No, he was not a friend of Burns. He had simply given to one in terror and misery, and now it appeared that what he had given was all that he valued in life.

Geraldi rode straight forward, while a small, cold smile came on his lips. The gate loomed before him. He put the mustang at it. They might smash through it and break both their necks. He hardly cared. But, when he gave the spur, the pinto rose clumsily, but high enough to clear. They thudded down on the farther side and raced on.

When Geraldi looked back again, he saw the riders of the posse scattering and rounding up the Grogan horses. But it would be whole minutes before those careering mustangs were cornered and caught and the pursuers remounted.

In the meantime, he could unroll miles between. But what did it matter? Wherever he rode, there was only one termination for his journey, and that was ruin. They would find something to seize, the hounds of the law. His land, his horses, they would have everything that was his, before long. He smiled again, that faint, small smile, and straightened the pinto down the trail.

Geraldi, horse thief! They had called him gunman, conjurer, trickster, gambler, safe-cracker, highway robber, in the old days. But now he was a horse thief. Mary, who knew the West and who loved it and its ways, how would her lip curl when she heard the tidings?

The way pitched sharply upward. He let the mustang fall to a walk. It was breathing hard. He leaned and listened, and noted the clean sound of the panting. He felt the big, honest thumping of the heart beneath his knee, and a curious satisfaction stole through the mind of Geraldi.

He came to the top of the rise and found himself on the shoulder of a hill that angled high up to the right. Before him was a broken country, half covered with grass and half thickened with brush. He could see the Grogan house, smaller than his hand in the distance to his left. Beyond the Grogan house were the mountains, heaping up in broad backs, in great shoulders and lofty heads.

The smile of Geraldi, as he looked at them, was no longer cold. This was his country. He knew it and loved it. He felt for it a sense of possession. It was almost as though he had exchanged his intimate right to the little patch that was his farm for a more diffused ownership of all this wilderness.

He turned and looked behind him. Far, far away through the golden light of the day's end, he saw the posse streaming — so far away that no sound of the pack bayed up to him. They seemed to Geraldi like little men, pygmies — fools to ride in chase of such a man as he.

Chapter Six

BACK TRAIL

In the dusk, Geraldi led the posse into the twistings of Bitter Spring Cañon. As the night fell, he sat his horse among the tangles of the rocks and watched the marshal go by with the posse, a weary group of men. The dogs had lost the trail, as it passed over the cold, iron surface of the stones that paved the cañon's floor, and now the marshal was shoving the tired brutes on ahead in the hope that they might pick up the scent again.

So, they went on, and Geraldi waited until the growling voices had died down. Then he turned and rode back down the ravine and aimed his course like an arrow for his own house.

All through the night he rode, and dawn was almost appearing, when, at last, he came in sight of it and saw the familiar angle of the roof above the trees. He came up with caution, dismounted, and went on foot toward the place. Now and then, the glinting starlight seemed to shift and waver on the black face of the windowpanes, as though, something were watching from within. But it was only a ghostly life that he sensed there.

He went up to the front door and stood for a

moment, breathing the sweetness of the honey-suckle vines that Mary had planted. They were blooming profusely. All through the day there was a humming of bees and of pollen-loving birds about the vines. But now all was still except for the thin whisper of the wind in the swinging tendrils and the soft touching of leaf against leaf.

A cow began to low loudly from the barn. It was the brindled heifer, whose calf was being weaned. He recognized its peculiar low note, and he smiled a little.

He stepped to the front door and found it locked, but locks were a vain protection against the magic touch of Geraldi. The picklock that he used was thinner than a toothpick, but in a moment the door was open, and he had closed it behind him as he stepped into the thick darkness of the hallway.

He knew every inch of the place, the position of every chair and table. He did not need a light to show him the way as he stepped to the room that was to have been Mary's and his own. He listened at the door, and then he heard breathing, but not the breathing of Mary. This was stentorous, the breathing of a man. As he listened, a cold iron of fear went through Geraldi's heart.

That door he opened also silently, and, like a ghost, he entered. The softness of the rug helped to deaden any sound his feet might make, but those feet fell as fall the feet of a cat.

He went straight to the bed. On the table

beside it, there should be the night lantern which he had placed there that same morning. He found it instantly, and, trying the shutter, he found that it had been lighted. So, loosing a ray as fine as the body of a needle, he probed the dark and finally whipped the streak across the body that lay under the bedclothes. He worked the light upward, and presently it showed him the face of Larry Burns.

He could have laughed bitterly at the sight of Burns lying in his own bed. But there was no laughter in Geraldi's heart at that moment. He simply widened the shutter, and, in the flow of the light, Burns wakened with a start and a groan. He sat up suddenly, reaching a hand beneath his pillow.

"It's I, Burns," said Geraldi. "It's Jimmy Geraldi. Don't grab a gun."

Burns collapsed upon the bed and laid a hand over his heart. "You might've spoken before you turned the flash on me, man," he said. "You might've done that. You pretty near give me heart failure."

"What's happened?" Geraldi asked.

"What's happened here?" replied Burns, sitting up again and yawning. "That don't matter. But tell me how you put the life into that mare and got her to last long enough to laugh at the marshal?"

"Let that be," Geraldi said. "Tex Arnold is riding a little north of the trail that he wants. But what I want to know is . . . what happened here?"

"Well, a lot of grief," said the thug, and yawned again. "Women are kind of foolish," he added. "And the prettier they are, the more likely they are to have no brains. That girl of yours, she's that way."

"What about her?" Geraldi asked, his lip curling as he listened. "Only, be polite."

"Aw, I'm polite," said Larry Burns. He yawned again and stretched his big arms. "You know the way it is?" he demanded. "I could sleep a whole week through and never stop once."

"I suppose you could," said Geraldi. "But I'm asking you a question. What happened here after I left?"

"A lot of grief, I told you," said the outlaw. "After you drifted out, everybody starts leaving."

"Everybody?"

"Yes. They all started off, except the girl. I heard them asking if there would be a wedding later."

"What did she say?"

"I didn't hear what she said," answered the sleepy Burns. "She was all right, in a way, but she was talking pretty low. I waited till the crowd had pulled out, and the dogs was sounding pretty thin and far away as a cloud on the edge of the sky. Then I went into the house and found her. She was setting in this room, with her hands folded, and tears on her face."

"Go on!" Geraldi urged harshly.

"It kind of upsets me, when I see a girl crying,"

said the thug. "I told her so. And I told her there was nothing for her to worry about, because you'd come back."

"What did she say to that?" asked Geraldi.

"She asked me if I were a friend of yours, and if I was the one who had taken you away from the house."

"What did you answer to that?"

"Well," replied the other, scratching his head, "I told her that I was a friend of yours, all right. And if I'm not, may I be blasted. I told her, too, that it was on account of me that you had gone away and left her."

"On account of you?" Geraldi said slowly. "Well, get on with your yarn."

"Maybe I ought to've said," answered the other, "that you had just stepped into my shoes for friendship's sake."

"You didn't tell her that?" asked Geraldi. He turned his back on the other, lighted a lamp, put out the dark lantern, and then sat down near the bed again. He made a cigarette and watched his companion with a curious detachment.

"I didn't tell her that," went on Burns. "You know the way that it is. A gent, he don't want to tell everything to a woman, particularly to a pretty one like that. I wanted to let her know. But then ag'in, I says to myself that maybe *you* wouldn't want the thing talked about too much . . . even to her."

Geraldi interjected at this point: "Didn't she press you to find out why I had left?"

"She didn't leave no stone unturned to find out," Burns responded. "When I come in here and asked for the horse . . . the way that you told me to do . . . she seemed pretty glad to see anybody that might know something about you. She kept saying to me, would you ever come back, did I think. And I tell her, of course, you will, you not being a fool. But she would always shake her head. She cried a good deal, too."

"She never cries," Geraldi said sternly.

"I don't mean that she went around bawling like a kid," said the other. "What I mean is that a tear would leak down, now and then. But she done most of her crying inside, I guess."

Geraldi put back his head to take a deeper breath. "You couldn't have told her that it was to help you out that I went off?" he suggested.

"Why, look here," Burns said, aggrieved, putting out a hand in protesting argument. "You know the way it is. If I begun to talk like that, I'd go on to have to tell her that I'm lined up for Salt Creek. I couldn't tell her that. Look at the shock . . . her finding out that she's alone in the house with a gent that's up for murder?"

His sincerity was clear, and Geraldi nodded.

"She wants to know if I'll be likely to see you again soon, and I say that I hope so," said Burns, in continuation. "So she says that she's taking a trip, and she'll leave a letter for you, and here it is."

He reached to a pocket of his coat that hung on a chair beside the bed, and from it he drew out an envelope that Geraldi tore open at once.

Burns was explaining: "She said that I could take any horse that I liked, but, after she drove off in a buckboard, I just figgered out that there was no safer place for me to sleep than right here. So here I come and done a flop in this bed, and I never slept harder till you showed up, Jimmy. I feel pretty near like a new man now."

But Geraldi was reading:

Dear Jimmy:

Just now it hits me pretty hard, but I'll get over it. I keep telling myself that time is a great healer. Saying that doesn't help very much for the moment, but after a while it will. Every day will be better, until finally I can stand it.

For a moment I wished that you had not gone away before saying good bye to me. But now I realize that you were right. If the cut hurts me . . . well, I put the knife in your hand. It's a lot better to have had the blow fall when it did.

Now I'm going away as far as I can go. I don't know exactly where, and I'm not going to tell you even when I find out. Because I know you're a tender-hearted fellow and that you may begin to pity me and so take up my trail.

But don't do that, Jimmy. If love couldn't keep you, I don't want pity to put you in handcuffs. The very best thing

for me is never to see you again. If I should, perhaps I couldn't prevent my silly heart from aching. But, meanwhile, I'm trusting to time, as I said before.

After all, I forgive you. I know it wasn't an easy thing for you to step out through that window. You're the sort that will always face the music, and I know that you quit in that way because you didn't want to stand in front of me and see the blow hurt me.

Good bye, dear. God be kind to you, and may the wild old life mean all to you that you hope. I have walked all through the house, and said good bye to every room. Now I'm going to try to put everything out of my mind forever.

Mary

Chapter Seven

FREIGHT PASSENGERS

It was not until Geraldi had changed saddles to one of his own horses and mounted that big Larry Burns, following him numbly about in the gray of the morning, seemed to realize what had happened and was happening now.

"You ain't leaving the place, Jimmy?"

Geraldi pointed to the stolen mustang. "I'm a horse thief now, Larry," he explained.

Burns blinked at him. "And what about the girl?" he asked, beginning to guess at the truth.

"It's all right about her," said Geraldi through his teeth.

"Hold on," said Burns. "I've busted everything for you. I've busted it like a bubble. It makes me feel like a hound. It makes me feel like a no-good dog, Jimmy! *You* a hoss thief! There ain't anybody fool enough to think that you'd be a hoss thief. Not you . . . not Geraldi. Jimmy, what can I do about it? I'll take the hoss. I'll cross your trail with it. I'll pull 'em after me. . . ." He closed his eyes as he spoke. He began to shudder from head to foot.

Geraldi leaned a little from the saddle and put

a hand on Larry's shoulder. "You take care of yourself and lie low," he said. "You watch yourself, Larry. If you have another rub, before long, you'll find yourself with the shakes. And that's the finish."

Larry Burns did not open his eyes. With them tightly closed, he could more vividly see the truth of what Geraldi had said. His brain whirled; there was a roaring in his ears. Yes, if a posse hunted him now, he would be an easy prey. When he opened his eyes again, Geraldi was at a little distance, riding off.

"Hey, Jimmy!" shouted Burns.

Geraldi turned and waved farewell and then, putting his horse to a lope, swung off down the trail.

He had made up his mind as to the direction Mary must have driven. Her will, when she left the house, was to go as far as possible from Geraldi, and in as straight a line, no doubt. The noise of the manhunt had faded toward the north and, therefore, she was most likely to take the southern trail. So he rode south.

He came to a small house near a crossing of the trail. It was a wretched place on the worst bit of the range. A few cows and mules grazed among the rocks; there was a scattering of sheep in an upper field, and in the corral an old man was standing. He had broad shoulders, a bent back, and very long legs. He looked like a standing crane, waiting for food to come to his feet.

Geraldi reined in his horse at the gate of the corral. "Hello, Pop," he said.

The old man waved a stiff arm in greeting, then he stalked slowly toward the gate.

"Pop," said Geraldi, "take this." He held out a paper and explained it. "That's a deed to my whole place and all of the livestock on it. It may not hold in the law, because it's not done by a lawyer, or signed before a notary. But I've written it out in full form, and I've made everything over to you."

The old man lifted his eyes, small and bright as the eyes of a bird, and fixed them on the face of the young man. He waited.

"I'm a horse thief now," said Geraldi. "They're chasing me, and, if they get a chance, they'll scalp me of everything I have. You move up to my place and take care of it. If ever I'm on my feet again, I'll come back and claim half of it from you."

"Suppose that I hang onto all of it?" asked the old man. "Suppose that I don't wanta give it up?"

Geraldi smiled. "I'll take my chance with you, Pop," he said. "Move up to my place. Drive up your cattle, too, and move in and make yourself comfortable. There's a good stock of grub. Help yourself to everything. Is it a go?"

"Why," said Pop, "any fool knows that a featherbed is easier lying than hard ground. I reckon that I'll move up. You don't need to worry none about the law gettin' any of your things out of my

57

claws. Not unless they got more law in their heads than I've got slugs in a riot gun." He grinned.

They shook hands, and with one word of farewell Geraldi was off down the road. He made steady progress until the middle of the morning, and then, as he came to a little village through which the railroad ran, he marked down two horses in a corral near the road. They were not the only ones in the enclosure. A dozen others were grouped there, but the two drew somewhat apart from the rest. They stood alone not only in their place, but to a horseman's eye, and Geraldi knew them for his own. Was Mary here, then?

A bare-legged young fellow with a great, ragged straw sombrero on his head sat on the top rail of the corral fence and regarded the pair with an unwavering stare.

"That's a likely couple of mustangs," said Geraldi.

The boy did not turn his head. "Them ain't mustangs," he said. "Them're hot-blooded hosses. If you got half an eye, you oughta be able to see it."

"Your dad raise 'em?" asked Geraldi.

"Bought 'em. Yesterday. Two hundred and fifty."

"That looks cheap," said Geraldi.

"Cheap?" said the young fellow scornfully. "Why, either one of the two of 'em is worth five hundred. Dad said so. And he knows a hoss from a cow, too. It was a girl done the selling," he explained briefly, and contemptuously.

"What made her so anxious to sell?" asked Geraldi.

"She liked a railroad better than a buckboard, that's all," said the young fellow. "You know the way that girls are. They got no sense."

The railroad? thought Geraldi. Turning his head, he glanced at the two silver streaks that the rails made, running down the valley. His eye flew along their course, and his heart sank. The horse he rode was good, but it could not keep pace with feet of steel, lungs of iron, or breath of steam. The very birds of the air could not keep pace with the monster that was bearing the girl away from him.

"Which is your pony?" Geraldi asked.

"Me? I ain't got none," the young fellow said bitterly. "Sometimes I get a ride on a mule, comin' back from plowing." He sighed.

Geraldi dismounted. "Take this horse," he said. "Keep it here. You don't need to handle it like silk. But don't lame it. Ride it with an easy rein. Don't use spurs on it, or it will buck you into the middle of the sky. Treat it well, and it will outspeed, outlast, and outfight every horse on your dad's place."

The young fellow, at last turning his head, ran his amazed eye from head to foot of Geraldi's mount. He, too, knew horses, perhaps more by instinct than by training. He tried to speak, but, once his mouth was opened, it merely remained ajar. He gaped, and he wondered. He shifted his amazed glance from the horse to Geraldi.

"Look-it!" he exclaimed. "I ain't worth to ride a hoss like that, that could jump over the moon, about."

"You ride it," said Geraldi. "One day I may come back for it. Perhaps never. If I don't come back inside of a year, that horse is yours."

The young fellow slid from the fence, but he was limp and hardly had the strength, as it seemed, to take the reins in his hand. But Geraldi did not remain to hear his words of gratitude. He walked swiftly down the winding lane, turned to the left to the railroad station, and there found the agent seated on a packing case, chewing a straw and turning wistful eyes down the magic brightness of the rails, looking to that point where they melted into the horizon glare and were gone in a shimmer and dance of heat. He gave Geraldi a side glance and returned to his staring.

"How're things?" asked Geraldi.

"Aw, sort of comin' and goin'," said the other. "Mostly goin'."

"Not much traffic here, I suppose," Geraldi speculated, "except when the cows are bein' shipped."

"The rest is mostly a blank," said the station agent, sighing.

"You have some passengers, though, I suppose," said Geraldi.

"Aw, one a week . . . maybe only one a month."

"Hold on," Geraldi said. "With a town like this, I'll wager there's more than one a week."

The agent looked at him more carefully. "You'd kind of think so, wouldn't you?" he said. "With a town like this, you'd think that the whole crowd would wanta pick up and leave altogether. But they don't. They stick on here. They got no sense. They're like the cattle they got grazin' in the field. There's only been one ticket out in ten days."

"Somebody got sick of this town?" suggested Geraldi.

"Nope. Not even that. Just a girl. Girls is a wandering lot, these days. But even her, she didn't go East. She just took a step deeper West."

"Going West gets into the blood," Geraldi proposed in a deprecating tone. "There's a lot more life to the East."

"Yeah, ain't there?" said the agent, looking with surprise and sympathy at Geraldi. "Kansas City is my best bet."

"But the girl went deeper West, eh?" Geraldi reiterated. "How far, then?"

"Five hundred whole mile," said the other. "Yep. Five hundred whole mile to a dinky little place called Neering."

"Neering?" echoed Geraldi. "Neering? Don't recognize that name. What would anyone want to go there for?"

"How could I tell?" said the agent. He seemed irritated by the question and again turned his

61

gaze toward the East, where the rails wavered out of view.

At the same time, a murmur seemed to be growing up out of the ground.

"Freight," said the agent in disgust. "And it won't stop here, I'll lay my money. Nothing ever stops here. I'm gonna quit this job. After five whole year, I'm gonna resign. The dog-gone railroad, it don't know how to treat a good man, at all." He looked around, but his recent companion had disappeared. Presently, the agent was on his feet, watching the tower of smoke appear, and then the rocking front of the engine that came thundering up the long grade.

The agent was right. The train did not stop at this small station. Nevertheless, it picked up an added burden. As it went by, a cat-like form slipped from the brush on the farther side of the tracks and leaped for a ladder, caught it, and swayed up to the top of a boxcar.

Chapter Eight

THE TRAMP BOSS

From the top of a boxcar to the padlock on the door is quite a distance. But a man who has no nerves may hang by his toes from the edge of the top and reach the padlock with his hands. Geraldi did that.

He had no intention of scouring from one part of the train to another, harassed by shacks, hiding between cars, jolting over couplings. He simply selected an empty, easily distinguished by its hollow uproar, and a minute later the padlock had yielded to his picklock, and he was ensconced inside.

It had carried baled hay, this car, and the hay had not been swept out — that part which friction had chafed free from the bales. So he gathered this hay together in a corner, and lay down upon it. The door he had left open, for the sake of the good air that poured through it, since the smoke was streaming away to the leeward on the other side of the train.

He relaxed. The strain of the ride had told on him, flexible steel that he was, and now he composed himself for a rest. He did it by degrees. He turned his will up the muscles of his legs and arms, first of all. When they were as flabby as pulp, he made the muscles of his neck limp. And then he concentrated, last, upon breathing easily, regularly, and seeing that there was no tension about his stomach and loin muscles. The art of sleeping is the attainment of perfect relaxation.

Geraldi, in thirty seconds, was as limp as though he had been asleep for five hours, and in thirty seconds more sleep actually followed.

When the train slowed down for a station, he wakened automatically, closed the door, and opened it again after the train got under way. He allowed thirty miles an hour for the train's progress. There were fifteen hours and more of travel, therefore, ahead of him, and he intended to sleep the bulk of that time.

He was not one of those nervous travelers who cannot face five hours alone on a train without a heap of newspapers and magazines to comfort him. Just as a camel can eat itself fat and drink itself full in order to prepare for a desert journey, so Geraldi knew how to lay up the strength that comes with perfect repose. He was laying it up now. With the door open, and the fresh air streaming in, he lay down once more, and in less than a minute he was sound asleep again.

This sleep did not last so long. For the train struck a long, laborious grade, up which it groaned at hardly more than a walking pace. In the midst of this grade, Geraldi was disturbed by

64

a noise other than the mechanical sounds of the train in motion. He wakened and sat up. Two men already were inside the open door of the car, and they were helping in a third. They were not a savory trio. They had "tramp" written large on their unshaven faces and on their tattered clothes. They were a part of that floating population which drifts with the railroad, hoping that clever wits will secure them against the ardors of work and ready for crime rather than labor.

Geraldi looked upon them with a peculiar disfavor. Then he reclined once more on his bed of chaff and closed his eyes. Presently he could hear one of them say: "Here's a drunk, clean out, and usin' the only bed in this here hotel."

"Rouse him up, Jerry," said another.

"I'll rouse him," said Jerry malignantly.

Geraldi opened his eyes the least crack, and, through the long lashes, he saw Jerry, beside him, poise himself and swing back a leg to kick.

The kicking leg drove forward, and it met, not the ribs, but the hand of Geraldi, and that hand, diverting the direction of the kick a little, twisted the foot to the side. It was not the force of his wrist that did the trick. It was rather the weight in the driving foot that did the thing. But the tramp named Jerry pitched suddenly upon his side and rolled in pain upon the floor of the car, beating at the boards with the flat of his hand.

Geraldi sat up and began to make a cigarette.

The two other tramps raised their comrade

from the floor. He shouted to them to let him lie and that he had broken his hip. But it was not a broken hip, or even a dislocated one. It was merely badly wrenched.

Geraldi gave him advice. "You'll be able to walk pretty well inside of three or four days," he said. "In the meantime, lie still and keep on your other side."

Jerry repaid him with a glowering glance, and then with a tide of profanity. "It was that damned *jujitsu!*" he shouted. "Crown that swine for me, will you?"

This appeal his two comrades did not allow to go unregarded. They were big fellows, all three of them. Little men are not apt to go on the road. Essential pride makes them wish to show themselves as good as the next fellow at anything from sewer digging to brain work. But your big man is your ideal loafer. His size is the diploma which attests his manliness, and he lounges secure in the knowledge of his bulk. Big, hardened by the bitterest sort of living, well accustomed to giving and receiving blows, the pair took position, one on either side of Geraldi.

"Soak him, Bob . . . soak him, Pete," begged Jerry, full length again on the floor and still groaning. "It was a dirty trick. He done me in with a dirty trick."

"We're gonna bust him in two," confided Pete, who wore a brush of shining red hair.

Geraldi looked from one of them to the other. He did not rise.

"Stand up, you fool," said Pete, who seemed the leader of the trio. "You're gonna take it, and you'd better take it standing."

Geraldi gave them warning. "Boys," he said, "if you start in on me, you'll wish that you'd dropped a keg of dynamite before you hit me. I'm not boasting. I'm telling you facts."

"He's a ring man," Bob said, impressed. "He's a boxer, Pete."

"He's only a damn lightweight," declared Pete. "Ain't I been in the ring myself? I never seen the day when I couldn't've taken on three like him. One in each hand, and one in the teeth. You . . . stand up!"

"Let him take it sittin'," Bob said, and hurled himself with elbows and knees at Geraldi.

With elbows and knees prepared, he struck not Geraldi but the straw on which Geraldi had been sitting. The latter had slid forward just enough to avoid that onslaught, and he repaid it with a tap behind the ear. It was not a hard blow. It was no heavier, say, than the stroke of a tap hammer. But it landed on exactly the right spot, and it unstrung the limbs of Bob as thoroughly as any Homeric spear could have done.

Then Geraldi rose to meet the third of the gang, the redoubtable Pete. But Pete, although he had served his time in the ring and was confident of his prowess, was also a man of caution. He had seen his two burly companions each undone by a single touch, as it were. He recognized magic when he saw it, and he was no man to depend upon mere flesh and brawn in such a case.

He passed his hand inside his coat. When the hand came out, it carried the flashing and curving length of a Bowie knife, and, with that, he made his lunge at Geraldi.

The latter stood like a statue. It seemed as though he were benumbed and could not make out that such a danger was before him. Or was it dread of the naked steel that paralyzed him, as it had paralyzed many a man before him?

Only at the last instant, he shrank a little, not backward, but down. He did not duck, but his whole body seemed to contract, and the knife-bearing hand, that had been directed at his throat, shot over his shoulder.

Geraldi turned with it. One might have thought that the sheer wind of the stroke had knocked him about, or the grazing force of Pete's bulky arm. He turned, caught the arm, and, stooping forward, he utilized his own shoulder lift and the weight of Pete's rush to shoot the latter clear of the ground and hurtling against the side of the car. With shattering force, Pete struck on his head and shoulders, then he dropped limply to the rattling boards of the floor.

Geraldi, taking the cigarette from his lips, looked down on the motionless bodies of Pete and Bob. Then he turned toward Jerry and found the latter regarding him with the eyes of one entranced.

"Both of 'em dead," gasped Jerry. He braced himself against the side of the car and shook out of his sleeve a slingshot that he grasped tightly in his fingers. Yet there was no hope of making a real defense in his face. Grimly, desperately, he waited for an onslaught against which he felt there would be no hope of effective resistance.

"They're not dead," Geraldi said. He went to the place where Bob lay, and, rolling the inert body from the chaff on which it lay, he composed himself in his former resting place. He continued to breathe deeply of the smoke and to regard the pair of fallen heroes.

"They're cold," said Jerry. "You gone and murdered the two of 'em. You'll hang for it, too."

"They're not dead. They're only groggy," Geraldi said calmly. "How's your leg?"

"Broke, pretty near," Jerry said. He stirred, and groaned again.

"I'll rub the twist out of it," said Geraldi, still puffing at the cigarette. "There's only a twist. That's all. The next time, you won't kick a sleeping man, Jerry."

"Sleeping wildcats is what I won't kick," said Jerry. "Who are you, stranger?"

"A tramp . . . like you," Geraldi said.

"Like me?" gasped Jerry. "You, like me?" He began to laugh. "You're velvet. I'm gingham," he continued. "There's Bob givin' a stir, sure enough."

Bob and Pete sat up at almost the same

69

moment. They held their heads. They looked wildly around them. And finally they united in staring at Geraldi.

"Sleight of hand!" broke out Pete hoarsely, at length, as he began to rub at his half-sprained neck. "He's one of these here sleight-of-hand experts, that's what he is."

"Sleight of hand? Sleight of hand, hell!" Bob said. "He's cracked my skull for me."

"Hold on, boys," Jerry interrupted. "I got an idea. We been wanting brains to lead us since they croaked Isaac. And here's the brains that we been looking for. This here is our new boss."

Chapter Nine

MIND-READING

This surprising idea did not find immediate favor with the other two rascals. They first looked from one another to Geraldi, and back again, considering.

"What's your line, bo?" asked Pete.

"You fellows ought to tell me yours, first," said Geraldi. "I think I've won a right to do the first listening."

Bob took out Bull Durham and papers and began to manufacture his smoke without looking down at the work of his fingers. He preferred to keep his glance fixed upon Geraldi's face.

"You bein' one of these conjurers and magicians," he said, "you oughta be able to read my mind and tell me what I am."

"Oh, I can tell you what you are," said Geraldi. "But it's hardly worth the effort to read your minds. I'd rather sit here and listen."

"You're a bluff, eh?" Pete said. "You think that you can put over easy ones like that on us, do you? Go on and mind-read. I seen it done on the stage, pretty good. But that's all faked. Well, there ain't any fake here. You never seen us

before, and we never seen you. You got nothin'
on us. Now you go ahead and read our minds,
will you? You start right in and tell me what I'm
thinkin' about this minute, will you?"

"The lock step," Geraldi said.

The head of Pete went back. It was plain that
he had received an unexpected blow.

"Looks like he stung you that time, Pete," said
Jerry. "I told you that he had the brains for us."

"Shut yer mouth," advised Pete. "Go on, will
you? You tell me some more. I'm thinkin' about
the lock step, am I?"

"Not now," Geraldi said. "You're thinking of
a crowd, and yourself working it."

Pete jumped to his feet. "Damn you!" he said.
"Have I got a window in my forehead that you
can look in through?"

"Practically," Geraldi answered, with his
small, cold smile.

"How would I be working it?" asked Pete.

"With your hands," said Geraldi. "Lifting out
of pockets, most of the time, hunting the
heaviest crushes, dipping in and out, getting
anything from a purse to a handkerchief. Because you don't mind the little things, old son.
You like 'em. You're willing to add grain to
make up your sack of wheat. When you started
in, on that first day. . . ."

"I've had enough of your bunk," Pete said,
blinking. "There ain't any more that I want to
take from you, kid." He drew back a little. He
dropped his head between his hunched shoul-

72

ders, and glowered up at Geraldi.

"All right," said Jerry cheerfully, wriggling into a more comfortable position. "Go on and read my mind . . . ouch!" As he moved, he hurt his twisted hip again.

"I'll fix that for you," said Geraldi.

He took hold of the injured leg below the bend of the knee, then he worked the fingers of his right hand into the tendons of the hip. "This will hurt a bit," Geraldi cautioned.

"If it'll get me walkin'," said Jerry, "what do I care what it hurts?"

He had hardly spoken when Geraldi jerked the lower leg suddenly to the side and at the same time drove his fingertips like steel points into the hip of the other.

Jerry uttered a brief howl, like a dog under the whip. The stroke of the pain was so great that sweat started out on his forehead. It was still rolling down his face as he flexed his leg and straightened it again.

"By thunder!" Jerry cried. "You've fixed it as easy as you spoiled it. How'd you do that?"

"Magic, of course," Geraldi stated. He held out his slender hands, palm up, as though to call attention to the smallness of his wrists and to indicate that with brute force there was little that he could accomplish.

"Go on and tell me about myself," Jerry urged. "How did I start in, will you tell me that?"

"It was the Army that turned you wrong," said Geraldi. "You were rather a loafer, but after you went into the regular Army, you got into bad habits, as they say. That was where you turned crooked."

It was Jerry's turn to gape.

"He's got you!" Pete exclaimed, rejoiced to see the confusion of another, matching his own.

"Who'd you ever know that knew me?" Jerry demanded, marveling. "No, it couldn't be that way. Look here, is there really anything in it? Can you read a gent's mind right through his forehead?"

"Of course," Geraldi said, smiling. "It's perfectly simple."

"If I went crooked, what was my lay?" demanded Jerry, leaning forward eagerly.

"You were almost always the outside man," Geraldi continued. "You got a small split, but you had the easiest job."

Jerry nodded his head. "That's straight," he said. "I never was any good on the inside. I didn't have the right kind of nerve for that. I never minded when I had some sky over my head. You got me right, though. How did you do it?"

"Magic, of course," Geraldi affirmed, still smiling.

"There's still me," said Bob. "Now you tell me what I am?"

He had a square block of a face, and pale, dull eyes, set too widely apart. They were now staring, like the eyes of a bull, straight at Geraldi. "You tick me off. It's my turn," he insisted, as

Geraldi looked back into those eyes with something of a shudder. "What's my lay?"

One word came slowly, lingeringly, from the lips of Geraldi. "Murder," he said.

Bob threw up a hand before his face. Between the fingers, the eyes, no longer dull, now burned at Geraldi. Suddenly he blinked and turned his glance away, as an animal turns, to avoid the steady eye of man, the master.

"My . . . God!" breathed Bob.

The other two said nothing. Whatever tricks of hand and mind Geraldi had showed them before seemed as nothing compared with this single word of revelation. They were even embarrassed.

"He's a dick," said Bob, muttering slowly to himself. "He's got us all framed. He's gonna try to turn us all in . . . and we gotta do something about it!" He glanced aside at his two companions, but both of them shook their heads. They had felt the hands of Geraldi in such a way that they would never forget.

"Hold on," said Jerry. "He ain't a faker. He'll tell us how he got that lot of dope on us. Will you tell us that, partner?" He appealed to Geraldi, and the latter nodded.

"Why, Jerry," he said, "it's all very simple. The look of you shows that you're not a born bad one, and nothing but the Army could have stiffened your back and squared your shoulders that way. As for the outside stuff, that was a guess. I took my chance that you worked the easiest lay."

"Well, that's simple, all right," said Jerry. "There's no magic in that. What about Pete, though?"

"Fellows learn to talk out of the corners of their mouths in the prison line," said Geraldi carelessly. "And a man who can roll a cigarette, without spilling a grain of tobacco and without looking at his work, has trained fingers. There are a few other little signs. They're not worth mentioning."

"And there's Bob," Jerry said, lowering his voice a little.

Bob lifted his glance suddenly, and the pale eyes hung with fascination upon the face of the other.

Geraldi pointed. "Look at his hands."

They were vast, red hands; across the fingers were many little pale streaks — old scars.

"He started as a butcher," said Geraldi. He looked deeply into the dull stare of Bob. "And he's a butcher still," he concluded. "That's all my magic amounts to, you see. Simply adding little signs together."

"It sounds easy," admitted Jerry, "but the simpler a thing sounds, the harder it is to do. I know that, all right. Look here, partner. Will you tell us something about yourself? What's your lay?"

"Magic," said Geraldi with another of those graceful gestures of his, palms up.

"Stage stuff?" asked Jerry.

"No. Real magic," Geraldi said. "The sort that opens padlocks and combinations on safes, and all that sort of thing. A little second-story work, now and then, gives spice to life. I've specialized in jewels at different times in my life. On the whole, I think you may safely say that I'm a man of the world. But magic is my line. No 'soup.' No dynamite. Magic to open any door. D'you see?"

The three gazed at him with a sort of despairing envy, until Pete broke out: "Well, all your magic ain't kept you out of riding the rods, just like us . . . or doing the rattlers on the boards of a boxcar. What's the use of magic when it winds you up there?"

"Magic is its own reward," said Geraldi.

"Look," said Jerry, pointing a stiffened arm at him. "Take us along with you. Let us work with you. Is that a go? Can you use us?"

Geraldi, before answering, turned his head a little, and looked straight and deeply into the pale eyes of Bob.

"Well?" he asked gently.

Bob crimsoned to the brows. "You know my lay," he said hoarsely. "You know my lay. You can take me on, if you want to."

"I can use all three of you," said Geraldi, "in the job that I have on hand now. I'll take you on, and I'll pay you a regular salary. Does that sound to you?"

"Hey!" shouted Pete. "No regular split? Just wages?"

"Good wages," said Geraldi. "Twenty dollars a day. Does that sound to you?"

"Twenty apiece?" asked Pete cautiously.

"Twenty apiece," Geraldi confirmed.

"And what sort of work?" asked Jerry.

"Every time," said Geraldi, "that you have to jimmy a window or use a blackjack, you'll get a bonus. Fifty for a window, and two hundred for a blackjack job. Does it sound to you?"

They did not answer. Each of the three was grinning widely from ear to ear, like starving men who hear a glorious promise of limitless banqueting.

Chapter Ten

OFF GUARD

Neering was one of those wind-blown cattle towns that are jotted down on the map, not because they are pleasantly located, but because they make convenient centers for a wide range. Ranchers came in their buckboards and carted out season supplies of bacon, flour, beans, coffee, and a few canned goods. There was a store, also, where they could buy saddles, hides of leather for the repair of harness, and such necessities. And the women could get cheap clothes, two years behind the fashions. Neering had a bank, also. It was a private bank, and it served the entire district. But the actual center of Neering's life was not in either of the two stores, or even in the post office, where a stove stood to accommodate loungers. The center of Neering's existence was in the hotel, and the center within the hotel was the dining room.

It was more like a restaurant than like a hotel dining room. And it was sometimes more like a bunkhouse than like a restaurant. When the winter winds were up, they poked long needles of icy cold through the chinks of the flimsy walls and whistled mockery under the window sashes. But still the dining room was the place of main resort, for, in the center of the place, stood a big round stove which had a rail like a bar rail around the bottom of it. On that rail, heels could rest while the sole of the foot was toasted. Around the stove there was also a circle of low-backed armchairs, clumsy, heavy, unbreakable. These chairs were in place all the year round, for the same people who came for warmth in the winter were apt to drop in for the cool of the room in the summer.

To complete the furnishings and make perfect comfort, there was a rack on which were hung newspapers of every age up to a year. They were collected from all hands, and the men were sure to look through the number of them with a yearning hope that, if luck were good, he would be able to find a paper from his home town. These newspapers were treated with astonishing reverence. Men who threw them on the floor, after reading, were severely rebuked by the others. When the edges of the sheets began to tear, sometimes Molly repaired them, using a piece of brown butcher paper and glue.

In addition to the newspapers, there reposed upon the floor a number of boxes of a good size, half filled with moist sawdust. They made the perfect spittoons — not beautiful, but easy targets.

As for the dining tables, they were ranked around the edges of the big room — a dozen tables, each capable of seating four. Sometimes all of those chairs were filled, and other guests were served with plates to hold on their knees, putting their coffee cups upon the floor. But this was generally only during the Christmas or the cattle-shipping season.

Now, at the corner table of the dining room, sat Geraldi. At another, nearer the door, sat a fellow with a cheerful face, who had come in walking with a slight limp. At another, was a man with flaming-red hair, and at a fourth sat a newcomer with dull, pale eyes, set much too far apart.

They had come in separately; they had sat down at separate tables. Molly, the waitress, regarded the three with distinct disfavor. They had a foreign, an Eastern look; and Molly felt toward the East and Easterners very much as the Irish are apt to feel toward the English.

But upon Geraldi, she looked with an instant liking. His smile was so candid, his dark eye was so open and frank and bright, and, above all, he seemed so young and delicate, that a maternal instinct swelled the heart of Molly. She could not help lingering when, as she put down his coffee cup, he looked up with a pleasant and a silent look of thanks. Why couldn't other men smile in this manner?

"What does smiling cost?" Molly commented aloud. "But they's a premium on it around here. The boys get the smiles blowed off their faces, before they've been in Neering very long. You

81

take a February norther, and it'll freeze the smiling muscles bad enough to keep a man's face stiff for the rest of the year. But you're new to this part of the range, ain't you?"

Geraldi said that he was. What was he intending to do? He hardly knew. He had heard that there was good hunting in these mountains. He might try his hand at it. Had he used a rifle? Yes, a little.

Molly grinned down at him. She herself was an uncommonly good shot; she owned a Winchester and a Colt revolver, and she knew how to use them.

"You wanta be sure that your eye is in," said Molly, "before you start out to bag a deer. The deer around here, they can smell a man a mile, and a rifle ten mile. The minute that they see you, they jump a furlong wide, and then they lay themselves out and hum. Good buck around these parts . . . he sails over the mountains like a dog-gone hawk. You're always shooting at five hundred yards, if you want to eat venison around here."

"I'll have to wish for luck, then," said Geraldi.

"You got some folks out here?" said Molly.

"No. I'm just seeing the country. My father thought it would be a good idea for me to rough it a little. He said it would toughen me a lot, being a little soft out of school."

"Yeah. It'll toughen you," said Molly sourly. "It'll toughen you, or it'll kill you. But watch your step around here. They're hard. Look at some of 'em around the room. Tough, ain't they? They've had their toughenin', and they've lived through it." She folded her arms. The powerful muscles of her forearms bulged formidably.

Geraldi lifted his eyes again toward her in a confiding fashion. "You know," he said, "it can't be as bad as all that."

"It's worse!" she said firmly.

"Well," he said, "I'm not a giant. But if women can come out here, I suppose that I can stand it, all right."

"Yeah," drawled Molly. "Women come out here, once in a while. I dunno why. They read about the West in books. They come out and think every cowpuncher is a cross between a prize fighter and the Prince of Wales. They get their eyes opened, though. 'Punchers are all right, but they need a good laundering, most of the time. There was one of them soft pieces of calico here yesterday."

"A girl?" said Geraldi innocently.

"Yeah. She was a girl, all right. One of the kind that makes the men pretty dizzy."

"Pretty?"

"Yeah. Pretty. More'n that. She steps in here yesterday and eats her ham and eggs and looks at me sort of blank and wild, like she envied me . . . like she wished that she had my job. I was sorry for her. But I asked her what brought her this far West. And all she said was that she liked it."

"Living in the hotel?" asked Geraldi.

"She done a fade-away," said the waitress.

"She steps out with her suitcase. I go after her a minute later, to ask her where she wants to get rooms, or is she going to take the next train out. And, by Jiminy, she's gone."

"Disappeared, eh?" Geraldi said.

"That's it. Disappeared. Somebody must've come by and picked her up."

Geraldi started, although very slightly.

"A little kidnapping job?" he suggested.

"Oh, no," said the girl. "Somebody seen her standing with the suitcase and offered her a lift, I guess, and she took it. That's all there was to that."

"It sounds a little strange," said Geraldi.

He looked down to the table. His brain was darkening and spinning like a top. To follow her to this point had been hard enough, but now, if Mary was whirled away into the mountains, by any one of a hundred winding roads and trails, how was he to follow her? Panic took hold of him. He fought it back as well as he could.

What was in her mind? Well, that was simple enough. She wanted to get away. She feared that he would follow her, and she was taking any road to leave him behind — any road, so long as it might be the most complicated. She would fly from him for weeks, perhaps, before she felt safe from pursuit.

"Looking for a job, perhaps," said Geraldi. "She may have gone out to work at a ranch. Cooking, or something like that."

"Her?" said Molly the waitress. "She didn't

look like work. But you never can tell. All kinds of folks get on the rocks. Maybe that happened to her. Have another slug of that coffee?"

"Thanks," said Geraldi. He watched the steaming liquid, night-dark, pour into the cup. "If a girl can keep smiling, she'll always pull through," he suggested.

"This one could smile, and wrinkle her nose when she smiled," said Molly. "She'll come through, all right. She's the kind that can pull through and wind up on the top. That's her way. She looked as though she'd been hit, but she still put out her chin and was ready for another whang."

Geraldi needed no further identification. This was enough. Still he could remember, most vividly, the faint wrinkling of Mary's nose as she smiled. It wrung his heart, now, to think of the picture. "I wish her luck," he said slowly.

"Oh, me, too," said Molly. "She was a lady. That's what she was. There was no side about her. She talked to me like I was a sister. You could see that she'd been high, and now she's low. But the right kind, they never get too low. They're always high enough to look the world in the face."

There was no better description of Mary than this, thought Geraldi. All that Molly had said was true, and yet far less than the truth, the fullness of which he alone could understand.

He thought back to the day when Larry Burns had whispered to him through the window and blasted his life. It seemed to him that his existence fell into two parts — all of that which had lain before the coming of Burns, and now the few days which had followed, each rich with misery.

But, when he stepped back mentally to that moment, he could not say that he regretted what he had done. He could not have refused the plea of Burns. A man in despair has a special right to all that other men may do for him. He could not have turned the man away. And, once he became Burns's champion, all the other events had followed as a matter of course.

For once in his life, Geraldi, as the waitress moved off to other guests, fell into a dismal waking dream. His eyes half closed. The cat-like watchfulness, that at all other times, day and night, was like an armor about him, now disappeared.

Out of that trance, he was roused by a voice behind him that said quietly, but sternly: "Geraldi, don't move. I've got you covered. I've got two charges of buckshot ready for the small of your back."

Chapter Eleven

A VOICE

Geraldi did not move. It was not so much the mention of a shotgun that deterred him, as it was the sound of the voice, for he recognized Marshal Tex Arnold, and, through that recognition, he was aware that it was time for him to play his cards carefully, one by one. He glanced across toward the door. It was opened at that moment, and into its aperture advanced two men, rifles in hand. He looked to the windows. There were two, and in each of them he spotted a pair of shoulders, dark against the sun.

"Easy does the trick, Jimmy," said Tex Arnold, behind him. "Do I tie you, or do you give me your word not to try to break away?"

Geraldi smiled. From the corner of his eye, he watched his three hired men. They looked on calmly, almost uncuriously, at what was taking place, and he wondered what confidence he could place in them. He saw Molly, too, thunderstruck by this scene of capture — the capture of her youthful tenderfoot. Well, it would be a slight lesson for Molly.

"I don't give promises, Tex," said Geraldi.

"You'd better tie my hands."

"Behind his back," said Arnold. "You, Durham, do the tying. It's a job that you ought to know."

"I've tied bulls," said another voice at the back of Geraldi. "I'll tie this lad so he'll never budge his hands apart. Not till you cut the rope, because nobody but me will likely be able to undo the knots that I throw into it."

Geraldi, without a struggle, placed his hands behind his back. They were seized at once, and the tying began, while Tex Arnold cautioned his man: "Slowly and carefully, Durham. You've tied other men so that they couldn't budge. But ropes won't hold this one. Ropes won't hold Geraldi." He went on, as the job of tying was completed: "Now take your place here. You're guarding him from behind. You're guarding his hands. Don't think of anything else. Just fasten your eyes on his hands. The moment that they begin to move, jam the muzzle of your gun into the back of his neck. Don't take any chances. Don't even blink, or he might be free."

"You're joking, chief," said the other man. "You're not serious. How could he get out of that rope without it was untied?"

"Durham," said Arnold, "you're a good fellow, and a fine hand with a rope. But I know Geraldi . . . in part. Here, Wendell! You go down to the station and find out when the next eastbound train goes through. We're going to sit right here with our man until the time comes to board that train." He added to the waitress: "D'you know those three fellows?"

"No," said Molly in a gasp, still staring at the face of the innocent Geraldi. "I dunno that I know 'em."

"I don't like the look of 'em," said the marshal. "Ask 'em to get out, will you?"

"Hold on," said Molly, outraged in a professional point of pride and dignity. "We never turned a hungry man out of this room."

The marshal chuckled. "Let 'em finish their meals, then," he said. "After that, they can go. Don't let a new customer in, though. I'm a federal marshal . . . I have authority to do as I please in a case like this."

"Mister," Molly said, "I've gotta do what you say. Only . . . what has that poor kid done?"

"This poor kid," said the marshal, "is James Geraldi. Did you ever hear that name before?"

She had heard it. She turned pale with excitement at the repetition of it. She gaped once more at Geraldi, and then retreated in haste toward the kitchen, to enlarge on what she had observed.

Tex Arnold took the place opposite his prisoner. "What happened, Jimmy?" he said. "Tired out? Having a nap? You let me fix things as though you were asleep."

"I was," said Geraldi. "Asleep with my eyes open. The first time and the last time, Arnold. That's what makes this your day."

The marshal relaxed a little in his chair. He

called another of his men — he seemed to have a full dozen at his call — and Geraldi was thoroughly searched. They took out from his clothes two revolvers, a little pistol that hung by a horsehair lariat, finely made, from around his neck, and finally, along with his wallet, smoking tobacco, and other small odds and ends, what seemed like a very thick knife.

The marshal picked it up, worked over it an instant, and the seemingly single knife dissolved into six leaves, each a small knife in itself. Tex Arnold took these by the handles and fanned them out on the table like a hand of cards. Then he picked one up and weighed it in his hand. "I've heard of 'em, Jimmy," he said. "But this is the first time that I've seen 'em." He shook his head. "I see they're weighted in the handles," he went on, "and that they're as sharp as needles. But still, it's hard to believe what Tom Rawlins told me."

"What did he tell you?" asked Geraldi.

"That you could hit a bull's eye no bigger than a silver dollar at ten paces with one of these knives, and do it nine times out of ten."

Geraldi smiled and shook his head in turn. "Did you believe that, Tex?" he asked.

"It's pretty easy to believe strange things about you, son," said the marshal. "But that went down hard, I admit."

"It's wrong as can be," Geraldi said frankly. "I couldn't hit a mark like that more than once in three times."

"The devil!" said the marshal. "Could you do it that often?"

"Set my hands free, and I'll show you," said Geraldi. There was a glint of amusement in his eyes, and he did not seem to mind when the marshal laughed.

"We'll keep your hands safe," he said. "Never mind your magic, Jimmy."

Someone returned with a report that a train would be leaving the town within a half hour. The marshal nodded with satisfaction. "That gives us a chance for coffee all around, and a little chat with you, Jimmy," he said. "Will you talk to me?"

"Why not?" said Geraldi.

"Why did you do it for Burns?" asked the marshal.

Geraldi shrugged his shoulders.

"He never was any great friend of yours," said Arnold. "And I don't suppose that he ever did you any great favors?"

"No," said Geraldi.

"That's why a good many men had sworn by you," said Arnold. "Because you're a white man to the core. It's a grand thing that you did for Burns. But it puts you in bad with the law. You know that?"

"I don't know what you mean," said Geraldi.

"You don't know that you led the posse off the trail of Burns to save his neck? Or that you rode across that tree bridge . . . a devil of a thing to do! . . . to save Burns's hide?"

"What's all this about?" asked Geraldi.

"Oh, you don't know, of course," said the marshal. "We didn't find Burns's horse, just after you'd changed horses? We didn't *see* you change? That kid in the tree didn't recognize you? No, I guess that was all a dream."

"I'm no dream interpreter," confessed Geraldi. "I don't know anything about that stuff, so don't ask me. I wanted to go for a ride, and I took the first handy horse. That's all. I tried the tree bridge, because it looked like a game to me. Then I borrowed one of Grogan's nags because the one I was on looked dead beat."

The marshal looked him in the eye. "You expect me to believe that?" he asked.

"No," said Geraldi. "It's not a very good story, but it's the best that I can rig up."

"It won't do, Jimmy," said Arnold. "They'll send you up for a long stretch for this business."

Geraldi nodded. But, for a moment, his face lost color, and his eyes were glassy with fear. He mastered himself at once, but the marshal had had a chance to glimpse more than enough. Fear was not what one expected to see in that handsome face. Fear, many a man had said, never had been shown by James Geraldi.

Yet the marshal understood. The bravest of the brave have ever some weak spot; that of Geraldi's was, no doubt, an overmastering dread of the prison bars.

"I'm mighty sorry for what I have to do," said Arnold. "I know that you'd given up the old life.

92

I know that you were living straight and that all of the old scores had been straightened out. But I have my duty straight before me."

Geraldi looked back at him, and the straight look of Geraldi was hard for any man to endure.

"You're not sorry, Tex," he said. "It's the greatest day of your life."

"You're wrong, Jimmy," said the marshal hastily. "But you see. . . ."

"I see what you see," said Geraldi. "Headlines two inches high . . . telling the world that Marshal Tex Arnold has caught Jimmy Geraldi and brought him to jail. It's the greatest day in your life, Tex. Be honest, and say I'm right."

The marshal flushed. To the core, he was an honest man. "Maybe you're right, Jimmy," he said.

"You're inside the law," said Geraldi, "but you know that you're working outside of it. You're arresting me for horse stealing. Yet you know pretty well that I'm not the man to steal a mustang. If the law was what you loved so well, you never would have branched off after me. You would have stuck to Burns's trail."

The marshal braced back his shoulders. "I'm not here to take a curtain lecture from you, Geraldi," he said.

"You'll take more than words from me, before I'm through with you," said Geraldi. "You haven't landed me in jail yet, and you're not going to. I may die quick, but I won't die in jail. Smoke that idea. It's worth tasting. If I get free from you and live, I'm going to make your life a little hell on earth . . . I'm going to let the world have a chance to laugh at you."

The marshal grew redder than before. His eyes flashed. "That's a sort of challenge, Geraldi!" he exclaimed.

"It's exactly that," said Geraldi. "You have me here with my hands tied. You have your guns in front of me and behind me. In spite of all that, I'm going to step away from you, Arnold. Then you can curse the day that you ever got ambitious and took up my trail!"

Chapter Twelve

UPSET

The marshal was outraged. He felt that he had given to his prisoner the best treatment and the greatest courtesy. In exchange, he was receiving threats, and his blood suddenly boiled. "If that's the way you look at it, Geraldi," he said, "we'll treat you the way you ought to be treated. Wendell, put that double pair of irons on his legs!"

The double irons were duly produced from a knapsack, and the two pairs of cuffs were fitted over the ankles of Geraldi. A very neat fit they were, too, very much as though they had been built to this order. The marshal regarded them with much satisfaction.

"They're not ordinary things, Jimmy," he said to Geraldi. "The best locksmith in Sheffield has been working for ten years to turn out a lock that no pick can handle. And here's the result. You'll never get that off, Jimmy."

"A little time," said Geraldi. "A little time and patience, Tex, and you'll see what'll happen. Remember that we have a good long train journey ahead of us."

"D'you think that we'll sleep on the way?" said the marshal. "No, no, Jimmy. No matter how strong this lock is, I'll never trust to locks alone to handle you. Now, if you don't mind, we'll start for the station." He shouted to one of his armed men at the nearest window. "Doc, get that buckboard from across the street! We can't expect Geraldi to walk very far in irons like these!"

In fact, as Geraldi got to his feet from his chair, it was seen that he could step only a few inches at a time.

"Give me a hand, one of you men," Geraldi said cheerfully to his guards. "The first thing I know, I'll trip and fall on my head."

One of them put an arm through Geraldi's in order to steady him, and so they started for the door that opened onto the street.

As they went, Bob, Jerry, and Pete, at their separate tables, looked earnestly at the procession, at the guns, at the slender fellow who was shackled and surrounded by guards. Bob turned his head, and, from the corner of his mouth, he whispered toward Jerry: "Where's his magic now?"

"The dance ain't over till you've paid the musicians," said Jerry. "You hang on tight, and maybe we'll see something."

It was the table of Pete of the red hair, however, that stood nearest to the door, and he, instead of staring at Geraldi's face, looked down at his feet, where the chains were dragging on the boards of the floor. In all his life, he never had seen a man whose chances looked so infinitely small as did the chances of Geraldi in this situation. But he had seen, as he thought, miracles performed by this man; and with his heart in his throat, he waited for another miracle now.

Geraldi, as he came closer to the door, said to the marshal, turning his head over his shoulder: "You haven't laid a bet against me, Tex."

"I'll lay you a thousand to five hundred that I land you in jail," said the marshal, raising his voice so that other men could hear. "After that, steel bars ought to hold you, Geraldi."

"I'll take that bet," said Geraldi. "Confound it. . . ." For, as he spoke, his feet tripped upon the short chain, and he went down as though he had been clubbed over the head. He hooked his arm harder than ever into the arm of his guard who was assisting him, and the suddenness of the fall knocked the man off his feet at once. Such was the impetus of the fall, that the two rolled over and over — or was it that Geraldi was subtly twisting his body on the floor? At any rate, they crashed against the legs of that table at which sat flame-headed Pete.

At that moment there were arranged before Pete a big soup dish half filled with greasy, thin soup, a platter scattered with the remnants of ham and half a dozen eggs, a stand holding vinegar and oil, a butter pat of liberal size, a bread plate, and a large cup filled with hot coffee, newly from the pitcher of the waitress.

When the impact came against the table of Pete, it knocked the thing over, and into the face of Pete, like a swarm of hornets, flew the dishes and food that had covered the table. The platter missed his eye by a hair's breadth; the vinegar cruet smote him fairly between the eyes with a force which only a prize fighter could have withstood; and, in addition, the scalding contents of the cup of coffee spilled over the broad breast of Pete and ran like liquid fire down his chest.

This was not all. For Wendell, the guard who was walking exactly behind the prisoner, excited by the sudden fall of the man, hesitated one split fraction of a second, and then fired — not at the two who rolled on the floor, but straight into the space where Geraldi had been standing. The result of this foolish act was that the slug came nowhere near to Geraldi, but the hornet's song of the bullet darted past the ear of Pete.

He was already prepared and aching for action. Not that he saw any way in which Geraldi could be delivered, but simply because he loved battle with a blind and a brutal love. Now, as this confusion and multiplicity of disasters came upon him, he let out a roar like a bull, and shouting — "Help! Murder! Murder! Don't shoot!" — he sprang across the toppling table and smote Mr. Wendell upon the side of the jaw.

It was a long time since Pete had stood up in a prize ring. He had lost a vast deal of the alertness and the speed that once had been his. But in a rough and tumble, where there is time to measure one's man thoroughly, the weight of his punch was greater than ever. It took Wendell off his feet and knocked him spinning sideways, straight across the knees of the marshal.

At that moment, Marshal Tex Arnold made a glorious picture of a real Western fighting man. His long, pale hair was flying back from his head as he sprang into action. His eyes blazed. A wordless cry, a battle shout, was parting his lips and straining his throat, and into his hands two fine new Colt revolvers had flashed. It was not an empty gesture, when he drew two guns. Others might be able to manage only one at a time, but the marshal, when time served, spent two patient hours a day manipulating the pair. He had acquired a great measure of ambidextrous skill, and the pair might mean two separate deaths to two enemies in the same instant.

But, just as he leaped to meet the danger, across his knees fell the weight of Wendell. There was nothing to be done about it. Even a trained football player could not have stood up against the shock, and the marshal, a sparely built fellow, went down like a tree, and rolled as he hit the floor so that one gun spun into a far corner of the room and the other, flying through the air, descended upon the top of the stove with such a shock that it exploded and sent a bullet straight up through the ceiling and through the roof above.

These were the things that happened in the first half second after Geraldi struck the floor.

But he himself was not idle. He cursed the guard who had fallen with him — jerked down in the tumble. He asked for help to be lifted to his feet, and, at the same time, his hands and wrists were busy inside of the ropes. As snakes writhe, so they writhed. It was cruel, bruising work, but it was an art that Geraldi understood. There seemed to be oil on his flesh. And the strong, well-hardened ropes seemed to be no better than stout elastic bands, for the hands of Geraldi were suddenly free.

Instantly he doubled up, as though he had been kicked in the stomach, and, so doubling, his hands were brought down to the lock that held upon his ankles the double irons. His fingers were not empty. They had touched the lapel of his coat and now, between thumb and forefinger, was a narrow, strong piece of steel, hardly larger than a needle. It entered the hole of the lock. It worked delicately but with lightning speed, and suddenly the irons fell from the ankles of Geraldi, while he still twisted and shouted for help.

So twisting, it seemed by accident that his feet came just under the jaw of the fellow who had tumbled to the floor with him. When his feet had that resting place, perhaps it was sheer instinct that made him kick out with all his might. The thrust almost broke the neck of the other, and sent him rolling straight under the feet of three more of the posse who had rushed into the room through the front door. Others were coming from the kitchen entrance.

"Help! Help!" shouted Bob, his eyes no longer dull, but red-stained with excitement, and, leaping from his table, the thrust of his legs, in rising, cast the table fairly in front of this fresh detachment.

Geraldi was under the tangle of the tables by this time, and through the mess of overturned chairs. He made straight for a window. Through that window another of the posse men was scrambling at that moment, holding out his rifle before him.

Geraldi sprang to his feet.

"Murder!" shouted Jerry. "Murder! Help!" A revolver flashed in his hand.

Geraldi snatched the gun away, and, as the posse man lurched in through the window and fell on hands and knees upon the floor, Geraldi dived through the window, headfirst.

It was enough to have broken the neck of another man. But he landed lightly enough on his hands, twisted sideways to his feet, picked up the revolver that he had dropped from the window ledge, and darted around to the back of the hotel. He knew what to expect there, and he found it. Half a dozen horses were tethered to a small hitching rack. As he ran, he judged them. The broad quarters of one promised weight-carrying worth. The deep bottom and the fine legs of another offered the ability to lope all day long, like a wolf on the blood trail. But there was one long, tall, spindling gelding with narrow shoulders, sloping hips, and legs that looked like hammered iron. This should be a sprinter, and a sprinter was what Geraldi wanted.

He was in that saddle with a single bound, loosed the knot of the lead rope with one touch of his fingers, and, wheeling the horse about, he drove it straight across country to the rear of the hotel, and dodged behind the barn.

The uproar from the hotel, at the same moment, emerged into the open air, and a great clamoring poured after the fugitive. But Geraldi was safely away.

Chapter Thirteen
POST MORTEM

They hunted Geraldi into the dusk of the day, but their hearts were not in it. Perhaps they would have done better, but the marshal himself had a wrenched hip and a bruised side from his heavy fall during the fracas at the hotel, and he could not sit the saddle with his usual iron endurance.

Therefore, they came back to Neering with empty hands. Their hearts were aching more than their bodies, however. For they had had fame in their grasp. There would have been enough glory for all of them, if they really could have landed Geraldi behind bars — enough glory to have crowned each of them with honor. What man would not have been proud to say: "Geraldi? Yes, I was there, when he was taken."

A man could have said that casually, and a whole room filled with men would sit up to listen. No bunkhouse obscurity ever could overwhelm such a hero with darkness.

But the prize was gone, and the hearts of the posse were empty as they returned to the hotel at Neering. The marshal made a little speech to them. As they sat in the dining room — now and then looking up toward the little half-inch hole that had been drilled in the wooden ceiling by Arnold's gun — as they sat there waiting for supper to be served to them, Tex Arnold said: "He's beaten me again. He's made a fool of me, the way he promised that he'd do. But we're going to make a fresh start. He's not very far away. I have reasons for thinking so. If you men stay on, I add two dollars a day to your pay. Don't answer me now. Think it over, and tell me in the morning. Wendell, you come up to my room with me, and we'll have something brought up. I want to talk to you."

For Wendell was his right-hand man. He was a plain cowpuncher, leathery hard, brown as a tanned hide, quiet, unassuming, but a fighting man of the first quality, and without fear. He had only become confused once in his life, and that was on this day, when he fired the bullet not at the twisting pair on the floor, but straight ahead, past the ear of the tramp, Pete. Since that mistake, a small spot of red had been waxing and waning in the cheek of Wendell all the day long.

He went up with the marshal to his room. The marshal began to stride up and down restlessly. Wendell stood stiffly in a corner.

"Sit down," urged Tex Arnold.

"I've done enough sitting," said Wendell harshly.

"Don't be hard on yourself," advised Arnold. "I'm as sick about it as the next one of you. I'm a good deal sicker, in fact. But it's not the first time that Geraldi has walked safely through trouble without a scratch."

"I was ticked off to keep a gun on him," said Wendell bitterly. "I was right there behind him. It was me that had the only good chance to put a slug through him!" His face twisted with pain and with shame at the recollection.

"Be easy on that," said the marshal, who was a man of some heart. "Sit down there. We'll have some food up here in a minute. Here it comes now."

It was Molly who brought it. Her look was downward toward the tray she carried — perhaps because of the great weight of the heavy crockery. She laid out the things on the plain pine table in the center of the room, put the lamp in the midst, and still her look was downward to the floor as she went toward the door. There, however, she lingered for a moment, with her red hand working the knob back and forth.

"Mister Arnold," she said, "is it true that he got clean off?"

"He's gone," said the marshal shortly.

"Without no scratch on him?" gasped Molly.

"Is he a friend of yours?" queried the marshal sternly.

Her head went back. Her eyes rose to the ceiling. "Ah, but wouldn't I want him to be?" she said. "Ah, but wouldn't I want him?" She fled from the room, crimson with excitement.

"There's women for you," observed Wendell bitterly. "They're always for the crooks. Always for the crooks that win."

"Not the women only," said the marshal. "What about everyone else? Every man is for the criminal. Because the crook plays a lone hand usually, one against a thousand. When you get a handsome, romantic fellow like Geraldi, of course, he's going to make excitement wherever he goes. He has more friends, Wendell, than any man in the West. He has them of all kinds . . . greasers on the border . . . Spanish gentlemen, too . . . respectable ranch men, miners, stray prospectors, wise old sheepherders, and all sorts of ordinary 'punchers on the range."

"What gets him all his friends?" asked Wendell.

"Because he takes his money from thugs, not from honest men," said the marshal. "He's a frigate bird. He's not a common hawk."

"What's a frigate bird?" demanded Wendell, slowly massaging the sore place on the side of his jaw where the fist of red-headed Pete had gone home.

"A frigate bird," said the marshal, "is the fastest thing that flies."

"Geraldi's fast," admitted Wendell.

"A frigate bird," continued the other, "is all wings and beak and talons."

"That's Geraldi," nodded Wendell.

"A frigate bird," continued the marshal, "lives on fish, but not on fish of its own catching. It stands in the middle of the sky and waits till a fishhawk has caught something worth having. Then down it comes out of the air, makes the hawk drop the prize, scoots on down, and snatches the fish before it hits the water."

"By Jiminy," muttered Wendell, "that would be worth seeing."

"And that's Geraldi. Robbing the honest men never was his line," said the marshal. "Not that he cared about their honesty, I suppose. But because it wasn't exciting enough. If he gambled, he gambled with sharks, and beat them at their own game, and, if he pulled a gun, it was on a gunman. If he stuck up a man with a fat wallet, you could be pretty sure that the wallet was lined with stolen cash. You know the story of Bill Keenan's money?"

"No, I don't know that," said Wendell.

"Bill Keenan," said the marshal, "was a fellow who piled up a fortune running drugs and dope and chinks across the border from Mexico. He always had to have a lot of cash on hand in case a big deal came through, so, in one of the largest banks in El Paso, he kept a cash box with never less than fifty thousand in it. Now, this fellow Keenan asked a favor of Geraldi, and Geraldi obliged. A pair of Keenan's own thugs had run away and taken ten thousand dollars' worth of dope with them. So Geraldi consented to try their trail. He found them, too. One of those greasers was never heard of again. Geraldi brought the other back, and the dope with him. But then Keenan, like a fool, decided to be economical, and he paid Geraldi only a thousand for the job."

"The crook!" said Wendell, heated by this tale, and the obvious injustice of it.

"That's what Geraldi thought," said Tex Arnold. "Besides, he said that he had hated to get his hands dirty with dope. He wanted to clean them. He cleaned them on Bill Keenan, you can be sure. He broke up Keenan's whole gang and business and cleaned him out of everything. But there was still that nest egg laid away in the cash box in the safe at El Paso.

"Well, one morning the cashier finds that the safe has been opened . . . the combination has been worked, and the door locked again. When the safe is opened for that day's business, he finds that a robber has been there, and the only cash box the crook has touched is the box that holds Keenan's fifty thousand."

"Geraldi did it?" asked Wendell.

"What other crook," asked the marshal, "would have stopped with the taking of a single cash box? There was a whole big fortune under his hand, if he'd wanted it."

Wendell gasped. "He beats me!" he said.

"He beats everybody," replied the marshal. "Still I've a hope that he won't beat me on this job."

"You're going to keep chasing after him?" asked Wendell curiously, and without hope.

"Until I've worn the skin off my soul," said Tex Arnold.

"Have you still got a hope?"

"I've got this hope, and I'll tell you about it.

Geraldi's home is broken up. The woman he was going to marry . . . the only girl he's ever cared about . . . has skipped out. And I know he's after her, and that it's her trail that has brought him to Neering. Now, then, he's a matchless scoundrel on a trail. But, after all, he has only one horse, one pair of feet, one pair of eyes. I can use twenty men to scour this country. I'll find the girl before he gets to her."

"What good is that?" asked Wendell.

"What good?" asked the marshal, with a grim ring in his voice. "It's this much good. It means that I have a constant trap for him, and bait in that trap that he can't keep away from. If we can find the girl, all we need to do is to sit down and wait. Sooner or later, Geraldi will come for her . . . and then he's our man for once and for all."

"Aye," said Wendell. "You may put the irons on him again, but what good are irons on Geraldi? You've seen what he does to them. What jail could hold him? What prison, even, could keep him inside?"

The marshal was silent for some time. Then he said abruptly: "We don't need irons on a dead man, Wendell."

The latter started, gaped, and then was still. He sat back in his chair, and a quiet fire burned in his eyes. He nodded. "He's gone and broke the law," said Wendell. "Now the law'll break him."

"By the way," said the marshal, "I've stowed

the three hobos in the town jail. They were working for Geraldi, I think."

"Them three?" said Wendell. "They're too low for him."

"A real artist can work with cheap material," said the marshal. "Let's eat before the food is cold. The three of them raved and raged. But they've got the marks of jailbirds on them. If I can't hold them on this day's business, I'll hold them on their records, as soon as I can look them up. We've bagged something, after all, in taking the three of 'em."

But Wendell shook his head gloomily. "What good are three sparrows," he said, "when you're out hunting for an eagle, Arnold?"

To this the marshal found no adequate reply.

Chapter Fourteen

A BET PAID OFF

All men of vigorous mind are endowed, above all, with hope. Marshal Tex Arnold was no exception to that rule. He had failed dismally on this day to secure a prisoner already in his hands. In the place of fame, he had secured merely a rebuff which would make of him a laughingstock in many quarters. He would be known as another of those officers of the law who had been good enough to capture many a lesser criminal, but who could do nothing at all with the famous Geraldi.

Yet, instead of sitting down to mourn, his mind was already busy with future plans. He ate his supper with his eye upon the future. As soon as the meal had ended, he brought out a detailed map of the country around Neering. On this map, every trail, no matter how minute, how old, how disused, how dim with time and neglect, was pricked down.

Then, in consultation with Wendell, he proceeded to split up the territory and divide the trails. To the most stupid, he assigned the most apparent roads. To the most intelligent, he gave the faintest trails. The most difficult of all, he assigned to himself, and the next in hardness went to Wendell.

The latter appreciated the assignment. "But," he said, "suppose that Geraldi has got to the place ahead of us."

"If he does," said the marshal, "perhaps the girl won't go away with him. He can coerce men with tricks and with guns, but he can't handle a woman in the same manner. She's run away from him. Perhaps she won't go back. Not, at least, until we've had a chance to locate them for ourselves, and close in on them. The next time that we sight Geraldi, there won't be any talk. We'll start shooting, and shooting to kill."

Wendell moistened his lips. "What will the law say to that?" he asked.

"The law," said the marshal, "knows that a man who can fade through handcuffs has to be held with lead. That's all there is to that."

Wendell considered a moment. "I suppose that you're right," he said at last. "It looks like a pretty rotten business to me, though. He's stolen a hoss. Why should we have to up and plug him?"

"Because it's the only way to get him," said the marshal. "And the law has to be obeyed. It's not for Geraldi himself that we're working, only. We're working to head off the fool ideas that may pop into the heads of a thousand wild youngsters, if they should hear of such yarns as this one . . . how Geraldi slipped through the hands of twenty men, even when his hands were tied behind him, and there were double irons on his legs. That's the sort of a thing that makes the law despised. That's the sort of a thing that puts thousands of crooks on the roads. We've done a lot of harm today, Wendell, and tomorrow we're going to undo it. We're going to start the combination that will catch Geraldi! I know it. I feel it in my bones!"

As the enthusiasm of the marshal grew, fanned by conversation, he really felt what he spoke. Some of the flame entered into Wendell. "If we get him . . . ," said Wendell.

"If we get him, you're a made man," said the marshal, with truth in his voice. "You could run for sheriff in your home county, and no one could beat you. You'd be able to laugh at the record of the best man-catcher on your range, if you could say that you'd helped in the catching of Geraldi."

The nostrils of Wendell flared out suddenly. He stood up. "Is there anything more, chief?" he asked.

"That's all. You go and take a good sleep."

"I'll go and sleep, if I can," said Wendell. "But I'll be dreaming about Geraldi."

"So will I," said the marshal.

He waved good night to his lieutenant. He even walked a few paces after him toward the door of the room, and he nodded as the door closed behind him. Then he turned back, saying slowly to himself: "I'll dream of Geraldi. There's no doubt of that."

"You won't have to, Tex," said a voice.

He started back. Seated in the chair between the two windows was Geraldi, now, as usual, filling up an idle moment in the manufacture of a cigarette. Yes, Geraldi himself was there!

Where had he been when the conversation was progressing? How much had he heard of it? Had he overheard all of the plans of Arnold? Or had he simply come in at the last moment — and how had he managed it? Through one of the windows. There could be no other way.

The marshal remembered the dizzy fall from those windows to the ground, down a sheer wall of boards. But there was a saying, oftentimes repeated, that Geraldi could climb wherever a cat could climb. This instance seemed the proof. There was another side to the situation. Geraldi sat there with both hands employed in the making of a cigarette. There was the marshal before him, both hands free to go for a gun. Yet the marshal did not reach for his. He knew, at the first insignificant gesture he made, those magic hands of Geraldi would flicker a gun out into the open from beneath his coat — and Geraldi, at such a range, never had to shoot twice.

The marshal was a brave man. Few braver ever had worn his honorable badge of office. Few had proved their courage more often. But now he hesitated, and with the hesitation came a greater opportunity for thought.

He was, of course, an expert marksman. He

spent his due quota of time in practice with his weapons. But not for an instant did he dream that he was a match for James Geraldi, Esquire. So he made no move and allowed his hands to hang quietly at his side.

"You won't have to dream about me, Tex," repeated Geraldi. "Because here, you see, you have a chance to see me without dreaming." He looked up to the marshal and smiled a little.

The marshal did not like that smile. He hated the innocence of it, and the calm of the eyes behind it.

"Jimmy," he said, "you're the bravest man in the world. I could stamp on the floor and fill this room full of armed men."

"Tex," replied the other, "you're the wisest man in the world, because you won't stamp. Am I right?"

"You're right," said the marshal. "You're a faster and a straighter man with a gun than I am. There's no glory in being shot to death, unless it serves a good cause. If you murder me, the law gains nothing. Neither do I. Neither do you."

"I knew you'd be reasonable," said Geraldi. "That's why you're such a success, old fellow. Brains, Tex. Brains!" He nodded. His enthusiasm seemed perfectly warm and real.

"Thanks," said Tex Arnold. He waited.

"You want to know what brought me in through the window, I suppose," suggested Geraldi.

"Well, I can wait to learn," said the other.

"Why should you wait?" said Geraldi. "I know that it's close to your bedtime. I know that you'll have a busy day tomorrow, hunting up my trail. . . ." His eyes flashed as he said this.

Still, the marshal sighed a little with relief. For this proved that Geraldi had not overheard the earlier part of the conversation between Arnold and Wendell. Otherwise, he would have known that it was the trail of the girl, and not his own, that Arnold intended to pursue.

Geraldi, having finished the making of his cigarette, brought out a match and lighted it. For the lighting, he leaned a little from his chair. The match was held in his left hand. The right was free, lying gently on his thigh. Arnold knew the meaning. Tensed like a hair-trigger, Geraldi was ready for the first move in a gun play. Still he was disappointed. The courage of the marshal was not of the outrageous sort.

"Go on," said Arnold. "What's your news, Jimmy?"

"News that you know already," said Geraldi. "News that you've lost a bet."

"What bet?" asked the other, amazed.

"The bet of a thousand against five hundred that you'd put me in jail," said Geraldi. "It seemed easy odds, then. You had my hands and feet tied. You had your armed men all around me. But still . . . you've lost the bet, it appears?"

The marshal cleared his throat. He was a careful man in money affairs. It was true that he had a good salary, and that he enjoyed a good

116

many bonuses during the course of a year. But a thousand dollars was not to be idly spent.

"I'll have you in jail, Jimmy," he said, "before the year is out. As for the bet. . . ." He stopped short. He could not follow the glancing swiftness of Geraldi's hand, but he could appreciate the fact that a revolver was now lying in it, the muzzle carelessly pointed in his direction. Yes, fairly covering his heart.

"You know, Tex," said the other, "that the best way to end an argument is to clinch it with nails. What do you think of this for a nail?" He smiled at the marshal again.

Tex Arnold was a man of sense. He looked at the gun, and he looked into the hard, bright eye of Geraldi. Then he nodded. "I guess that's the nail that ends this and seals the box," he said. He added: "I have to reach inside my pocket to get at my wallet, Jimmy."

"Don't bother," said Geraldi. "Don't trouble about that. Just make the move very slowly. Nothing but a fast move will be telegraphed to my trigger finger. Take it easy. Move it slow. That's all, old son. I'm watching all the time."

He spoke soothingly, and the marshal did exactly what he was bid. The motion of his hand was no faster than the movement of an automaton. Slowly he drew forth the wallet and laid it on the table. Slowly he opened it and took out a thick sheaf of bills. Part of it was his own money. Part of it was government financing. Out of the sheaf he carefully plucked forth ten bills of a hundred dollars each. There remained three or four times as much in the stack that was left, and from it Arnold looked curiously toward Geraldi.

"No, no, Tex," said the latter, smiling, as he left his chair and picked up the thousand dollars of the bet. "A fair bet, but no robbery. Your cash, but no government cash for me, old son."

He stuffed the bills carelessly into his outer coat pocket. He made a gesture with the revolver, and it disappeared — just where it went the marshal's practiced eye could not be sure.

Geraldi walked to the door. "And so, good night, Tex," he said.

"Until we meet again," said the marshal.

Each smiled at the other. Then Geraldi glided through the door, and was gone.

Chapter Fifteen

THE GANG

Once Geraldi was outside the door, the marshal did his best. He plunged into the hall with his two revolvers in readiness. He rushed to the head of the stairs, rousing the hotel with his shouts as he ran. From the head of the stairs he saw a lithe form darting across the landing one story down.

He fired. He could almost have sworn that he had sent a bullet ripping through the leg of Geraldi, yet he was not quite sure. It encouraged him, at least, to go hurtling down the stairs in pursuit, but he had no further glimpse of Geraldi.

As the others of his posse crew came tumbling from their rooms, the marshal reached the front door of the house, wrenched at the knob of it, and found it locked. At the same time, a scamper of hoofbeats fled down the street.

Tex Arnold had taken a good many rebuffs from Geraldi before this, but this one almost raised his temperature to the bursting point. He damned the hotel, the door, the lock that held it, and the scoundrel who had just manipulated it from the outside as he fled through.

But the marshal pursued no farther. He only examined the hallway and the stairs carefully to make sure that no blood appeared upon the matting. When he became aware that not a splash of red was showing and that Geraldi must have escaped unwounded, Tex Arnold gave up his latest hope.

He ordered his men back to their beds. He told them that they might as well try to catch the devil in his native hell as to attempt to catch Geraldi after a flying start by night.

No one argued. It was a tired crew of manhunters that turned back into the bunks at the Neering hotel, and so Geraldi cantered his horse down the street, undisturbed.

He went straight to the jail. It was the only new building, the only strong one in Neering, and the only one that was built of stone. It was made like a turret almost, being somewhat rounded at the corners, and with one small window set into each side of it, like a single eye in the forehead of a monster. It was one story, compact, and powerful. The walls were three feet thick, and they had been built by Mexican masons, than whom the world can offer no better workmen. Inside this wall there was a single block of cells, composed of the finest tool-proof steel, the bars placed close together, yet at a sufficient distance so that a single guard could look into all the cells at once.

The town of Neering did not put all its faith in padlocks or locks of any other kind. It simply trusted to the watchful eye of a guard. Two men handled the jail. They worked the matter exactly as sailors manage the same thing at sea, in four-hour watches. Since the new jail was built, Neering never had lost a prisoner. It had cost the county a good deal of money to build that jail, but the ranch men had gladly raised the sum. It was a sort of insurance against cattle rustling and horse stealing. Since the jail was built, crime had fallen away to the smallest proportions. Still, one or two prisoners were generally in the jail, awaiting trial or serving short sentences. There were four, all told, in the little building on this night. Geraldi dismounted, threw the reins of his "borrowed" mustang, and walked up the four steps that led to the front door. On this he beat loudly with his hand.

"Hello?" called the wakeful guard within.

"Hurry up and open," said Geraldi.

"Open for what?" asked the guard.

"Open for Geraldi!" said the latter.

"Great Scott!" cried the jailer. "Have you really got Geraldi out there?"

"Geraldi's here, all right," he said.

"This'll put Neering on the map!" exclaimed the jailer, and instantly he thrust back the bolts with a great clanking and turned the key, then leaned hard against the massive door and thrust it open. He stumbled out, lantern in hand, straight against the muzzle of Geraldi's Colt. He was no fool, that guard. He looked straight into the face of Geraldi and knew his man, so he simply hoisted the lantern and backed into the jail again. Geraldi followed.

In the distances of the cell room, half lost behind the bars, like objects dimly seen through a heavy downpour, he could see men rising from their bunks. There was a glint of the lantern light upon red hair. That was Pete, no doubt.

Geraldi took the jailer to the nearest cell, which was vacant, opened the door of the cell with his picklock, thrust the guard inside, and locked the door upon him again. He already had fanned the man and taken from him his pair of Colts.

"I'm sorry for you," said Geraldi.

The jailer sat down on the bunk in the cell and shrugged his shoulders. "You don't have to be sorry for me," he said. "You know how it is. I'd be a joke and a laughingstock if anybody else had made such a fool out of me. But so long as you're Geraldi, it doesn't make any difference."

Geraldi quickly turned toward the cells.

He heard Pete saying: "Here he comes, fellas. I told you that he'd come. He's a white man. Jimmy, how's things?"

Geraldi freed him first of all. He turned loose the other two, as well. The fourth occupant of the jail now shook at the bars of his cell, rattling the lock of the door.

"Hurry up!" he gasped. "It's my turn. I seen you, Geraldi. Let me get out of here!" He was a tall, yellow-faced man, a little stooped in the shoulders.

Geraldi came closer. "What are you in for, brother?" he asked.

"Me? Oh, for nothing much. They just framed me and slammed me in," said the other. "They got nothing much on me. Here, Geraldi. Gimme a touch of your hands on this door, and turn me loose, will you?"

Geraldi peered more closely still. He saw that the tall man was not shaking the door purposely, but his whole body was shuddering nervously from head to foot. His great, white, long-fingered hands were locked frantically about the bars of the door. His mouth twitched, and his eyes blinked in the ecstasy of impatience.

"Hello, partner," said Geraldi over his shoulder to the jailer. "What's this fellow in for?"

"Aw, he's just waitin' for his trial," said the guard. "They got him red-handed, when he was runnin' a coupla cans of opium up the country."

"Opium?" said Geraldi.

"Two dinky little cans," muttered the prisoner. "But they'll soak me. What difference does it make? The dopes have gotta have their stuff, don't they, or they'll go crazy? There's a thousand gents runnin' the dope in. You know that."

"I know it," said Geraldi, "and I wish that the whole thousand were piled in here with you, and then the whole jail sunk, like a cageful of rats, in a trough." He turned on his heel. "Come on, fellas," he said to his three tramps.

"Wait!" wailed the opium-runner. "Geraldi! It ain't impossible. You ain't gonna turn me down

123

and not give me my chance. Is it possible?"

"I wouldn't give you a hand," Geraldi said over his shoulder, "if it meant simply to help you out of a mud puddle. Fellows like you are the inside lining of hell, stranger. And that's where you belong, and that's where you're going." He walked on.

"Geraldi, you've got a lot of sense," said the jailer. "That one is a rat . . . just a rat!"

A shout of terror and rage came from the abandoned smuggler. Bob snatched a gun from Geraldi and whirled.

"Shut yer face," he said through his teeth. "Shut yer face or I'll croak you, by God. I been wantin' to, all day long. I been wantin' to get my claws on your dirty throat and twist it for you. Shut yer face. If you make another noise, I'll come back and kill you, if I have to hang for it afterward!"

The noise of the tall man ended abruptly, and through the door went the trio, with Geraldi bringing up their rear.

Instantly, from within the jail, there began a double clamor. One voice was that of the jailer, now true to his job and yelling for help. The other voice was the fiendish shrieking of the dope-runner, as he realized that he was definitely left behind.

Geraldi herded his men straight across the main street and down the mouth of the next lane, leading his horse behind him. They could hear, as they went, windows being wrenched up with a groan, and the slamming of doors, as Neering was roused by the uproar from the jail. But Geraldi cared little for that. In a moment they were on the verge of the town, well screened around by tall shrubbery, and here Geraldi paused.

"It was the neatest thing that I ever seen," said Bob. His voice trembled with delight and with excitement. "I never seen it better done. I never heard of a better thing done. 'Here's Geraldi,' says you, and the fool opens up the door . . . and Geraldi walks in, all right. Sure Geraldi walks in. You never told him no lie, I guess."

All of the trio laughed. They were rubbing their hands as though to warm them, there was such a chilly thrust of pleasure in the memory of how they had been delivered from that formidable little jail. Geraldi stopped this outpouring of congratulations, saying: "Here's three hundred dollars for each of you. Two hundred is pay for what you've done for me. The other hundred is to buy a horse. You go straight on up this road, and you'll come to a small house. Wake up the owner. He lives all by himself, and he has horses . . . good, tough mustangs. He'll sell to you for a hundred dollars apiece, and ask no questions. Then get saddles and bridles from him. He has a lot of cheap, old, second-hand junk, but the saddles will do for you. Then, tomorrow, I want you to line out on the road and do some trailing for me. I'll tell you where to hunt and what for, later on. But I want to know first, if the three of you want to work for me still. If you don't, take your money and slide out. There'll be no hard feelings on my part."

Bob answered first: "If either of 'em tries to sneak out on you, Geraldi, I'll sap him over the head. That's all that I'll do. But neither of 'em will. They're both with you, and they're for you, just the same as I am. Geraldi, you couldn't pull us away from you. Not with a crowbar. We're your gang!"

Chapter Sixteen

THE LEAN-TO

When the marshal laid out the plan according to which his men were to comb the countryside, he had assigned to Wendell the most difficult task of all, and that was to wander by broken trails, or by none at all, over the rough country that lay high up, close to timberline. But he knew that Wendell was the most patient of trailers; in fact, Wendell rode for two days, steadily, searching as though he were hunting not for a woman, but for a small jewel that might be concealed in any crevice of the rocks.

It was a raw, bleak day, the second of his traveling, with a wind that cut down from the snowcaps above and worried Wendell's lean body to the bone. His cheeks turned blue. His nose was as red as a torch, and his eyes were bloodshot by the cutting of the breeze. But it never occurred to Wendell to turn back, or even to shorten his ride on this bitter day.

He was now traveling on the very verge of the timberline. Far below him, the dark pine forest was drawn like a robe over the knees of the mountains, but where he journeyed, the trees pinched out, and he saw deformed willows and other hardy growers that staggered and stumbled along the ground, dwarfed by the cold and tormented out of shape by the prevailing wind.

To Wendell it seemed that the world was filled with human beings just as deformed as the trees past which he was riding. There was Geraldi, for instance, who, by his magic, walked through walls of steel — who could charm dragons and make them his friends, if he chose. Instead, he had thrown everything away in order to join the longriders of the range and move from crime to crime. It seemed to Wendell that the matter was clear. Geraldi and his ilk were the wolves. The majority of men are the poor sheep, patient and helpless before the slaughterers, except that, here and there, such faithful watchers and warders as Marshal Tex Arnold appear and drive the wild beasts away.

He, Wendell, aspired one day to be such a man. The lonely life did not oppress him. The infinite labors and the small pay could not deter him. He told himself that what lured him to the grim service was a sense of patriotic duty to his country and to his fellows. But down in his heart there was another reason, and that was the temptation of danger.

Danger is to most men either a poison, or a mere spice for life, but to a few it is meat or wine or both. So it was to Wendell. So it is, to be sure, to all of those men who ride on the rim of civilization, hunting for adventure, trying to assign good reasons for service and duty to explain what is really no more than the rich impulse of the blood. Pirate or admiral, guerrilla or conqueror, the blood is likely to be the same, although the actions may differ. But Wendell was that highest type of the Westerner, hard-handed, clean-minded, honest, honorable, and ready to fight a grizzly with his bare hands if the need arose. Still, the impulse that drove him through the mountains was the very love of danger, and he knew it not. The full peril, however, was clear to his mind.

He had seen Geraldi escape from the posse in the hotel. He knew how Geraldi had walked into the jail and out again, taking three prisoners with him. Nothing appeared to be impossible when this conjurer put his mind and his hand to a task. Now he, Wendell, was hunting for a woman, who was to be bait with which Geraldi might be caught. He, Wendell, was to help in the setting of a new trap. And to break from that trap, if once it were closed upon him, Geraldi, this time, might use bullets.

The picture rose dimly before the mental eye of Wendell — he saw the gun in the slender hand of Geraldi, the muzzle jumping and jerking as the cartridges exploded. He saw the faint, cold smile upon the lips of the man; he saw the gleam of the dark eyes. He, Wendell, was standing opposite the destroyer, pouring in shot for shot. He, Wendell, was falling to the ground, still shooting. He, Wendell, lay bullet-torn and dying, but still firing at the other.

The picture went out from the mind of the hunter, for he remembered his mission. There could be no daydreaming, if he were to succeed in his task.

His horse climbed a bare knoll and at the top stopped, unbidden, so powerful and so icy cold was the sweep of the wind. Wendell bowed his head to meet the blast, and, bowing his head, he found himself looking down into a shallow ravine up which marched a host of brush and some trees of very fair size.

He took the first way into the hollows, not that he felt it necessary to search the place, but simply because even his leathery strength winced, for the moment, and he wished to find some shelter against the probing cold. Once beneath the rim of the walls, he had his instant reward. The wind was shut away. Only its voice mourned through the upper air, and into the hollow the full, bright force of the sun came streaming.

Wendell took off his gloves and chafed and wrung his hands together, while the weight of the sun, like a kindly hand pressing upon his shoulders, gradually thawed his body and reached the vital spirits. The mustang stopped shuddering. It was possible for horse and man to breathe freely and deeply, their loins no longer pinched by frost.

However, he decided to work up the gully. If he went down, he would be longer in this pleasant shelter, but he would also be leaving the terrain which the marshal had instructed him to search. So, giving his head a shake, like a faithful dog about to plunge out into the winter cold at the heels of its master, Wendell turned the head of the mustang up the valley and urged it forward.

The horse seemed to understand, as well as its master. For a moment it balked, but the gathering of the reins and the premonitory touch from the rowels of the spurs were enough to start it on again. They wound slowly with the windings of the narrow ravine. It seemed to the hunter a pleasant place, indeed. It was not only sheltered from the wind, but both wood and water were at hand. The stream that ran down it was the merest trickle, but it would be sufficient for man and beast. Here and there, came small natural clearings, where the ground was covered with a fine grass that seemed admirable forage. The mustang was so tempted that it was continually trying to stretch out its head and, using up the slack of the reins, would take a bite at the turf.

The vigilance of the deputy marshal was laid to rest by a warm, an almost drowsy, sense of release and comfort. So it was that he almost rode by a lean-to without noticing it. In fact, he was well past before he turned his head, aware that something unusual had drifted through the corner of his eye. Then he saw the thing clearly. The dump heap and the mouth of an old mine shaft appeared under the rim of the ravine wall, and just below this was the house. House it could hardly be called, but rather a hut or a lean-to. It was made of logs huddled together in the most careless fashion, and it had the look of having stood unoccupied for years. However, there was a heap of brush over the top of the shack, to act as a thatching, and this seemed to have been newly put in place.

He turned the mustang promptly about. It was not that he had any real hope, because, of course, no young girl would be found in a place as remote as this one. However, he turned his mustang and went to explore. The door of the shack was open. He beat on it with the butt of his quirt, and got no answer except from a flying echo that leaped across the ravine and dimly back again.

Wendell dismounted and went inside. The place was occupied, certainly. The bare earthen floor had been carefully swept into tidiness this same day — the marks and scratches made by the brush broom were still upon the floor. In the corner there was an Indian bed made of supple willow branches, woven together. Blankets, neatly folded, lay across the head of it.

Wendell leaned to examine the construction of the bed. It was not Indian craftsmanship. He was sure of that, at least. It had not the exquisite precision and strength of Indian work; this was the improvisation of some neat-handed amateur. However, the bed looked comfortable enough.

A slicker hung from the wall; there was a homemade table — half-squared logs were lying across two sawbucks — and on the table lay a sewing kit.

He leaned to admire the completeness of this. He himself always carried a sewing kit, of course, but he never had put in so many kinds of thread or needles so small. He admired again. He told himself that he could take a leaf from the notebook of the proprietor of this cabin.

Yonder in a corner was a canvas carryall, bulging with a number of unpacked articles. He went to it and stooped to open the roll, but then he changed his mind. A certain decency and respect for the will of an unknown man stopped him. He even blushed a little as he went back to the door.

There he stood in the broad, comfortable shaft of the sunshine and allowed the warmth to soak through his body as sleep steals through a tired brain. His muscles relaxed. His shoulders suddenly sank — he realized he had been carrying them hunched very high. So he made a cigarette. He began to think of Geraldi. Geraldi was never tense. Geraldi would face danger or cold or heat without permitting a single muscle to contract. Such tenseness of the muscles caused fatigue, lay on the brain like a burden of worry, and made accuracy of touch or speed of movement impossible. No, Geraldi was always relaxed, at ease, comfortable. He, Wendell, must study how to imitate that master.

He was thinking of Geraldi, still, when he heard the clanking of ironshod hoofs coming over rocks in the upper reach of the ravine. The deputy marshal hastily withdrew with the mustang into the screen of brush near the house.

Perhaps this was a foolish precaution, but one never could tell. Men who chose to live so far from the fringes of society might be honest prospectors, sullen sourdoughs, or outlaws as dangerous as wild animals, and far more cunning. He tried his revolver and gripped it several times, to make sure of the numbness having passed from his fingers. He dropped the fuming cigarette to the ground and stepped on it. For one taint of tobacco smoke in the air would be too gross a warning.

Then he saw a solitary rider coming slowly down the valley toward the house.

Chapter Seventeen

THE FIND

As the rider came nearer, Deputy Marshal Wendell's heart leaped into his throat, for he saw that it was a woman. As she came still nearer, he realized that it was a girl, whose age and whose beauty matched the marshal's description. She was the age for which the marshal had told him to look. She had the beauty of which the marshal had spoken. At length, she was quite close, and he remembered the last words of Tex Arnold: "Brown as a berry, with a glow shining through her." That was a perfect description of her as she came riding down toward the lean-to.

She had killed a deer, a big one. The four quarters were bound across the mustang she rode, and now, dismounting, she untied the fastenings and lifted the heavy burdens, putting them on the ground.

It was then that Wendell came out from the brush, leading his horse.

She turned on him as a cat turns, whipping the rifle from its saddle holster. She was all alight and prepared for battle, but Wendell smiled.

"I ain't here to find trouble, ma'am," he said.

"You gave me a start," she replied. "Coming out of the bushes like that, I mean. But it's all right." She hesitated one instant, studying him with a frown that was masculine in its intensity. Then, with a nod of reassurance, she slid the rifle back into its holster.

Wendell came on and began to help her. He stowed the meat away by hanging it to the tips of three trees, three supple saplings that bowed far over with the weight, but lodged it in the air above the leaping powers of cat or wolf. The fourth quarter was to be prepared for cookery.

They went about the meal with silence and industry. He did not wait for an invitation to share the meal. He simply set about chopping wood and building the fire, while she was busied with the carving and cleaning of the meat.

The fireplace was out of doors, composed of a circle of handy stones, and the draught in it drew well. Very shortly they were sitting about roasting gobbets of the meat at the end of long, sharpened branches. Over the center of the fire the coffee pot was blackening and beginning to hiss and to steam.

Still in silence, they ate their meal. It consisted merely of the roasted meat, of salt, and of the black coffee. But it was a good meal to the taste of the deputy marshal. He was hungry as only a man can be who has subsisted for two days on hard tack and cold water, for he had traveled light and was proud of his mileage. Tex Arnold himself had taught him how to do it.

When they had finished eating, the sun was westering rapidly, and up the cañon — that at this point turned well toward the occident — a flow of rosy golden light was streaming and staining the treetops and all the rocky faces of the ravine walls. The fire had died down. A thin arm of smoke was rising from it to the place where the upper air currents snatched at it and knocked it to nothingness.

Wendell offered the girl the makings. She did not smoke. She merely put her back against a rock, stretched her legs, and relaxed.

She was tired. She had been out all day, stalking deer. Finally she had had this stroke of luck. A very lucky stroke, she said, for the deer was two hundred yards away and running hard when she tried a snap shot that broke its back. Now it was good to have meat stored up for the future days. She had not had a good, square meal for days, she said.

"Up here with your husband? Or is he off on a trip?" asked Wendell.

She looked him mildly in the eye. "I'm up here alone," she said.

"Up here alone?" he echoed, with well-simulated surprise. "All alone . . . here at the end of the world?"

"Oh, you know how it is," she said. "My father found this mine. He always wanted to come back to it. But then he died, and I promised him that I'd give the thing a look."

"So you came alone?"

"There was nobody to come with me," she said.

If she were Geraldi's promised wife, then Wendell knew that she was lying, but her glibness fascinated him.

"Who was your father?" he asked.

"Pete Wyman," she answered. "A lot of people called him Arizona Pete. Maybe you knew him?"

"I've been in Arizona a lot," said Wendell. "I guess I've known half a dozen by the name of Arizona Pete. What did he look like?"

"Biggish, sort of," she said. "He had a blond beard that split in the center. When he rode, half of his beard fanned out over each shoulder. You'd remember him, if you ever saw him."

"No, I don't think I ever met him," said Wendell. "What took him off?"

"Curiosity," answered the girl.

"Eh?" said Wendell.

"He went into a shaft to see why a shot didn't explode. After he got in close, the shot went off. And that was the end of him."

"Mighty sad," said Wendell.

He looked her straight in the eye, and she looked straight back at him.

"All we could collect of him was hardly more than a memory," said the girl. "But we buried all that we could find."

Her callousness shocked Wendell for a moment, but then he told himself that this was entirely a fiction, that was why she could speak of the horror so glibly.

"What sort of pay dirt have you found here?" he asked her.

"It's all patchy," she answered. "There's some streaks of wire gold that would make a man rich in a month, if it held out. But it doesn't hold out. It's all in handfuls. I think Dad was dead wrong about the place."

"You never can tell," said Wendell. "The old-timers were right one time out of four. That was enough to make a lot of 'em rich. Was he a real old sourdough?"

"He was sour enough," said the girl. She yawned.

"How long will you be here?" asked Wendell.

"Oh, I don't know. What's your business, stranger? Looking for lost sheep?"

"No," said Wendell, feeling that he would match lie with lie. "I'm one of the lost sheep, and they're looking for me."

"Hold on," she said. "What d'you mean by that?"

"You know," said Wendell. "Too much whiskey and too many guns. That's what was the matter with me." He drew hard on his cigarette. He raised his face and blew the smoke carefully into the air. He was proud of his lie, and he saw how he could use it.

"You bumped somebody off, then?" said the girl.

"I dunno," he said. "The way they're hunting me, you'd think so. He was looking for trouble, this Canuck that I'm telling you about. He was looking for trouble, and he kept right on riding me till he collected all that he wanted. I was sorry about it. I'm not the fighting kind. I take things easy. But he kept on asking, and finally he did a little damning, so I pulled my gun and started to work."

"Dropped him?" she asked, with uncommon indifference.

"Yeah. He dropped, all right. That was the bad part . . . what came then. I found out that he didn't have any gun on him. So I saw that it wouldn't be self-defense in front of any jury, and I started riding. I wish I hadn't. I wish that I'd stayed and faced 'em out. But I started running. And here I am."

"What's your name?" asked the girl.

"Bender," he replied.

"That yarn of yours is a bender, all right," she said, and she laughed at him, merrily, without restraint.

"What's the matter?" asked Wendell. "Don't you follow what I been saying?"

"Listen," she said. "I've seen a lot of tough ones. You never dropped a man when you were tight. Don't tell me that!"

"Didn't I?" he said sullenly. He felt that it was an offense to his manhood.

"You bet you never did," she said. "Not with a look like yours. You're practically antiseptic, I guess."

He stared back at her. She stared straight back.

"It's all right, Mister Bender," she continued. "I shouldn't have called you like this, I suppose. Only, the words popped out. Forgive me."

"Sure," he said. But he was uneasy. He scowled at the dwindling column of smoke and felt his face grow hot.

"What is it?" went on the girl. "What brought you all the way up here to the end of the world, as you call it?" She was smiling and very much at ease.

"Something that I can't talk about," he said. "The mine, let's say."

"This mine?" she asked.

"Yeah. Call it that."

"Did you know it was here?" she demanded.

He looked straight at her. "Did you?" he said. "Did you, before you stumbled onto it?"

She started, then sat up straight. "Why do you say that?" she asked.

He, in turn, pointed toward the mouth of the old mining shaft. "D'you mean to tell me that you've been down in there?" he asked her.

"Of course," she said, but with caution in her face.

"And you worked it a little?"

"Yes. A little."

"Ma'am," he said, "I don't want to embarrass you any, but that windlass hasn't been turned for years. And the rope on it's rotten. How could you have worked it?"

She was silent. He was relieved to see the color come flooding up into her face, in turn. Then

141

she shrugged her shoulders and smiled. "Well," she said at last, "that makes us even. One lie apiece." Suddenly she laughed.

He could join that laughter without trouble. Because, as he watched her and as he saw the courage and the embarrassment struggling in her face, a great triumph welled up in him. His last doubt was gone. This was the girl. He, Wendell, had succeeded in finding what the marshal and all the rest of the posse had failed to do.

This was Geraldi's girl, this was the bait, and around her must be set the trap to catch the great outlaw.

Chapter Eighteen

A VISITOR IN THE NIGHT

There was nothing more for Wendell to do at the moment. All he could manage was a careful survey of the place. Then, since it was nearly the time of sunset, he said good bye to the girl and left her. She offered him some venison to take on his way, but he refused the gift. Already he felt more than a little guilty, since, having accepted her hospitality, he was planning to betray her or, at least, Geraldi.

When he had a foot in the stirrup and the mustang waited with ears put back for the pressure of the man in the saddle, he said to her: "It's a lonely life up here all by yourself."

"I like it," she said. "I've had enough crowds. I like this all pretty well, in fact."

He looked from her to the gathering blackness along the face of the ravine wall. The place seemed as wild as one could wish or imagine. Even the most solitary old sourdough might have hesitated a little at the thought of remaining there alone.

"Besides," she added, as though interpreting his thought, "I have a friend along with me." She

143

whistled, and the mustang she had ridden back to camp lifted its head from the spot where it was grazing and turned quickly toward her. "He's my lookout, you see," said the girl.

She was still smiling when Wendell swung into the saddle. He took off his hat and gave her his best bow. He wished her luck and good company, and rode straight on up the ravine. She had asked him where he was heading, and he had told her that he wanted to cross the range. He would camp higher up, for that night. But, when he came to a place where the walls shelved back and the horse could climb them, he cut away to the left, and presently he was making the mustang scamper down the long slopes toward Neering.

He must find the marshal at once. That was clear. He had found the bait. It was only necessary, now, to arrange the trap. His blood was so heated at the prospect he forgot the cold wind that laid a hand of ice in the very small of his back.

Then he entered the forest, and the wind was shut away, but, at the same time, the light fell off until he was riding in a sudden twilight. It was almost utter darkness before he swung into the well-marked trail in the lower valley, pointing toward Neering. Once pointed in that direction, he burned up the last strength of the horse to make good time to his goal.

Far later, when the dark had closed in, and

when the stars had wheeled for several hours out of the east and shining hosts had sunk in the west, and when the cold of the mountain night had settled strongly through the ravine, and when the wind was dead and the frosty damp came upward from the ground, then Geraldi came down the cañon from the region above the timberline.

He had worn out two horses that day, although he had tried to save and cherish each. But the nervous energy that was driving him forced him on, hour after hour. The tough mountain mustang that he had secured by exchange from a small ranch was now stumbling and staggering in the darkness, too weary to use its wits or its keen natural senses.

So he came down to the place where a single eye of red gleamed at the side, under the brow of a cliff that walled in the ravine at this point. Geraldi gave the ray one glance and knew that it was the final spark of a campfire. He dismounted, went to it, and discovered, only then, the shack behind it, and finally the outlines of the structure of the windlass at the mouth of the old mining shaft.

He was ready to halt. He had gone as far as the horse would take him, and this was a place sufficiently far away to be secure, as it seemed to him. If he found hospitality here, it was not likely to be from a man who had ever heard the bare name of Geraldi. So he stood in the dark doorway — for the door was open and the sweet, cold air of the night filled the little room inside. Geraldi rapped on the door, after he had waited there a moment.

An instant later, out of the darkness, the voice of Mary spoke to him. "Who's there?"

The shock staggered him. He put out his hand and gripped at the wall of logs. It was as though an apparition had started up before him out of the ground. Something caught in his throat, and he began to cough.

Then said the voice of Mary, perfectly calm and sure, without fear: "I'm alone here. But you can build up a fire and sleep near it. There's plenty of wood left handy. If you want to cook, light the lantern . . . you'll find it there at the right of the door, hanging on a hook. I'll show you where the provisions are. There's nothing but venison and coffee and salt."

Venison, coffee, and salt! The miracle of his finding her hardly matched, for that moment, his hunger. It was a very strange thing. Suddenly all seemed well in the world. He had Mary again. It was only the hunger that obsessed his mind.

He said not a word, but he fumbled until he found the lantern, pried up its chimney, scratched a match, and watched the flame jump on the wick. The chimney went down again with a small screech. Then he shaded his eyes, and looked about him.

He saw the damp and naked poverty of the shack. He looked from the saddle on the wall to the opposite corner, and there he saw the girl, rising on one elbow, with the swathing of blankets around her. Her tousled hair dripped across her face in streaks. She was frowning against the light. She looked to him older and far paler than she had been before, although this doubtless was no more than the effect of the lantern light. Suddenly she sat bolt upright and peered.

"Jimmy!" she exclaimed.

He nodded. The lantern light began to waver violently, and only by that token did he realize that he was trembling.

"You're tired and hungry, Jimmy?" she said.

"A little," said Geraldi.

"You go out and build up the fire," she said. "I'll come out and start the cookery."

He left the lantern hanging on the peg and went into the open. For a moment he did not stir to kindle the fire, but he looked vaguely about him, vaguely yet knowing that the scene would never fade from his mind. Not a tree, not an outline of the cliff, where its head jutted against the sky, not a star above him would be forgotten; just as a photographic plate receives an image, so his mind received that scene.

He was still shaking a little. He had to force himself to think about the gathering of the wood and the rekindling of the fire. This was almost dead, and he had to put some dead leaves over the last coal, blowing upon the small heap until the rising smoke half choked him. Then he laid on small sticks, blew again. Finally the flame came up with a flicker and a dance, appeared, died, appeared again, and at last the true fire showed itself in a stiff, steady tongue of yellow.

Upon this he could build more carelessly, and presently he had a good fire going. He made it larger than was needed for mere cookery; he wanted the warmth of it for his own shuddering body. Even the horse, too weary to think of grazing, came and stood close by the kindly heat, pricking its ears, its eyes shining brightly.

Geraldi saw this with a sharp pang of pity. He stripped away the saddle and, with a twist of pine needles, he rubbed the mustang down. Then he hobbled it in a patch of good grass that the slant-wise gleaming of the fire showed to him. So attended, it began to graze at once, and Geraldi nodded with satisfaction. If it fed as heartily as this, he could be sure that it would be fit for travel the next morning. But why travel so soon, for that matter? Why not remain here and rest for a time?

He turned back toward the fire and found that the girl was there. She had dressed in haste, tying up her hair in a ragged knot at the back of her head and throwing a blanket around her shoulders so that she looked like a squaw. In the firelight, he saw the strong, shapely hands at work, spitting lumps of the venison, and the glistening of her eyes as she turned her head. He went back to her slowly, letting this picture sink gradually deep and deeper into his mind.

"Fill this up with water," she said to him, and handed over the coffee pot. He took it in silence and filled it from the brook. Some of the water spilled over his hands, and it was colder than ice, he thought. He came back with numb fingers, and with a greater cold commencing in his heart.

It was her utter calm that troubled him. But he decided that it was best not even to think of her. It was far better to eat, first, and then to smoke. Afterward, they might talk. Perhaps it would be wisest of all to wait until the next morning, and then the talking would be calmer and wiser.

He sat down cross-legged on a half-rotten stump of a tree, near the girl, but at such an angle that he could see her face without turning his head. She went on calmly with the turning of the spits. He looked keenly at her. She was neither pale nor flushed now, he could see. She was as calm as though he were a small child, and not a man at all.

As he settled the coffee pot in a convenient place to take the flames, her eyes met his. It was the meeting of a single instant, yet she did not snatch her gaze suddenly away. Instead, she allowed a faint smile of kindly recognition to come into her eyes.

Geraldi was on his feet instantly, and then, kneeling beside her, he took her in his arms. She looked straight up into his face. She did not flinch, but the smile was no longer there in her eyes. He kissed her, and her lips remained cold and insensitive at the touch of his. There was no resistance, but neither was there the slightest yielding. He drew back from her, amazed and hurt.

"You're all shaking, Jimmy," she said in the calmest of voices. "Shall I get you a blanket to put around your shoulders? It's a pretty cold night."

"Aye," said Geraldi. "It's a cold night, but I'll get on without the blanket."

Chapter Nineteen

IMPLACABLE MARY

He fell into a muse, looking now at the fire, now at the fumes that rose from the cooking meat, and now at the slender, firm hands of the girl. But only now and again did he venture to lift his glance to her face. It was utterly and placidly content, so far as he could see. The faint half smile that appeared on her lips was not for him. It was merely the normal expression of a healthy young girl, pleased with the world around her. Bitterness and fear grew up in Geraldi.

The meat was cooked. The coffee was beginning to steam as he started to eat. He had been very hungry a moment before, but now his appetite seemed to have failed him. That luscious meat, dripping with good juices, was to him no more than tasteless wooden chips.

His eyes tried to feed on the beauty of the girl, but it was a barren pasturage. She was far from him. She was so far, in fact, she could look straight across at him and consider him with a grave and impersonal manner.

"What's the matter, Jimmy," she said. "Isn't it good?" She canted her head critically. She frowned in sympathetic anticipation of his reply in just such a manner as a mother might look at a child.

"My God," said Geraldi, "how far you are from me, Mary?"

"Why, Jimmy," she answered, "I'm in touching distance of your hand. I'll tell you what . . . you're not getting enough salt on that meat. That's what the matter is. It's tasteless to you."

He stopped eating, and stared at her.

"You could understand me if you wanted to," he suggested.

"Coffee is what you need," she said. "That'll warm you up. You're blue under the eyes. You've ridden too far today. I can always tell by the look under your eyes. You shouldn't press yourself too much, Jimmy."

She was pouring the coffee as she spoke. Geraldi took the cup without a word and began to sip it. The heat and the steam rose to his face, stung his throat, loosened the muscles of his entire body. Tears came into his eyes. He was afraid to look up at her, for fear that she might think that it was weak sentimentality.

Tears in the eyes of Geraldi? Well, women were such subtle foxes that they were likely to suspect anything. He was more and more ill at ease. He had felt that all he needed was a chance to come within touching distance of her. But he saw now that he was entirely wrong.

"Something's happened to you, Mary," he

152

said, looking down at the fire.

"Yes," she said.

"What is it?" he asked.

"I can't tell you," she replied.

"You can't tell me?" He checked himself and set his teeth hard, for he had heard the ring of fear and pain that had been in his own voice. It was not fair to speak to her in this fashion. But it was amazing that she would make no effort to expand her idea a little. A decent courtesy appeared to call for this.

"You're trembling, Jimmy," said the girl. "I'm going to get that blanket."

She was half risen, but Geraldi said hastily: "It's not the cold, Mary."

She relaxed in her place again. "Try some more coffee," she urged. "You're tired. That's what's the matter."

"It's not that, either," he said. "I want to talk to you."

"You'd better wait," she answered. "Wait till you've had some sleep. A good, long one. I know that look in your eyes. Wait until you've slept, will you? Then we'll talk about everything."

He looked steadily at her, wondering. His wonder was so great that he forgot all self-consciousness. "You've changed a lot," he said.

"Yes," she answered.

Only the single word, spoken without haste or bitterness, with finality, as though it had been a whole paragraph of explanation, sufficient in itself.

"You know, Mary," he said, "why I faded out of the picture the other day?"

"I guessed," she said. "Your friend had something to do with it. The fellow with the prison look."

He felt that this answer was sharp enough, but he was prepared to take shrewder blows than this.

"Larry Burns," said Geraldi, "was standing outside our window. When you left the room, he spoke to me. He was running for his life. The dogs of the posse that hunted him were barking up the valley. He had the irons on his hands. He'd ridden two hundred miles in two days. He looked at me like a dog asking for a drink of water . . . a starving dog. There wasn't any time to make explanations to you. It was just touch and go, with every second counting. You understand?"

"So you jumped through the window and took his horse and led the posse away. Was that it?" she asked.

"That was it," said Geraldi.

Now that he looked back at the thing, he felt no shame. He felt, instead, a pride. He waited for commendation. But she remained silent, looking into the fire, with the attitude of one who has heard a thing by no means really surprising.

He explained: "It was the devil. The mustang that Burns had been riding was done in. His knees were shaking. But I managed to get away. I

154

rode across that tree . . . you know, the one that fell across the creek?"

"You *rode* across it?" she said, lifting her glance suddenly.

"Yes," he said, and waited for the comment.

"You took one chance in ten," said Mary.

That was all. It seemed to subtract all the glory from his achievement. It made him merely a reckless daredevil, a professional risker of his neck, as it were.

"Well, the chance panned out," said Geraldi. "There was nothing else for it. Farther on, I had to change horses with the hunt in full sight behind me. I took one of Grogan's nags. You know the pasture where he's keeping them now?"

"Yes. I know the place. That made you a horse thief, Jimmy." Still how calmly she spoke.

"That made me a horse thief," he agreed. "And it was Marshal Tex Arnold who was heading that posse. The one thing he's been dreaming about for years has been a chance to hunt me down. He has his chance now, and he's making my trail hot."

"I know Tex Arnold," she said. "He'll give you a good time, Jimmy."

"Good time?" he echoed.

At this, she made a wide gesture with both hands — not a sudden gesture, but as though appealing to his common sense about a very apparent thing. "Oh, Jimmy," she said, "you know how it is, really. You know what you love. If there were only two or three *more* Tex Arnolds, then you'd be having a perfect time. Now, look me in the eye and tell me true."

"I know what you mean, Mary," he said. "You think that the call of the old life is too much for me. You think that Larry Burns was only a symbol, and that sooner or later, married or unmarried, I would have broken away?"

"I don't think it," she said. "I know it."

"You're wrong," said Geraldi.

She shook her head.

"You're wrong," he repeated. "Mary, Mary, if you knew the fear and the sickness I suffer from when I sit here so close to you and feel that you've pulled far away from me in your mind . . . if you knew how miserable I am, and how I want nothing in the world except to have you. . . ." He stopped himself short. "I don't mean to whine," he said slowly.

"I know how you feel," she said. "It was the nearness of the thing. You like to finish a job that you've started. And you were about to marry me. Oh, yes, I understand perfectly. We were beginning to shine on one another like a pair of lamps, that day. We were melting like bad candles on a hot day." She laughed a little, without affection, without hardness. The thing seemed to amuse her thoroughly.

"It doesn't seem a funny thing to me," said Jimmy. "It was a sacred thing to me. Do you think, Mary, that I didn't love you, or that I love you less now?"

"No," she answered thoughtfully. "I think you care a bit about me. But it's as it should be. A man . . . a real man . . . ought to love his work more than he loves his wife. Of course, that's the proper attitude."

"Do you think," said Geraldi, "that I've ever put my farm and my horse raising before you, Mary? Great Scott, do you think that for a moment?"

She shook her head. "There's my point," she said. "There's the whole point that I'm trying to make. The farm would never hold you. No, you'd rate me above the horse breeding, I think. Although that's fine enough to fill the minds of most men. But farming isn't your real work."

"What is?" Geraldi asked, frowning.

"Fire eating," said the girl. "Walking on the air, magic, gun plays, and all of such things are your real business. That's what makes other people look up to you. That's why you're a great man to them. Oh, I know all that, of course, and I'm not in the least wondering that you should prefer that sort of life. Not in the least bit, Jimmy. Only, when I finally saw the thing clearly . . . just the other day . . . I knew that it wouldn't do to mix the two ideas."

"What two ideas?" asked Geraldi.

"Home and hanging," she said.

It raised him to his feet. She leaned a little toward him. Pain for the first time had come into her face.

"I'm a woman who has to have children," she

said. "They're in my blood. And I'll never give my children a father whose hands are not clean. I thought that you'd washed the old crimes away. Then my eyes were opened. It hurt a good deal . . . it was like looking at the sun, you know. But I've looked. I've seen the truth. And nothing will ever change that for me."

Geraldi stared at her across the fire, and, as the golden glow beat up against her face, he saw something both resigned and noble in her eyes. He knew, then, that the time for persuasion and explanation had passed between them.

Chapter Twenty

FAREWELL

In Geraldi there was an odd mixture of emotions. He felt, strange to say, first and above all, a greatly wounded pride. She had loved him. She had been on the very verge of belonging to him forever. For he knew that a nature as deep, as ardent, as bold, as true as hers would, once committed, cling forever to the course she adopted. Virtue, in all women, if it is glorious, is also cruel. It chooses one road to one end. From the way of the girl, Geraldi now found himself cast out. He spent some time contemplating the fire.

"Tell me now, Jimmy," she said. "What are you thinking of?"

"Magic," said Geraldi.

He looked up at her with an odd, twisting smile such as never had come to his face before. And she understood. He was one who had taken from life what he wished to get from it. He had been the conqueror, the strong hand, the sure touch. He had mastered men as he mastered the combinations of complicated locks. But now he was foiled and baffled.

"Magic," said Geraldi again. "I wish this were

something that I could use my hands on. But here's a combination that I can't solve. Tell me in one word . . . is this the end between us?"

She answered him carefully, not as one speaking in pique, but with due consideration. "This is absolutely the end," she said.

He took the blow as he was, standing, braced to receive the shock of it. Only he shook his head a little, not that he was denying her decision, only that he wished to clear his head. He was stunned, and she saw it.

She went on: "You know, Jimmy, I'll never feel that I have a right to pity you. For a couple of days, I was pitying myself. That's stopped, too. I don't get tears in my eyes, when I think about what has happened to me. I'm not going to get tears, thinking about what has happened to you. I suppose that you still care for me, Jimmy. It hurts you a good deal . . . this thing?"

"Yeah," drawled Geraldi. "It hurts a little. Thinking of what's to come hurts, too. You'll be finding some other man who'll take you up. A better man than I, of course. But still, that will be a knife between my ribs."

She said nothing. She continued to study the fire. "You know, Jimmy," she finally said, "that I don't think you ought to stay here long."

"Does it bother you, Mary?" he asked her.

"There was a chap up here this evening," she said. "I gave him a meal. He ate with me. He had a good, clean look about him. He was a real man. He looked capable of some action, too.

But he told me some lies."

"What sort of lies?" asked Geraldi.

"Lies about who he was and where he was going, and all that sort of thing."

"Well?" said Geraldi.

"That fellow was on a trail," she said. "He may have been on my trail . . . why, I don't know. But there was a look about his eyes, as though he were glad that he had found me. Now, Jimmy, does the marshal know that you've been following me?"

"He knows that," said Geraldi.

"Then," she said, "if they know that much, they may try to find you where they've found me, may they not?"

"They might," said Geraldi.

"If I were you," said the girl, "I'd saddle and start down the ravine right now."

He hardly seemed to hear her. He was looking straight before him, over her head.

"Well, Jimmy?" she said.

"It's all right," answered Geraldi. "I'm pulling myself together. That's all. I'll be gone in a moment. I keep thinking that there's something that I may be able to say to you. I keep feeling that there's some magic word that may turn the trick. Suppose I were to try to tell you, Mary, how much I love you."

"I wish you wouldn't do that," she said very gravely.

He did not stir. He remained there, standing, and she, watching him, felt such a rush of tenderness and love and pity that the tears stung her eyes. She shaded them with her hand and frowned at the fire.

So there came a long moment of silence between this exceedingly strange pair. It was not broken first by a word from them. Instead, they heard from the cliff just above them the long, ringing neigh of a horse. It was answered from another, straight down the ravine, the echoes picking up the sound, giving it depth and a powerful ring.

Mary sprang up.

But Geraldi, without moving, merely answered: "Well, there they are, after all. Tex Arnold makes his moves fast, doesn't he?"

The girl looked wildly, swiftly around her. It was the height and the steep faces of the cliffs that she was measuring. She pointed. "Do you see, Jimmy?" she gasped. "It's a closed bottle. You couldn't get out of this pit except with wings. Hardly with wings, even. They're down in the valley. They may be up the valley, too. But that's the way to go. Hurry, Jimmy. For heaven's sake, hurry!"

"Oh, there's no hurry," said Geraldi. "Not a bit. Tell me a little of your plans."

"What are you talking about?" she cried. "Jimmy, are you trying to drive me frantic?"

He shook his head. Calmly, thoughtfully, he continued to gaze past her and above her head. "No, I'm not trying to bother you, Mary," he said. "I'm only thinking."

She ran to him. She caught him by the arms and shook him, with all of her strength. "Jimmy," she said, with a break coming into her voice. "Jimmy, Jimmy, don't you see? They're closing up the valley? They'll have you sealed in . . . they'll be hunting for you here . . . they'll form a cordon across both ends of the ravine."

"I'm just wondering," he said. "I might wait for them here."

She gasped, and was silent for a moment. Then she said: "What do you mean?"

"No, I won't wait for them here," he said. "There's no reason why you should see ugly things happening."

"You're going to fight?" she asked him. "Is that what you mean?"

He made a slight gesture with one hand, a small, impatient, proud gesture. "You know, Mary," he said gently, "a fellow doesn't mind being hounded about for a time. But after a while it's a bore. I'm a little sick of Marshal Tex Arnold, making his reputation out of me. He's bothered me before. He's had his ropes on me. Now I'm tired of it. I don't think that I want to run away any longer."

She grew white, and he saw it.

"This sounds like bravado," he told her. "I don't mean it that way."

"Here, Jimmy. Give me both your hands."

"Well, here they are," he said.

She took those hands, slender as the hands of a woman, almost, delicately made. They were

163

cold, now, cold as ice. But even in spite of that, she could sense the nervous power, the accuracy that lived in them.

"Jimmy," she said in exasperation, "look at me."

He looked her fairly in the eye.

"No, don't think of something else," she said.

"I'm not," he answered. "Now I'm thinking of you."

"I've hurt you," said the girl. "You're sullen, just now. That makes you glad to have a chance to fight. But don't do it. You've kept your hands clean before. I mean to say, your dead men have deserved to die, Jimmy. They were gunmen, crooks. But if you kill one honest man, doing his duty in the eyes of the law, you'll break my heart . . . because then you'll live forever under the shadow of the law. You know that. Promise me!"

Geraldi smiled at her, and the smile made her shudder.

"I don't see why I should make promises to you, Mary," he said. "We're living apart from one another. Your plans are your own. You won't tell me about them. My plans are my own, too. I don't see why I should tell you about them. Only, I can tell you that I need a little excitement just now. I've been a farmer long enough. I would have been one forever, to make a home for you. But that's behind me, and now I want a change. Even a doctor would prescribe a change for me, I think." He smiled again, the cold, small smile that had shrunk the heart of many a fighting man who had stood before Geraldi.

"Is that all you'll say?" she asked breathlessly. "You won't try to get away? You won't even saddle your horse?"

"No, I'll walk down the valley," he said.

"Not down!" she begged of him. "You've heard the horse down there. They've already closed that way."

"I'm not running away, exactly. I intend to walk down that way," replied Geraldi.

"Jimmy," she pleaded, "without a horse!"

"That plug of mine is tired," he said.

"Take mine. It's still fairly fresh," she urged.

"Take a woman's horse?" smiled Geraldi. "No, I can't do exactly that. Not when there are so many better horses belonging to men around us. Tex Arnold always rides a good horse. I wouldn't mind taking his along with me to-night."

She moaned, and placed her hands over her eyes.

"No, I don't mean murder, either," he said. "At least, I hope not. But if they crowd me too far. . . ." He paused, and she understood. "Good bye, Mary," he said.

The tears began to streak down her face. She held out her hands, but he took only one of them, and, bending over it, he touched it with his lips twice.

She shook her head. When her eyes were clear, she saw that he was walking down the ravine, stepping lightly, easily. In the walk of the man, his grace, his cat-like power appeared. When he came to the brook, he sprang across it.

Now he stood on the verge of the firelight, where it glimmered faintly upon him, and upon the bulky forms of the trees behind him. There he took off his hat and waved to her, and then, turning, in three strides he was lost in the forest.

Chapter Twenty-One
THE DUNDERHEAD

Geraldi was not far down the ravine when he heard a rapid fire of rifles breaking out far behind him, and he knew that the upper mouth of the ravine was now watched. These shots were answered from lower down. Finally, distant choruses of triumphant shouting reached the ears of the hunted man. Geraldi paused. He was, at that moment, in the midst of a rather wide clearing, so that he could look up and out past the tops of the trees and see the black and ragged rim of the cañon walls on either side. The vague silhouette of a horseman journeyed along one wall. Two more he spotted on the opposite side.

They had taken no chances. There must be scores in the small army that Tex Arnold had rallied to make his man trap. It was typical of Arnold. He was thorough. He moved as a general who is not willing to risk defeat if human caution can prevent it.

Geraldi tightened his belt a notch and smiled in the dark. It was a closely woven net which was dragging the cañon for him, but it requires the best of nets to catch a slippery eel. His heart raced, but not with fear. Suddenly, looking up to the face of the sky, powdered and whitened with stars, he asked himself if he really would prefer some other place in all the world? No, for this was his happiness, to stand straight before the bright eyes of danger.

He heard voices below him, and then saw the gleam of firelight that was thrusting long, tremulous fingers of red among the trees. He understood at once. They were kindling watch fires. They would not try to sweep the cañon for him during the night, but in the daylight they would commence, when their eyes could search every treetop above them as they worked gradually forward. That was the cunning wit of Tex Arnold again. Geraldi recognized his man by these tokens.

Far behind him was Mary, waiting, listening to these sounds, watching the glow of the fires. He wondered what went through her mind, and what pain, if any, was in her heart. He could understand Tex Arnold and the rest of the manhunters. All men seemed, to Geraldi, slates upon which the writing was clear and bold. But the women were a different pattern, and what passed in the mind of the girl he could not guess.

He had thought that he knew her. He had thought that he could look into her as deeply as the eye penetrates through clearest well water. But he was wrong. She, by an act of pure will power, had ruled him out of her life, put him at a distance, and barred him away from her with a wall he did not know how to attempt to pass. There had been no tremor in her. It was he, Geraldi, who had appeared the weakling when they met.

He put that melancholy thought away from him. There was something else to be thought of now. Perhaps she was right. His work was more to him than any woman, perhaps, and here was a task to fill his hands ideally.

He stepped forward until he could see the row of the twinkling fires stretching across an irregular clearing. He could also see the ragged silhouettes of men carrying armfuls of brush to heap on the flames or pile in reserve. He could hear the thudding of axes as more durable fuel was cut down. It was like moving against the front of an army. When he was closer, he found some shrubs dead at the root. They gave quite readily when he pulled, and he heaped up a mass. Then he raised it, an armful so great that it blotted him out, and went forward with it, through a gap in the dark masses of the trees.

He avoided the nearest fire. He went slanting onward toward the next. Through the interstices of his burden, he could see the other workers. They were armed to the teeth, all of them, and, besides those who worked, there were others employed only with their weapons. These guards stood well back from the line of the fires. He saw that most of them carried shotguns, and even the heart of Geraldi sank a little.

A man may take chances with rifles and revolvers, but shotguns are a different matter. A charge from a shotgun snatches the dodging snipe out of the air. What chance has a man to escape the load even when it is fired by the rankest amateur? So Geraldi reasoned, as he partly carried and partly dragged his burden toward the fire. Then, rounding it, he unloaded what he had carried upon the great heap of the reserve fuel.

He stood back. The grass on the ground at his feet had been burned. He leaned, touched the charred grass, and then smeared his blackened hands across his face. There were other sooty skins around him — fire tending is the dirtiest job in the world.

"Throw some more on the fire! Throw some more on the fire . . . you!" said an arrogant voice, approaching him.

He saw the gesture of the pointing arm, too, and Geraldi obediently picked up what he had just added to the pile and started toward the fire with it.

"Not all of that!" yelled the other. "I never saw such a fool! Whatcha wanna do? Start a forest fire?"

Geraldi obediently dropped the lower part of his load and cast the remaining half high into the flames. They had been weltering low, up to this moment. But the brush that Geraldi had brought was very dry and highly inflammable. It seemed to explode into brilliance before it had well touched the body of the fire, and the draft whirled into the air, high above their heads, a shower of sparks and whole tips of branches, transformed into white, glowing wires.

There was an instant shout from nearby: "Who did that? Who did that? What fool threw on that stuff?"

"Here's the dunderhead!" cried the man who had given the orders to Geraldi before. "The same fool that brought this stuff in!"

"Hai! Bring him over here!" called the second, who seemed in command. "We don't want any weak wits along with us now. Not when we're after Geraldi. One bad rope in the net, and Geraldi slips through the gap. Bring him over here!"

"I'll bring him. It's only a kid. It's a fool of a kid," said the first. He said this as he set his big grasp upon the slender arm of Geraldi and dragged him forward.

The hat of Geraldi was broad of brim, and he was glad of the shadow it cast. He was glad, furthermore, of the black which was smeared upon his face, for he had recognized the voice of the second speaker and now he could recognize his face as well. It was Tex Arnold, in person, supervising the blocking of the ravine from side to side, with guns, with fire, and with many a watchful eye.

Beside Arnold, who had no weapon drawn, a watchful 'puncher stood with a sawed-off shotgun hanging in the crook of his arm. From that moment, Geraldi paid more heed to the bearer of the riot gun than to the marshal himself.

"Who are you? Who took you for this job?" demanded Tex Arnold angrily of Geraldi. "Did Wendell hire you?"

"Aye," said Geraldi.

"Say that again . . . who are you?" asked Tex Arnold, starting.

Had he recognized the familiar voice of Geraldi? The latter was taken with a convenient fit of coughing, the sobbing sounds appearing to tear his throat and to bend him double.

"What's your name?" asked Arnold again.

An indecipherable sound came from the throat of Geraldi, still partially bent by the apparent spasm and wiping tears from his eyes, as it appeared.

"Why, he's some half growed-up kid," said the first fire guard. "Wendell was a fool to take him on." He added: "I'll throw him out on his ear. You get your hoss, and pile out of here, brat."

"Aye, sir," said Geraldi humbly. He stepped past the marshal, toward the shadowy line of horses which appeared among the brush and the trees, half seen. Three steps more, and he would be safe in the obscurity of the underbrush.

"Hold on!" shouted Tex Arnold in a loud voice.

Geraldi's muscles twitched, but he remembered the riot gun in time. The keenest wit and the boldest heart in the world dared not take chances with the spreading fan of lead that burst from the mouth of such a weapon. So Geraldi turned, taking as he did so one more step to bring himself closer to the protecting shadows of the brush.

"Hold on," repeated Arnold. "There's something about you that I know. Keep that shotgun ready, Mike!"

"I got it ready," said Mike.

"I've asked you three times for your name," said Tex Arnold. "Come back here and tell me who you are. Mike, see that you keep him covered!"

"I've got him right inside the barrel of the gun," said Mike, with a calm conviction that shrank the heart of Geraldi.

"Out with it," said the marshal. "What's your name?"

"Geraldi, you fool!" shouted the other. Even as he spoke, the revolver winked in his hand, exploded, and a bullet ripped through the thigh of Mike's leg.

Mike fired. But the shock of the half-inch slug had twisted him a little, and the buckshot rattled through the brush a yard from the head of Geraldi.

Tex Arnold's own revolver was in action now. He made sure to spit the fleeing, slender body of Geraldi straight through the center of the back, but just as he pulled the trigger, Geraldi, like a flying snipe, leaped to the side.

The .45-caliber slug was spent in vain, and Geraldi leaped on toward the line of the tethered horses. Even here, the deliberate precautions of the marshal were in evidence. Over the line of horses, he had placed an intelligent, a brave, and a watchful guard. That man was walking up and down the line, swinging his rifle in his hand. But now he heard a sudden uproar of shouting from the line of the bonfires, and the excitement was too great for him. He lurched in that direction, heedless of the shadowy form that slipped through the brush toward the horse line. So Geraldi gained twenty vital steps before pursuit began.

As he ran in, he scanned the horses with an eager eye. Much, very much, would depend upon the selection of horseflesh which he made upon this day. Yonder he saw, at the end of the line, a gray horse upon which the broken firelight laid a finger, here and there, and seemed to be probing a silver mist. Well, gray was ever a favorite color with Geraldi.

That one he chose — that lead rope he slashed — into that saddle he leaped and heard, as he wheeled the horse away: "Tex! Tex Arnold! The devil's got your horse!"

Chapter Twenty-Two
SOMEBODY

Talk ebbed and flowed in a leisurely fashion along the verandah of the Sapphire Saloon. There were twenty stout chairs standing side by side along its ample length, and on a Saturday afternoon, such as this, the chairs were mostly occupied.

Only, from time to time, someone would yawn and say — "Let's liquor up." — and with grudging consent the entire line would heave slowly up and trail through the swinging doors of the barroom. There they had their drinks briefly and came out again, blinking, gasping a little, and apparently as startled as owls by the brilliance of the sunshine. Some said that the proprietor of the Sapphire knew just how to startle the oldest drinker in the world, because he put in a dash of lye to give his whiskey an added potency.

After issuing onto the verandah the entire line would sink down again, and the talk would begin to ripple slowly from end to end of the line. As the current flowed along, most men put in a word, a comment, or a whole sentence to swell the course of the gossip. There was only one break in the smoothly flowing tide, and that was when it reached the slender man at the farther end of the verandah. He neither commented nor offered remarks.

This shortcoming was forgiven in him. For one thing, he was reasonably young. For another, he was a stranger. For a third reason, he had the look somewhat of a tenderfoot, although it was noted that those slender hands of his manufactured cigarettes with remarkable skill. But he rarely spoke. He hardly seemed to listen, but gazed with rather melancholy eyes across the misty width of the valley and at the blue and brown of the mountains beyond.

After the last exodus from the saloon to the verandah the tide of talk began again, as usual, and flowed up and down the verandah somewhat as follows.

"Henry Clay Tucker's got a new cook." It was a solemnly bearded man who pronounced this. "I seen her at the station when she got off the train."

"I've heard she's a looker."

"Yeah, she can look."

"Tucker never has no she-cooks."

"Mostly he has chinks."

"Well, he's got a she-cook now. I've seen her."

"At his house?"

"Yeah, hangin' out some dish towels on the line in the back yard."

"Was she a looker?"

"She was kind of far away to see her face. She

looked made right, though."

"What does looks matter? Looks is the bait, and time steals it."

"Yeah. Take 'em at forty and what's left?"

"Wrinkles and alkali dust!"

"Calico means trouble."

"Yeah, even to Geraldi."

"Who said Geraldi?"

"I said calico meant trouble even to Geraldi. That's what busted him this time."

"He ain't busted."

"He's on the trail again, though."

"But he ain't busted. Ask Tex Arnold if he's busted."

"He'll get busted some day, and women has done it."

"How have they done it?"

"It was a girl that started him off this time. He was all settled down."

"I've heard about that. It was his wedding day."

"And the girl, she up and slides out a window and runs away on him."

"She took the silver with her, too."

"Yeah, and his spare hard cash, too."

"She left him flat."

"He'll have her hide for doin' that."

"Naw. He ain't that kind. He's easy with the ladies."

"Geraldi's smart. He made a clean fool of Arnold."

"He ain't smart enough to fool the women. This one, she made a fool of him. He thought he was gonna marry her. Haw, haw, haw!"

The slender man at the end of the line drew hard and long upon his cigarette, but as usual he said nothing. He merely narrowed his gaze a little as he looked out across the valley.

"Yeah, the women can fool even Geraldi."

"And he can fool all the men."

"They say that Tex Arnold's been asked to resign."

"Nope, but he's offered to resign."

"He oughta!"

"Don't be a fool, son. Nobody's much worse off because Geraldi's beat 'em. He beats everybody."

The slender man at the end of the row of chairs crossed his knees and began to swing his foot with a light, irregular, impatient rhythm.

"They wouldn't take the resignation of Tex Arnold."

"They better not. He's a good man, all right."

"They don't come much faster than Tex, with a gun."

"Except Geraldi."

"Aw, leave Geraldi be for a while, will you?"

"That's what you say. You know what he last done to Arnold?"

"You mean up in the cañon?"

"Yeah."

"I've heard about that."

"I was talkin' to one of the boys that was there. He told me."

"What did he say?"

"They had Geraldi all ringed around. He didn't have no chance. They had a solid line of bonfires. He didn't have no chance at all."

"What did he do then?"

"Why he runs up with a pole and vaults over the fire."

"Go on!"

"That's what you say. But this other gent, he seen it."

"I don't believe it."

"That's what happened, though. And where Geraldi lands is right on top of Tex Arnold. And he rolls off of Tex into the brush. That's how he gets away."

"Whatcha think of that?"

"And Arnold's hoss is the one that he rides off. A gray."

"A bay hoss, you mean."

"No, it was a gray."

"It was a bay hoss. I heard that clear and straight."

"What sort of looking gent is Geraldi?"

"Smallish, I've heard say."

"Biggish. Long and lean. Regular smart Westerner. Texas type."

"That's because he wears high heels onto his boots. But he's really small."

"He lifted eight hundred and fifty pounds of cast iron junk onto a scales. That's how small he is."

"He done it with a trick, then."

The slender man at the end of the row said:

"Who is Henry Clay Tucker?"

He said it softly to his companion, and his neighbor answered: "Aw, he's the father of a young fellow that's just gone off and joined up with that murdering Doctor Hayman gang. He's a rancher out yonder on the Dole Road."

"Seems to me that I've heard of him," said the other.

"You might've. He's the unluckiest man in this here county."

"Unluckiest?"

"I'll tell a man! First he ups and loses his wife, right young. Then their daughter, she dies. Now the boy, he goes and joins the Hayman gang."

"What for?" said the inquirer.

"Why do kids go wrong?" replied the other. "Maybe because he got tired of sitting at a table across from his pa's sour face. Which it sure would turn sweet milk with one look, and no mistake."

The man beyond, who had overheard the conversation, said: "It was a gambling debt."

"Go on!"

"It was. Young Jack Tucker, he does some gambling with Pete Borrow, and Pete takes him down the line and trims him good. He owes Pete a hundred and fifty bucks. He can pay only half of that. Then he goes home and asks his old man for the rest of the cash, and the old man won't give it to him. So then he goes and sells himself to Hayman, and Hayman buys him in, and pays off the rest of the debt to Pete."

"Is that how young Jack rode up to Willow Trail?"

"That's how. Jack was always wild, but he was always straight. He'll go to hell, now."

"Sure he will. Hayman takes 'em all to hell along with himself."

The man at the end of the row was speaking again. "Hayman is the fellow who robbed the Wells Fargo safe and killed the three guards, isn't he?"

"Yeah. That's Hayman."

"Single-handed?"

"Yeah. That's Hayman. He's done more'n that, single-handed, when his back was against the wall. He's sure death."

Another who had overheard the last remark broke in: "There would be a man for Geraldi to tackle."

"He'd be too hard on Geraldi."

"Yeah, he'd be too hard for anybody."

"A good pile too hard."

The man at the end of the row stood up and stretched his supple body delicately, carefully, as though he wished to try and test every muscle. He stretched as a cat stretches, limb by limb, and yet without too much gesticulation. Then he sighed and shrugged his shoulders more comfortably into his coat. After that he made himself a fresh cigarette, lighted it, and, crossing the verandah, he went down the steps between the two watering troughs. He went down the line of the horses and paused before a tall, finely made gray gelding.

"Look out, there!" bellowed the man who wore a heavy beard. "That buckskin'll kick the hat off your head!"

"You mean this buckskin?" asked the slender stranger. With wonderful ignorance he laid his hand actually upon the hip of the buckskin in question.

"That's the one!" thundered the bearded man. "He'll have your head off in another second."

The stranger smiled. "It doesn't seem to be his kicking day," he replied, and, pressing in carelessly between this horse and his own, he untied the lead rope, mounted, and passed off up the road.

A little silence spread along the verandah.

"Now who's he?" asked the bearded man, muttering.

Heads were shaken, and in the silence that followed, someone muttered: "Well, he's somebody!"

Chapter Twenty-Three

TUCKER'S RANCH

When Geraldi was free of the village, he put the gray into a long, raking canter and did not draw up until he approached a nest of poplar trees at a culvert. There he drew rein and whistled.

Red-headed Pete immediately stepped into view and blinked at Geraldi.

"How are the boys?" asked Geraldi.

"Sleepin'," said Pete. "They're done in. I'd be sleepin', too, except that my nerves have got the jumps. I'd like to have about a quart of red-eye to quiet me down."

"Pete," said Geraldi, "you're going to have enough jack to buy a whole tankful of red-eye before you're through with this. Have you got everything else that you want?"

"Yes," said Pete, "except a free trail."

"You want the world with a fence around it," Geraldi replied. "What's the matter with you, Pete? If there's a marshal and a posse looking for the three of you . . . and me, too . . . it's all the more reason why we should enjoy our riding. That's the salt on the egg, Pete. You can't eat eggs without salt, can you?"

Pete grinned dubiously back at his employer.

"All right," he said. "I know you, Geraldi. At least, I know the title page and how the first chapter begins of you. I guess nobody else knows much more. What's the news?"

"I think that I've located the girl again," said Geraldi.

"Hey! Near here?"

"Yes. At a place owned by a fellow named Tucker. Out yonder on the Dole Road. I may be wrong. I'm taking a long step. But I have a mighty good idea that I'm right."

"You mostly are," said Pete. "I never thought that you'd pick her up again this quick. But if she's there, maybe the marshal is there, too."

"No, not as soon as this," said Geraldi with conviction. "Not unless she's told him where she went."

"Do we ride that way with you?"

"Wait until the boys have had their sleep out," said Geraldi. "Then you trail along up the road. Cut over yonder off the main trail. I can see cow paths through those hills. Ride over yonder, and I'll try to pick you up before dark."

Pete scratched his head.

"Listen, chief," he said. "Mostly you're right. But whatcha gain by trailin' around after a girl that's turned you down? Ain't it better sense for you to take the three of us and turn us onto a job where there's real money to play for?"

Geraldi listened in patience. Then he said: "Let me work my own trail, Pete. Do what I've told you. Do you want higher pay?"

"Me?" said Pete. "Higher pay for just settin' around with nothing to do but dodge a few slugs of lead a couple of times a day? Why, Geraldi, we've hardly got enough to do to keep us warm. All we've got to do, mostly, is to keep from bein' turned cold forever."

Geraldi smiled. "Do what I said," he suggested. "Remember, Pete, that there's a bonus for you, all three, when I finish with you, and a bonus that will make your head swim."

He left Pete with these instructions and sent the gray at the same long canter, sweeping up the road. Where it branched, he turned onto the long, meandering stretch of rutted, hoof-beaten ground that had been pointed out to him as the Dole Road. Thus he came to the ranch house of Henry Clay Tucker.

It was not an ordinary ranch house. It was inhabited by people who had not deliberately cut down all of the trees around the place for the sake of getting easier firewood. Instead, the trees had been allowed to grow, and now they spread a fine shade. There was even a fresh coat of paint on the house. It glimmered dazzling blue-white through the gaps among the trees.

Geraldi went in through the corral gate, tethered his horse at the hitching rack, opened the garden gate, and allowed the weight to slam the gate behind him. He walked down a narrow, board path that creaked beneath his tread. Tomatoes were planted upon either side of it. The vines grew high and were tied up on tall racks. The tomatoes were still only small green beads at the tops of the vines, but they were swelling on the lower stalks.

So he came to the side of the ranch house, and there, on the side verandah, which was now the coolest place, he saw a tall, gaunt man sitting with overalls stuffed inside coarse, heavy boots — a gaunt man with a face like iron and gray, remorseless eyes. He looked up from the newspaper he had been reading and gave Geraldi a long look.

"What brought you here?" he said at last.

"Dinner time," said Geraldi.

The rancher stirred a little in his chair. Then his upper lip curled as he pointed toward a formidable woodpile in the back yard. A sawbuck and a pair of axes — one for chopping and one for splitting — stood beside it, and the ground was whitened with chips.

"Bums get no hand-outs here. They work for their grub," said the rancher.

"Yes, sir," said Geraldi. "I work for my chuck. But my hands are soft, Mister Tucker."

"You know my name, do you?" said Tucker.

"Everybody around here knows your name, Mister Tucker," replied the flatterer.

But Tucker was not flattered. "You chop wood or you go hungry," he said.

He shook out his paper with a loud rattling and resumed his reading with a frown of concentration.

"You know, Mister Tucker," said Geraldi, "that there are all kinds of work. There's card work, for one thing." A pack of cards appeared in his hands. He flicked them with a rattle.

Tucker looked up with a somewhat distorted grin. "You're a real sharp, are you?" he said.

"Yes, sir, in a modest way," said Geraldi.

"Deal out four hands," said Tucker. "Make 'em a straight, a full house, and four of a kind. I'll take the four of a kind."

Geraldi shuffled the cards without lowering the pack to the floor of the verandah. Then, in a steady, flashing stream, he made the cards shower into place in four neat stacks of five each.

Tucker turned them over. All was as he had demanded. At his own feet lay four aces. He kicked the cards away from him. Then, another impulse coming over him, he leaned a little from his chair. "A smart thing like you," he said, "ought to be able to make a fortune, if you have tricks like that up your sleeve. How do you happen to be out here, begging your way along the road?"

Geraldi shrugged his shoulders. "You know how it is," he said.

"I don't," said Tucker.

"Well," explained Geraldi, "if you deal yourself four aces around this part of the world, the boys pull their guns."

"And you don't wear one?"

"Not to kill with," said Geraldi. He smiled a flashing smile at the rancher. At the same time he began to juggle the cards. Six at a time spun into the air, whirling rapidly, and descended again surely into his fingers. Then one walked, apparently of its own accord, up his extended arm, and hopped off to fall back into a waiting set of fingers. A shower of cards spun up over his back and descended with equal infallibility into his grasp. As he juggled, he talked.

"You've spent years on that," said Tucker.

"Years! All my life," said Geraldi.

"You might have made some honest money in the same time, with less effort," said Tucker.

"Why?" asked Geraldi. "The honest money goes into a bank. And your children spend it for you. But crooked money is spent as fast as it comes in."

"And leaves you nothing!" said Tucker.

"It leaves you a good time," said Geraldi. He added suddenly: "How many good times have you had, Mister Tucker?"

"That will do," said Tucker, straightening.

"I beg your pardon," said Geraldi, collapsing the spread of cards suddenly into a tight pack, "but truth is like murder."

"It will out. Is that what you mean?" asked Tucker, scowling.

"Aye," said Geraldi, "and it hurts almost as much. I ought to get a dinner for telling you this much truth, Mister Tucker."

"Dinner's over," said Tucker.

He fell to dreaming, as it seemed, looking steadily, gloomily away from the younger man, brooding over the shadows that were spread under the trees.

"But there's something cold in the pantry," suggested Geraldi.

"Pantry?" said the other, suddenly recalling himself. Then he waved his hand. "Go back there and knock at the kitchen door. Tell the cook to give you whatever she has ready. She'll have something. Tell her to sit you down at the dining-room table and feed you. Now don't bother me any more!"

"Thank you, sir," said Geraldi. He walked around to the back of the house. He did not go at once to the kitchen door, however. Instead, he paused for a moment with one hand resting against a wooden pillar of the rear verandah. His heart was racing. After a time he rallied himself and raised his head, walked up the steps, and tapped at the kitchen door.

"Who's there?" sang out the familiar voice of Mary.

"A tramp," Geraldi said huskily. "Looking for a hand-out."

"You'll have to see Mister Tucker," she answered, not recognizing his voice.

"I've seen him," said Geraldi more clearly. "He sent me around here to see you."

She knew his voice this time, for now the door was snatched open, and she stood before him pale, with staring eyes. "Oh, Jimmy, why have you come again," she whispered.

He made one of his quick, flashing gestures. "Because I'm hungry, my dear," he replied.

Chapter Twenty-Four

WILLOW TRAIL

She looked at him in despair.

"Mister Tucker said you'd let me sit down at the dining-room table," remarked Geraldi. "But I'd as soon stand in the kitchen with you, Mary."

She held the door open, and, as he passed, his face came close to hers. He could see that she did not wince, and the thoughtfulness did not alter in her eyes. The color was already returning to her face. He could see that he had not gained greatly by the shock of his sudden appearance.

She said nothing for the moment, and neither did he, but watched her going about the business of preparing food for him. She brought out from the pantry a boiled ham and whipped a butcher knife sharp on a steel before she started shearing off large, thin slices. She broke three eggs into a frying pan and scrambled them with cream and butter while the coffee pot sat on the hottest fire the stove offered and began to simmer.

She put the eggs on the back of the stove and cut white bread for him, and finally sat him down at the dining-room table in front of this food. Then, as he ate, she stood opposite to him, leaning her hands upon the back of a chair.

"Sit down," said Geraldi.

"I'll stand," she answered. "I can always think better, standing."

"I haven't come here to worry you," Geraldi said.

She looked straight back at him in this new, considering, cold manner of hers, and he found that he could not endure the weight of her eyes. He returned to his eating, his appetite sadly diminished.

"How are things on the trail?" she asked him.

"Oh, Arnold is still on the job," said Geraldi. He smiled a little, a smile that flashed in and out and was gone.

"Poor Arnold is having a bad time," said the girl. "I don't think he'll ever manage to handle you, Jimmy. Not for a long time, at least. Are you enjoying it?"

"I'm enjoying nothing without you," he told her.

"Be honest," she said.

He looked back at her. Color began to heat his face. He felt like a small boy at school. "Well," he admitted, "it's true that I'm enjoying it a little. We went through a long, quiet time, Mary. Besides, I've got to have something to keep my hands full just now."

"So you've come here," said the girl. "You know that they'll find me . . . and they'll find you again, too."

He shrugged his shoulders. "I had to see you, Mary," he said.

"Why?" she asked him.

The bluntness of the question staggered him. He saw that she was steady as a rock while she watched him. "Do I have to explain that?" he asked her.

"You'll say it's because you're fond of me, Jimmy."

"Yes. I'll say that."

"Is it showing fondness," she asked, "to put me in the fire like this?"

"Are you in the fire?" said Geraldi.

"As long as you're in danger, being close to me. Of course, I am."

"I had to ask you a question. I don't intend to hound you around the world, like a fool," Geraldi said. "But there's a definite question that I have to ask you."

"Then ask it," she said.

"Are you through with me forever?"

"Yes," she said without hesitation.

He pushed his plate away and concentrated on his coffee.

She, leaning across the table, took his Bull Durham and wheat straw papers from the pocket of his coat and began to make a cigarette for him.

"I don't believe you, Mary," he said.

"Why not?"

"You're not the sort to love a man . . . and you did love me once . . . and then push him out of

193

your mind in a few days with a gesture, and little more."

"It hasn't been easy. I haven't said that it was easy," she protested.

"You care about me still," said Geraldi. "Now, Mary, look fairly and squarely at me, and tell me the truth."

She met his eyes. There was sorrow in her look; he could not read the other emotions.

"I won't lie to you, Jimmy," she said, "and, therefore, I won't answer that question. I don't want to talk about it any more."

He finished his coffee, accepted the rolled cigarette from her, and lighted it from the match she struck for him.

"Listen to me," said Geraldi. "You're in bad shape, Mary. You're thin. You have big black circles around your eyes. Why is that?"

"I can't sleep," she said. "I haven't slept since I came to this place."

"Why not?"

She gestured toward the side verandah — one window of the dining room looked out upon it. They could hear the slow rumbling of Tucker's rocking chair as it moved back and forth under his weight.

"It's because of him," she answered.

"Because of Tucker? What's he to you?" asked Geraldi.

He stared at her, amazed, suspicious, but Mary shook her head and smiled back at him.

"There's a lot of the silly little boy in you,

Jimmy," she said. "I'll tell you what Mister Tucker is to me. He's a human being, and a grand one. He's the salt of the earth. He's the kindest heart I've ever known. And just now he's in the middle of hell."

"Why?"

"Because his son has gone wrong. His boy has run away and joined the murderer, Hayman."

"I've heard of that," said Geraldi.

"And that's the end of things for poor Mister Tucker. He's slaved all his life for his family. He's pretty comfortably well off now. But what does it mean to him? The boy's gone. Now he sits and tries to read newspapers and think. There's nothing left for him. He hates the face of his ranch. He hates the work on it. He hates even to look at his cattle in the pastures. All that he's done has turned to ashes. That's why I can't sleep, Jimmy. The pain that's in him is getting into my own heart. You wouldn't wonder if . . . here, you can see for yourself."

She stepped back and reversed a picture that was turned to the wall. Geraldi saw the enlarged photograph of as handsome a young fellow as he had ever seen, a boy with the look of a man, and a man's decided jaw, and a man's keen eyes. His youth showed about the mouth only — that infantile look that will remain until pain has stiffened the upper lip.

"You can see for yourself," she said softly, giving a cautious glance toward the verandah as she turned the picture again.

"I see," said Geraldi. He dropped his head and stared at the table.

"He was straight as a string, but as wild as a hawk. I've talked to the 'punchers on the place about him. They all love him. They all say that a finer young fellow never stepped. Until Geraldi came into the picture!"

Geraldi sprang up. "That's a cruel thing to say, Mary," he cried to her. "That's twisting the knife in the wound, don't you think?"

"Well, I don't mean to do that," she said. "But Jack never would have run wild, it seems, if he hadn't heard so much about you."

"I never saw the lad in my life," said Geraldi.

"Of course not. Seeing and really knowing might have cured him. But hearing makes things big, you know. He's had you in his mind like a knight of King Arthur's. He has a stack of newspaper clippings and magazine articles about you. After he'd made a hero of you, he made something glorious out of your wild life. He was talking about freedom and such rot. Oh, Jimmy, it's not so much what fellows like you do. It's the trail that you blaze for lots of others."

Geraldi began to walk impatiently up and down the room. At last he stopped before her. "If it's laid at my door," he said, "suppose that I undo the thing that's been done?"

"Undo what, Jimmy?" she asked him.

"The boy. Jack. Suppose that I bring him back before he's gone wrong?"

"He's gone wrong already. He's joined the

Hayman gang. I told you that."

"He's committed no crime, so far as you know. Before he does, I may find him and bring him away."

"Away from Hayman?" said the girl, frowning at him. "Jimmy, you know well enough that men don't leave the Hayman gang, except when bullets set them free."

He immediately waved the impossibility away. "I'll tell you what, Mary," he said, "I've given you trouble and sorrow enough. Now let me have a chance to buy my way back to where I stood with you before."

"Buy your way, Jimmy?" she said.

"Buy my way," he said, repeating the words firmly. "Not with cash, but with young Jack Tucker, safely delivered here, without a stain on his hands or his reputation."

"If you brought back Jack Tucker," said the girl, "the gang would murder him within twenty-four hours. They've done similar things before. Every man who goes up the Willow Trail goes for good, if he's accepted."

"I've heard of the Willow Trail before," said Geraldi. "What is it?"

"Oh, it's the course of the long draw that runs north toward Kempton Mountain. It fills with water once or twice a year, and the willows grow along the side of it. Fellows who ride far enough up that trail are sure to meet some of the Hayman gang, winter or summer. And they're either turned back, or they're taken in as members. Everyone in the countryside seems to know about the Willow Trail."

He nodded. "I'm offering you a bargain, Mary," he said. "You've willed me out of your mind. You've set your will against me. If I bring back Jack Tucker, will you open the door to me again?"

"Your life for his life, Jimmy?" she asked. "Is that what you're offering to me?"

He wondered at her unmoved gravity of voice. As he stared at her, a sudden new thought came to him. "No," he said, "I'll not make a bargain. What I want from you no man can bargain for. Either the giving is in you, or it's not. Only, tell me this . . . it's mighty little that you care for me now, Mary. Isn't that true?"

How straight and steady her gaze could be.

"That's a thing that I'll never talk to you about, Jimmy," she said. "I've made up my mind, that's all. As for what may be in my thoughts, I can't talk about it, and I won't."

He hesitated. Then he spoke slowly: "If newspaper chatter about me is what has turned Jack Tucker's head, it's my duty to try to turn him straight. I'll make no bargain with you, Mary. I'll say good bye and start along the Willow Trail."

He held out his hand to her. She took it in both of hers.

"Jimmy," she said, "I'm afraid I'll never lay eyes on you again. I feel it in my heart. Yet, I can't ask you not to try to save poor young

Tucker. If you save him, you've saved his father, too. God bless you. No other man in the world would even think of trying such a thing."

"Good bye," repeated Geraldi. "The trail isn't ended . . . it's hardly begun. Only tell me . . . if I come back, will I find you here? You won't cut and run again?"

"Why should I run away?" said Mary. "If I took wings, you'd manage to find faster ones and catch me again."

Chapter Twenty-Five
DANGER AHEAD

When Geraldi started the gray horse down the road again, it seemed to him that the face of the world had changed. The burn was gone from the sun; the blue of the sky was paler. It was like the difference between summer and winter. For he knew that he had taken into his hands a task to which all others he had attempted were as nothing.

It made his heart both small and cold to contemplate what lay before him. Yet he was resolute. For he remembered the very last words that the girl had spoken to him as he left the ranch of old Tucker.

"Jimmy, if ever I come to you again, it will make no difference what you may be or what you may do afterward. I'll stay with you forever. Only now, I've wanted to give us both a fighting chance at a new life."

He had not even wished to kiss her. But he had looked at her with a melancholy pleasure, and then gone off down the creaking boardwalk toward the corral.

Now, as he jogged the gray down the road, he

looked north at the blue-brown vastness of Kempton Mountain, furrowed and scarred with intricate intertanglings of ravines and cañons from its monstrous shoulders to its many knees that sloped out toward the plain. To the shoulders it was darkly forested. Above these there appeared a vast face of stone with features set off in purple shadows. Above was the eternal cap of snow.

Somewhere yonder, probably, he would have to fight out the battle to save young Jack Tucker. How he would act he did not know. It was a problem that, if he could solve it at all, he would have to manage at the touch and go of a moment's notice. Planning ahead would do little good.

He came again to the poplars, and there was Pete in full sight, sitting on the bank and smoking a pipe, over the bowl of which he closed his big fist to shut out the wind, sailor fashion. Geraldi drew up beside him.

"You know Kempton Mountain?" he asked, pointing.

Pete rose to his feet, apparently amazed.

"Is that Kempton Mountain?" he asked. "Where Hayman hangs out? Sure, I've heard of his hole-in-the-wall country. To think of me sittin' here and never knowin' that was Kempton Mountain!" He pulled off his hat and scratched his red head. It was almost like a gesture of awe and worship.

"Yes," said Geraldi, a little amused, "that's

201

Kempton Mountain. That's where you three are heading."

"Not me," said Pete with definite determination. "I ain't going near Hayman. Anybody else, sure. But not Doctor Hayman. Nope. Not me!" He smiled in the enthusiasm of his resolution. "Fire," went on Pete, "is nice and cool to handle . . . but the Doctor is pretty warm. When he touches, he takes off the skin and all the flesh, down to the bone."

"You three," Geraldi said, "will go up there on the straightest line you can make it. You're not going to be bothered by Doc Hayman. You ought to have heard that the Doctor never troubles his neighbors. He believes in a peaceful home. That's what he believes in. When he wants his fun, he rides for it. There's only one dangerous trail toward Kempton Mountain, and that's the Willow Trail. Keep off that and you're all right. Go right up to the town of Kempton itself. It's a village somewhere in the woods. There are a couple of logging camps near it. Then you three scatter out and get jobs in the camps. I may need you, and need you badly. What for, I can't say as yet. I have no definite plan, but I think, if everything works out as I want it to, the four of us will earn some money. Mind you, Pete, I'm not promising. But when I speak of money, I mean several thousand for each of you. Ten thousand . . . twenty thousand, even."

"Twenty thousand!" said Pete, his eyes

flaming. "I'd go to Kempton Mountain . . . I'd go and pull Hayman's chin, for that much money. Twenty thousand dollars, did you say?"

"That's what I said. I don't know. It might be thirty thousand. It might be a hundred thousand, for all I know. But the game's big and the game's dangerous. You tell the other boys. If they don't want to take the chance, they can drop out. But I'd like to have you, Pete, at least. And I think that Jerry would tag along with you."

"Jerry'll stay. So will Bob," declared Pete. "We all of us'll stay. That's because you've brought us luck, easy work, and plenty of eats. A man'd be a fool that didn't stick by you, Geraldi. A hundred thousand? Why, everybody's gotta die some day. And why not die takin' a shot at something worth dyin' for? If I had a hundred thousand. . . ."

"How would you blow it in?" asked Geraldi curiously.

"Blow it in? Blow in a hundred thousand?" echoed Pete. "I wouldn't blow it in. I've blowed in up to fifteen thousand. Because that ain't no capital to work on. But with a hundred thousand that's different. I'd go back to New Jersey. I know the farm that I'd buy, and the line of cows that I'd put in. A dairy is what I've always had in the corner of my head. I can see the cows, walkin' on the grass. I can hear 'em lowin'. Y'understand me, Geraldi?"

The latter looked earnestly at his helper. "I understand you a little," said Geraldi. "There's different stuff in you than I thought. Pete, put the proposition up to the boys."

"Yes, sir," Pete replied. "Once we get to Kempton, will you get in touch with us?"

"I'll get in touch with you. There'll be a general merchandise store there, I suppose. I'll hunt you up there. One of you come into the store every evening. When I want you, I'll go down there and try to locate you."

"Easy," said Pete. "How long will it take to work up this lay?" His eyes shone with a foretaste of wealth.

"A day, a month, or a year," Geraldi responded. "I don't know."

"A day, a month, or a year," said the other. "Well, I'd rather wait the year. Then it's more likely to work through. The things that you wait for and work for, they're the things that are worthwhile. A hundred thousand for a day's work . . . why that's no good at all. Not likely to be good, I mean to say."

Geraldi nodded. "Fill the other boys with the same idea," he said. "You have a brain in your head, Pete. You and I can do things together."

"We can open the dog-gone work like an oyster," Pete said with confidence. "I got the wrists, and the fingers, and you're the cuttin' edge of the knife!"

"Good bye," said Geraldi.

"Hold on. Which way are you travelin' to Kempton Mountain?" asked Pete.

"I don't know. But an easy trail," said Geraldi.

"I don't want to arrive with the rest of you. When I see you in Kempton, if I manage that, pretend that you don't know me. I'll communicate with you in secret. You understand?"

"Like it was read to me out of a book," declared Pete.

"So long, Pete."

"So long, Geraldi. We're gonna have luck fit for the four of us."

Fit for more than the four of us, Geraldi thought as he moved away on the gray horse. *Because if we have only the luck that's fit for us, how long will we be left alive?*

He continued down the road for a little distance until he was sure that he was lost to the observation of Pete. Then he left the highway and struck across the fields until he came to the Willow Trail.

Chapter Twenty-Six
THE FAT MAN

It was an appropriate name. The bed of the draw made a broad and usually a comfortable road; the willows grew, scattering along the banks, or else filled shallow marshlands in dense groves. It was a commodious road in more ways than one, for water that was perfectly good for drinking most of the year stood in pools at intervals along the way; and among the willows a hungry man could generally knock over a rabbit with his first shot. The Willow Trail, therefore, offered both a road and maintenance on the way. There were other features about it, too. All through the summer heat of the day, Geraldi heard the cooing of the wild doves, deep, soft, sorrowing notes that lived in the air and seemed to float through the thin shadows beneath the trees. They gave the music to the Willow Trail.

But they were not the only birds. Now and then a hawk swayed close above the heads of the trees. The hunter was on the alert for small game; how many a song was ended by the stroke of the talons? Far higher than the hawks, dwindling in the air, the buzzards floated on their untiring wings and brought in grim thoughts.

As Geraldi rode on, he could see the trails that came down through the banks to the water holes. Fox, coyote, and wolf came in their due places. Here again would be a series of trails made by deer, and by antelope. Bobcats and mountain lions left their signs along the way, and sage hens criss-crossed the muddy edges with their tracks. Where there was water, there must be good hunting for beast and man. Tooth against tooth, and claw against claw, was the order of the day. Geraldi smiled as he thought of this.

He himself was going as a beast of prey among the hunters. A light foot and swift eye he would need to save himself from the danger. In the meantime, he put the gray along at a good stiff pace, keeping mostly to a trot, until, when he looked up between the willows that lined the banks, he saw that he was close under the foot-hills of Kempton Mountain.

Here, turning a wide bend, he found a pool of water larger than any he had yet encountered. The reason for its size was apparently a trickle of water that flowed from a spring on the eastern bank. Near the spring, seated on a willow stump, a fat man with a round, good-natured face, a battered hat, a pair of overalls girt about his hips, and a loose coat that fitted like a slicker was patiently extending a long rod over the dark pool and waiting for a fish to bite. Geraldi drew rein, and the other looked up with a pleasant smile and a nod.

"Howdy!" said the fat man.

"Hello," said Geraldi. "How are they biting?"

"They ain't biting yet," replied the other. "They're just makin' up their minds. A fish is like a girl. It takes a terrible lot of persuading before it'll come out in the open."

"I've noticed that about girls," said Geraldi.

"Yeah. And it's true about fish," said the fat man. "But it takes a thinker to catch a thinker."

"You're a thinker, then?" Geraldi said.

"Nothin' but," said the other with a smile that disclaimed all seriousness in this remark. "I'm a setter and a thinker. The more than I set, the more that I think . . . and the more that I think, the more that I set. It works both ways, like a two-edged axe."

"You've picked a good spot," said Geraldi. "Thinking in the shade on a day like this is the only right way of thinking, I'd say."

"Yes, sir," replied the fat man. "I been here, watchin' and communin' with a big, fat trout that's lyin' down there thinkin' of the spring flood, and fannin' himself with his fins, and layin' his back in the broadest patch of sunshine that goes down into that pool. He's a thinker, too, but him and me ain't yet agreed."

"Maybe you're thinking in Spanish," Geraldi suggested.

"I dunno but what I might be," replied the fat man. "I been down there through quite a piece of Mexico. Have you?"

"I've seen a little of it," answered Geraldi.

"Did you like it?"

"Yes. It has a pretty nice, lazy feeling," said Geraldi.

"Yeah. But it's dangerous," replied the fisherman. "You never can tell when there's a knife or a gun behind your back. There's too many eyes in the middle of the night to suit a gent like me, what has nerves and such things."

"I'd never guess that you're nervous," Geraldi stated.

"Wouldn't you?" said the fisherman. "That's because I'm kind of fat. It's a terrible thing the way that fat folks are misjudged, take them all in all. Because they got a layer of fat under the skin, folks think that the ends of their nerves are all covered up and buried. But nerves, son, they come right through to the skin."

"That's something I'll remember," Geraldi assured the man. "You grow so nervous that I suppose you have to come off here by yourself to quiet down?"

"That's exactly it," the fat man said. "I gotta be off by myself, thinkin', and out-thinkin' the fish, if I can. By the time that I get this here pool all persuaded the way that I am, I'll be feelin' pretty good."

"You live around here?" asked Geraldi.

"Yeah. I live back that way. I got a small place. It ain't much. But it's quiet. Only trouble about it is that I gotta ride a long ways to see fish. That's a likely hoss that you're ridin'."

"Yes," said Geraldi. "He's a good horse. He steps out, and he lasts pretty well, too. No better than yours, though. Yours can move pretty fast."

The fat man frowned curiously, and then he turned his head. His horse obviously was not in sight. He looked back at Geraldi. "What makes you say that?" he said. "You ain't seen my hoss, have you?"

"No," Geraldi said. "But I'll swap horses with you blind."

The fat man frowned again. But his good nature could not be repressed. A smile seemed to be bubbling in his throat, and it had to find his lips.

"You're a kind of reckless young feller, ain't you?" he asked.

"Not a bit," said Geraldi. "No. You have a pretty fine horse back there." He waved his hand.

"I ain't sayin' that it is, and I ain't sayin' that it ain't," said the fat man. "But I sure envy a gent with X-ray eyes that can look through fifty yards of brush and trees and see the hoss behind 'em."

"It's not an X-ray eye," admitted Geraldi. "But, you know, they say you can tell the lion by his claw."

"What might you mean by that?"

"Well, one thing leads to another. That's all I mean by saying that."

"Meanin' that I lead up to a hoss, son?" The smile froze upon the lips of the fat man as he asked the question.

"Look here," Geraldi said, "when you see the wagon, you can tell what sort of a horse ought to be hitched to it. When you see the man, you can tell what sort of a horse he needs, too."

"Wouldn't a plow hoss fit me pretty good?" asked the fisherman.

"A plow horse could fit you pretty well," Geraldi said frankly. "But he couldn't move fast enough to suit you, I think."

"Humph," said the other. "You seem to know a lot, young feller. You'll be tellin' me the color of my hoss pretty soon."

"Yes," said Geraldi. "I think that you'd like 'em pretty high in color. What about a pinto?"

"Eh?" grunted the fisherman, so astonished that he lowered the rod until the end of it splashed in the surface of the water.

"Yes," said Geraldi, "I'd say that your taste would run to a red horse with a big white patch on his left side."

The fisherman half rose from the stump, and only slowly settled back upon it. "You know me and my hoss, do you?" he asked, his eyes narrowing.

"Never saw you in my life," Geraldi assured him. "But as I was saying, one thing leads to another. You tell the lion. . . ."

"Oh, damn all that," said the fat man, his smile quite gone. "You were saying that I'd want a hoss that could travel some, too?"

"Why, of course, you would" answered Geraldi. "Anyone could see that."

211

"I dunno how," said the other.

"By the scars that the wind has left on you," Geraldi tried to explain. "Isn't that clear?"

"The scars that the wind has left?"

"Why," Geraldi went on, "it's a plain thing that you would never have picked them up in a fight, because you don't like fighting. You left Mexico to get out of it, apparently." He gave the fisherman the most genial of smiles as he continued fluidly. "That nick out of your ear looks as though a Forty-Five caliber slug had kissed you there. The little white mark down the side of your face might have been made by a knife in a fast hand. But, knowing that you're a peace lover, I take it for granted that it must be the wind that left the marks on you. If the wind did that, you must have been riding on a rather fast horse. There's nothing mysterious about it, you see?"

"Yeah, I see," drawled the other. He dropped his head and stared for a moment at the black face of the pool, but it was plain that he was not considering fish or fishing, for a full yard of the pole was now immersed. "I see," repeated the fat man. "You're kind of a thinker yourself."

"Oh, no," said Geraldi. "I just watch one thing leading to another."

"What led you to my hoss?" said the fisherman.

"The red hairs on the inside of your right knee and the white hairs on your other trouser leg."

The other looked down at his legs with a start.

212

He scowled as he stared back at Geraldi. "You got a telescope sight fitted into your eye, son?" he asked.

"No, it's just practice in looking at little things," said Geraldi.

"You're one of these here mind-readers, I guess," said the fat man, his smile now turning into a sneer.

"Some people say that I read minds pretty well," admitted Geraldi.

"What's in mine right now?" asked the fisherman.

"A name," said Geraldi.

"Eh? What name, then?"

"Hayman," Geraldi responded.

The fisherman threw his pole to one side and rose suddenly to his feet. "Who the hell might you be?" he demanded.

"A friend of yours," said Geraldi. "A friend in the making, as you might say."

"And just what d'you mean by that?"

"I mean that I hope to know you better. Because I like thinking men, I expect we'll be friends."

"Thinkin' is all damn' well and good," said the other, "but thinkin' and lookin' around a corner is a might different matter. I ain't accustomed to it, and I dunno that I like it. What have you got me sized up for?"

"A good left-handed shot and a hard man to beat in a poker game," Geraldi stated.

The left hand of the fat man shot inside his

coat, but it remained there. He was looking with a steady interest into the muzzle of Geraldi's gun, held waist-high, with an easily bent elbow, and so thrusting out before him.

"Besides," said Geraldi, "a thinking man, and a man who thinks fast enough to have two thoughts about any important thing. I hope the second one has come to you now, partner."

The fat man, some of his high color gone and his brow contorted, gradually, inch by inch, withdrew the hand that had dived inside of his loosely fitted coat. Then he shook his head. "Young, feller," he said, "I'll tell you something about yourself."

"I'd like to hear it," answered Geraldi.

"You beat the devil," said the fisherman.

"No," replied Geraldi, "but I might be useful to the devil, if the one you mean is named Hayman."

Chapter Twenty-Seven
UNDERSTANDING

The moment that the hand of the fat man was withdrawn from his coat, the gun of Geraldi disappeared. When it was gone, the fisherman started to jerk his own back in his original gesture, but he changed his mind at once. The smile reappeared upon his face, but this time it was rather a grin than a smile.

"Supposin'," he said, "that I was to reason from a claw to a lion, what kind of thinkin' would I do about you, stranger?"

"You would say," said Geraldi readily, "that you've met a young man on a gray horse, with nothing but time on his hands and a lot of willingness to spend it. You'd say that he has a pretty empty wallet and no great desire to work to fill it. You'd say that he liked to take short cuts and hates the longest way around to a good thing."

The fat man, for the first time, frankly and heartily laughed. "You're a rum kid," he said. "What might your name be?"

"Why, I've been called Manhattan Jimmy by a lot of people," he said.

"Manhattan," said the fat man, "if there

wasn't all this water betwixt us, I'd like to shake hands with you."

"Thanks," said Geraldi. "And how are you called?"

"Some call me," said the other, "just plain Fatty. Some call me Double Deck Joe. And there's some who have called me Juggling Joe. There's been some printed posters around that call me Joseph Decker. Those posters was printed by friends of mine that wanted to give me some free lodging, with board thrown in. But I always been so busy that I ain't had the time to go and answer the invitation."

Geraldi smiled in turn, for the first time during this odd interview. "I understand you, Joe," he said. "I'm glad that I'm not going to be introduced to Hayman by a green hand."

"Who said that I was going to introduce you to Hayman?" asked the fat man, instantly serious. "I dunno you, kid."

"That's because I take some knowing, as the mustang said to the man on the ground," answered Geraldi. "But you see that I'm a friendly fellow, Joe. And I hope to have a good word from you to Hayman."

"For all I know," said the other, "you might be a government agent."

"If you think that," said Geraldi, "you haven't looked at me twice. Look again, Joe."

Double Deck Joe looked and nodded, with his stretching grin that placed a great fold of fat before either ear. "You're a smart kid," he admitted. "What did you do to the gun of yours? Chuck it up your sleeve?"

"No," said Geraldi, "I just palmed it. I just soaked it away in the palm of my hand. That's where I usually keep it in case of accidents."

"How many bullets do you carry in your gun?" asked the fat man.

"There's nothing under the hammer but luck," said Geraldi. "I never carry more than five in each gun. Do you?"

"No, son, I wasn't born yesterday," said Double Deck. "But I've seen fools young enough to take their chances with a hair-trigger. I was just askin' in case."

"There's no reason why we shouldn't ride up the rest of the Willow Trail together, is there?" asked Geraldi.

"Gimme time. Don't you crowd me," said Double Deck Joe. "I don't know you yet. I've seen you juggle a gun, but I ain't seen you do no shootin'."

"That hawk hasn't either," Geraldi said.

The fat man looked up, and he saw a wide-winged hawk sliding over the top of a tree a good fifty yards away. A revolver barked at the same instant, and the hawk tumbled down. Before it struck, Double Deck Joe looked back at Geraldi, but the hand of the latter was empty again.

"Slick!" Joe commented. "Damn' slick. The slickest that I ever seen. I guess that you wouldn't need much introducing, son. You could do your own introducin', I reckon. Now wait till I get my pinto, and I'll ride up the Willow Trail with you, and mighty glad to." He waved his hand and, leaving his fishing pole behind, hurried off into the brush.

Geraldi, the instant that the other was well inside the brush, leaped from the back of the gray gelding, crossed the pool with a single cat-like spring, and in a moment was gliding through the same bushes.

There was this difference, that, whereas Double Deck Joe had entered the brush with much crashing, Geraldi slid through it as though the dried bushes were a soft mist. All noise had ceased before him, also, and presently he made out a shape slipping back through the greenery, stealing softly along. He saw that it was Double Deck Joe. The glint of steel appeared in the hand of the fat man, and upon the lips of Geraldi came that small, cold smile that had chilled the heart of many a man before this day. He stepped soundlessly behind Joe.

"Hunting grizzlies, Joe?" he asked.

Double Deck wheeled and found the muzzle of a Colt thrust deep into his stomach. He blinked, as though the face of Geraldi were a blinding light. "By the thunderin' holy Moses!" he gasped. "You ain't as young as you look."

"Put up your gun, Joe," said Geraldi, "and put it up slowly and carefully."

"Manhattan," said the other, "I'm gonna put that gun away like it was all made of one entire diamond."

He suited the action to the word. At the same moment, Geraldi's weapon disappeared.

"I was just gonna look and see," said Double Deck Joe, rather high in color at the moment.

"Of course, you were," Geraldi said. "Don't think I misunderstand. You might say that we never knew one another until this moment, Joe. Mightn't you say that?"

"Of course, you might . . . and so might I," declared Double Deck. "Now come along with me, and we'll stay together. You give me kind of a shock, speakin' out sudden behind my back that way."

He gave Geraldi a long, earnest look, and suddenly he began to roar with laughter. "I've certainly gone and made myself into a hell of a fool, ain't I?" he suggested.

"That's not half what you might have made of me," said Geraldi.

"No, no," protested the other. "There wasn't anything serious in my mind. Just sort of an idea to throw a chill into you, Manhattan. That's all, on my word."

"Why, Joe," Geraldi asked, "I'd trust your bare word against a whole stack of books any day."

Double Deck Joe laughed again, but there was something forced about his present mirth. "Drop it, son," he said, and led the way back through the bushes and into an opening, where Geraldi saw as fine a mustang as ever leaned against a bit or tried to kick the head from its master's shoulders. It was a pinto, as he had intimated. Although it was not tall, its long, low build suggested carrying power ample even for the bulky frame of the fat man. In its legs there was the promise of speed, moreover.

"I'm still standing behind that offer," said Geraldi. "I offered to exchange blind. I'm still offering, after I've seen the horse. You've got to admit that the gray has the looks."

Double Deck Joe ran his hand fondly down the neck of the pinto. "Looks in women and looks in hosses is all right," he declared. "They make a quick marriage and they made a quick buy. But gimme the girl with the ugly mug every time, because they's likely to be something inside of her head. And gimme the hoss that I've tried, the way that I've tried this double-coated son of Hades. He ain't pretty, but he lasts pretty good. You keep your picture hoss, Manhattan, and I'll keep my pinto, because now and then I need him, and, when I need him, I need him bad."

"He's got you all wind-scarred, though, as I pointed out a while ago," said Geraldi.

The other laughed heartily. "Manhattan," he said, "you're all by yourself. There ain't another that's right to stand beside you. You speak like one that had ought to know."

They went back to the bed of the Willow Trail, where Geraldi mounted the gray in a single bound. He thought, even while he was in the air, that the sinister left hand of Double Deck Joe had flickered toward the inside of his coat — and then had been hastily withdrawn as the fat man changed his mind. Geraldi rode close behind him, saying, as they started: "Listen to me, Joe."

"Manhattan," said the other, "I'll listen to you like you was Bible, if you want to know."

"You can believe me this time," Geraldi said. "I want to tell you about a queer, nervous disease I've got. It's landed me in a lot of trouble, in my day."

"You tell me, son," Joe said. "Here I am, all listenin' like a kid to a fairy tale."

"It's this way," said Geraldi. "When I see a man make a move toward a gun, my hands get so nervous that they're likely to jump out a gun from the palm . . . where I keep 'em hidden, you know . . . and they're likely to start shooting. It's a nervous disease."

Double Deck Joe looked steadily and firmly into the eye of the younger man. He said not a word.

"I'm just telling you, in case . . . ," Geraldi said.

The far man heaved a sigh. "I see how it is," he said. "But you'll have no more trouble with me, Manhattan. And God help any of the boys that ever get fresh with you . . . excepting the Doctor. Even Hayman himself might have to hump himself a mite to beat you."

"Oh," said Geraldi, "I'm not boasting. I hate trouble, Joe. I was just telling you in case. . . ." He paused again, and Double Deck Joe looked at him with that broadening grin that obscured half of his face and more.

"You don't have to tell me nothing, boy. Seein' is a lot more convincin' than hearin'. I've gone and seen with my own little bright eyes enough to hold me for a while. Manhattan, you're my friend. I wouldn't have you anything else. Not if I had an insurance policy up to half a million. That's how much your friendship means to me."

Chapter Twenty-Eight
THE HIDE-OUT

Far up the Willow Trail they rode, and, when it vanished, they passed through a wood of scrub pine, climbing rapidly, and so reached at last a wooded hillside on which stood a small shack with a chimney, crazy with time, leaning at a crooked angle above it. In front of the cabin, in the full glare of the sunshine — except where the triangular shadow of one treetop fell across the board — five men were seated about a table, playing cards.

They gave not a glance to the newcomer, and Double Deck Joe led the way around the house to a shed and small, fenced pasture. In that pasture Geraldi saw twenty head of horses, the worst of which was worthy to bear the burden of a prince. In their small heads, in their great, deer-like eyes, in their slender legs, hard as hammered iron, he saw the signs of their blood and respected them for it. When he turned in the gray among them, the new horse seemed a shaggy and cold-blooded thing in comparison.

"Pretty, ain't they?" Double Deck Joe asked, lingering at the fence for a moment and cocking his head affectionately to one side as he gazed at the beauties. "Them are the little sheep that bring in the wool for Doctor Hayman. You take Hayman . . . he's a kind of a scientific farmer. He plants his crops in his own head, and he harvests 'em with Colts and nitroglycerin . . . and these here is what takes his laborers back and forth to the job. He believes in savin' time. Save the hoss and spoil the man is one of his ideas. Why, he takes care of his workin' men like a father."

"That's a touching idea," Geraldi said, still watching the gray and comparing it with the matchless, silken beauties among which it was straying.

"We'll go back to the house and see if the Doctor is on deck," said Double Deck Joe. "Some of the fellows is gonna have a surprise out of you, Manhattan." He chuckled deeply in his throat. Then he added, gripping the arm of Geraldi gently: "But don't you go takin' no chances. The weakest gent in this lot is made with double timberin' inside and out. A bullet-proof lot is what they are."

Geraldi said nothing. He had consorted with rough fellows many a year before this. However, when they rounded the corner of the house and he had a chance to run his eyes over the lot before him, he felt that his initiation into the ways of the wild was just taking place. They were not particularly ugly. It was in their eyes that he read them, and in the straightness of their backs. Those eyes, when they rested upon another face, dwelt for a moment, quietly, coldly, reading the mind as well as they could. Such a glance was an insult, and such glances were constantly being exchanged at that card table.

"Say, fellers," said Double Deck Joe, "where's the Doctor?"

No one answered until the question was repeated. Then a lad with a pale, cold face at the farther end of the table, without looking up from his hand, answered: "He's sleeping."

"We gotta wait a while," said Double Deck Joe. "When the Doctor sleeps . . . which he don't do much . . . it's a dangerous thing to wake him up. I'd rather step into a cave filled with red-hot rattlers, speakin' personal. Which it won't hurt us none to set here a while in the sun."

He squatted on the ground as he spoke, but Geraldi, before he sat down, saw a burly form appear in the door of the cabin, and he recognized Larry Burns.

He winked, but it was a long moment before Larry mastered the amazement that had appeared in his face. In the meantime, Geraldi was staring back at him. He saw that something would have to be done with this pause. For Joe had looked sharply up at him, wondering at the delay. Geraldi walked straight up to Burns.

"Seems to me that I've seen you somewhere before," said Geraldi. "Have I?"

Larry Burns swallowed hard. "Seems the same thing to me," he said. "Maybe not. Maybe so. Maybe in a crowd, somewheres."

"That's likely," said Geraldi. "I've been crowded now and then." He laughed a little. Turning with Burns, he walked over to Double Deck.

"This here is Manhattan Jimmy, and that's Larry Burns," said Double Deck. "You fellows ain't met before?"

"We think we've seen one another," Geraldi said. "How about Chihuahua, Larry? Ever been there?"

"In El Negro's place?" said Burns. "You were buckin' faro!"

"That's it," Geraldi agreed. "You staked me to a ten spot when I went broke."

"And you built the ten into a hundred and quit. I remember now," said Burns.

They sat down in a small semicircle, one on either side of Double Deck Joe.

"How long has the Doctor been asleep?" asked Double Deck.

"Coupla hours," said Burns.

"He'll be up and around then, in another minute or so," said Joe, "because two hours is about his limit."

"Yeah," drawled Burns, "you'd think that there was something on his conscience."

He and Double Deck chuckled. Geraldi remained quiet.

"We're about even all around," said a voice at the card table. "Let's quit this game. It's too damn' dull. Everybody's playing too close to his chest."

There was a general agreement, and the stools and the rude chairs on which they were sitting were pushed back. The pale-faced young man stood up.

"That's Dick Kennedy," said Double Deck.

As Dick Kennedy stretched, he said: "Let's get some excitement around here. I'm tired of this here convalescent's home. Here's a hundred says that I got an odd number of coins in my hand." He drew out several coins, rattled them in the hollow of his double palms, and then clapped them down on the table under the flat of his hand.

"Who takes me?" demanded Kennedy impatiently.

A man with several days' growth of beard on his face, an unkempt fellow with rosy cheeks above the beard, answered in a husky voice: "I'll take you, Dick. You got an even number under that hand."

"That's Jungle Murphy," said Double Deck.

"I've heard of him," Geraldi answered.

"Who ain't?" asked Double Deck.

The fame of Jungle Murphy was spread far and wide. Safe cracking was his long suit, and he had worked in many great hauls.

Dick Kennedy raised his hand and revealed five silver coins. He thrust them back into his pocket as Jungle Murphy tossed two fifty-dollar bills into the air. With one hand Kennedy caught this bird in full flight. The other hand he thrust back into his pocket.

"Two hundred this time," he said, drawing out his hand again and slapping it down on the table. "Who takes me, odd or even?"

A lean fellow who talked from one side of his mouth, a man with a pockmarked face, answered: "I'll take you, Dick. They're even again."

"That's Bud Maker. He's a tough *hombre,* that one," remarked Double Deck. "Now watch him win. He was born with the luck, I tell you."

In fact, when the hand of Kennedy was raised from the table, it was seen that it had been covering four coins, and he counted out two hundred dollars to the other.

Geraldi looked on curiously. Even for a gang of thugs who might have made a recent haul, they seemed absurdly flush and careless about their money.

A small lad who could not have been over twenty stood up from his stool at the table and whistled a thin, long note.

"That's Angel Ray," said Double Deck. "He's the worst young devil I ever seen. He could get fat on poison."

Geraldi looked again at the boy. It was the most beautiful face he ever had seen, womanish in its refinement, child-like about the mouth and cheeks. The hand of Angel Ray was like the hand of a girl. Only his eyes were steady, calm, possessing a gravity that seemed to deny the rest of his features.

"You'll never get that blue jay back here into

the clearing," said a big, swaggering fellow who was always lounging his shoulders back into his chair, but never seemed able to settle them comfortably.

"That's Stew Malone. He's a good fellow," said Double Deck. "They're all good fellows," he added rather hastily. "But Stew's better than the most of 'em. Ain't he, Larry?"

"Sure. Stew's all right," Burns agreed.

His eyes were on the face of Geraldi, from time to time, not insistently, but as though he wished to get a signal. Geraldi gave him nothing except an almost imperceptible shake of the head.

Angel Ray was whistling again, a quick, sharp note, like that of a bird in distress. "I'll get him back," he insisted. "He'll come to me the way he'd go to the devil on Friday."

"What money you got behind that idea?" asked Dick Kennedy, his pale face colder and harder than ever.

"Whatever you want," replied the smaller lad.

"How does five hundred suit you?" Kennedy asked.

"I'd rather have five hundred of your coin than a thousand out of anybody else," said Angel Ray. He whistled again.

"There's my five hundred," said Kennedy, putting a number of bills on the table and weighting them down with a pipe that lay nearby.

"My word's as good as your put-up," answered Angel Ray with a sort of gentle insolence that Geraldi liked. "I've got five hundred against yours, Dick." Once more he whistled. There was no response from the woods.

"How long you going to take?" Kennedy asked with a cold-lipped sneer. "If you take all day, he might chance back this way, of course."

"I'll take sixty seconds more," snapped Angel Ray, "you short sport!"

"We'll take up the sporting business a little later," said Kennedy with iron in his voice. "Somebody hold a watch."

"There's twenty seconds gone . . . half a minute . . . forty seconds . . . fifty," said Stew Malone.

The whistle of Angel Ray shrilled again, breaking sharply off in exact imitation of a terrified bird pursued by some hawk. At that instant, over the tips of the farthest trees, the gaudy blue jay slid into sight and dipped well down into the clearing.

"One minute up!" said Stew Malone.

Chapter Twenty-Nine
DOC HAYMAN

Kennedy picked up his five hundred dollars and passed it to the boy. Then he said: "There was a little something said about short sport a minute back."

"I said it," promptly answered Angel Ray. He actually smiled at the larger man.

"I wanted to hear it twice," said Kennedy. "That'd make it dearer to me."

"You're a short sport," Angel Ray said gently. "You're a damned short one."

"Well," answered Kennedy, "suppose that we take a walk and have a talk about things."

"I never refused a walk in my life," said Angel Ray, "to any man or any girl. Uphill or down, old son. It's equal to me."

"Hold on," broke in Stew Malone. "You know that the Doctor don't like this sort of a business, don't you? You know that pretty damned well, don't the two of you?"

"Yeah, I know it pretty well," Angel Ray responded. "But this bum, he's been waiting to take a fall out of me, and now he's going to get his chance, the big frozen face!"

"You know what the Doctor says," said Stew Malone solemnly.

"The Doctor be damned!" exploded Kennedy. "I'm gonna have it out with this putty-faced fool! He's been badgerin' me for a month."

"Kennedy!" said a voice from the door of the cabin.

All heads turned. All expressions altered to something of alarm. Geraldi saw in the doorway a man of middle height, rather stockily built, with a great head on his shoulders and a Napoleonic face, filled with thought and with resolution. Whatever the morals of the man, the strength that showed in his face was enough to make him the ruler of this crew. Geraldi knew instantly that this was Doctor Hayman.

"Yes, Doctor?" said Kennedy, coming to attention like a soldier.

Geraldi could guess that this stiffness in Kennedy's back was due to the chill that was running through his spinal marrow. Some of that cold was working in Geraldi's own backbone.

"Now, my boys," said Hayman, "I've told you before that there is to be no quarreling here. Every man of you is good enough to be the friend of every other man, or else he would not be in my company. I've warned you, almost once a month, that there is to be no fighting . . . chiefly because I don't want you to do the work of the sheriffs and marshals, with all their posses. Pleasant reading for the papers, if people heard that any one of you was dead. I don't want them to have that sort of reading . . . at my expense. Now, then, I give you my ultimatum . . . I've told you before that in the case of a fight, I'd talk to the survivor. I tell you now, the next time I hear loud voices and wrangling, I won't wait for the fight to start. I'll come for the two . . . or the three . . . who are engaged, and I'll come shooting."

He made one step from the doorway as he said: "You're the youngest and the most worthless pair in this lot. I've had better lots than this, too. But you're the worst. You've broken my sleep with your cursed noise. If I didn't have a heart as gentle as the heart of a lamb, I'd slaughter the pair of you now. I've half a mind to do it now."

He made another step forward. Angel Ray stood his ground, although his pink cheeks had now whitened, but Dick Kennedy retreated a step, and his glance wavered to the side, as though he were searching for a refuge of some sort.

It seemed to Geraldi that the black, burning eyes of the Doctor carried a hypnotic influence. He was glad that they were not directed toward him. He began to steel himself, even now, for the encounter.

The Doctor made another step forward. He waved his arm. "Get out of my sight, the two of you, and let my eyes have a rest from the sight of your faces for a day. Don't show yourselves back here for twenty-four hours. That's all!"

They turned on their heels like frightened schoolboys. Only, as Angel Ray reached the corner of the building, he spun about again. A gun was already in the hand of the Doctor, but he did not fire. Angel Ray had not attempted to draw a gun.

"I won't be talked down to like I was a pup," said young Ray.

The Doctor said nothing. He merely looked, and Ray suddenly turned on his heel again and hurried out of sight.

When he was gone, Doctor Hayman made his gun disappear with a subtle speed of hand that startled Geraldi. Even his cunning eye could hardly detect the sudden up-flick of hand that shot the gun under the Doctor's coat.

Then Hayman turned to Double Deck Joe. "I told you never to bring in a new man till I'd seen his face," he said.

Double Deck got to his feet. The knees that raised him were unsteady. "This here lad is an exception, Doctor," he said.

"I make no exceptions," said the Doctor. "I make my rules, and they're obeyed. If there are exceptions, I make them." He turned to Geraldi.

The latter sat cross-legged. He lifted his head a little, and met the eye of Hayman. He was prepared for a shock, but all his mental preparation was not sufficient, at first. He felt his own eyelids widen. Then, steeling himself, he met and endured the gaze of the other. The eyes were dark as night, with a light far back in them, like the gleam of a reflection upon far-off water. Certainly there was some hypnotic quality about the man's glance.

Geraldi felt perspiration steal out on his forehead. He had encountered strong, brave, and subtle men before, but he knew that never before had he met the like of Hayman.

"Stand up," said the Doctor.

Geraldi did not move.

"Stand up," said Hayman coldly.

Suddenly Geraldi felt that the very air was surcharged with electricity. All eyes were bent with a still and fixed attention upon him. Then, mastering himself by degrees, half his mind given to the tingling readiness of his right hand — for his position was a cramped one for a fast draw — he said: "This isn't the schoolroom, Hayman." He was proud of the steadiness of his voice.

The latter waited for a moment. A veritable fire came into his eyes, and Geraldi was ready for the instant draw. But then the flame died down again, and greater, contemplative thought was in the face of the other. He began to nod.

"You're right, Double Deck," he said. "I forgive you. This is an exception. What's his name?"

"Manhattan Jimmy."

"What else?" asked Hayman sharply of Geraldi.

"The rest is for the family Bible," Geraldi stated.

A quick smile appeared and disappeared upon

the lips of the Doctor. "Will you come inside with me, Manhattan?" he said. Turning, he walked toward the cabin.

Geraldi got up and followed. He followed quickly, aware that not a hand, not a foot, not an eye of the others had stirred, and the very air seemed frozen in that sunny clearing before the cabin. Then, as he passed, he noted that Larry Burns was wiping his forehead. He put that down to the credit of Burns. The man had been capable of suffering for a friend. But it made him wonder a little.

Larry knew him well. At least, Larry knew what he had done, and of what he could do, and yet Burns had been frightened for his sake. What sort of man, then, was Doctor Hayman? What had he revealed of his latent powers to Burns?

With that cat-like step which some few people in the world already knew very well, Geraldi entered the cabin behind the other. He was sorry that they had gone inside, for the cabin seemed poorly lighted, drenched with shadow, compared with the brilliance of the outdoors. He wanted all the light that he could get upon the face of Doctor Hayman.

In the middle of the room, the latter turned, and Geraldi noticed, or thought that he noticed, an odd thing — that the black eyes of Hayman were as brilliant in the shadow as they had been in the sun. Or was it only a potent imagination that made them appear so to Geraldi? He sharpened every sense. He became almost tremulously alert. He was prepared for anything. Then he realized that this was wrong. He would wear himself out — while Hayman remained totally at ease. So Geraldi began to force himself into an attitude of more ease.

"You're sweating, Manhattan," said Hayman.

"Yes," said Geraldi instantly and frankly. "You're a hard man to meet, Hayman, and you're a hard man to go against. That's the truth."

"It's the truth," said Hayman. "I'm a hard man to go against. There are few that have been foolish enough to try it, my friend. You've come here to join me?"

"I've come here to look you over," said Geraldi.

"To look me over? People don't look me over, Manhattan. They join, or they. . . ." He waved his hand. "You've looked my men in the face," he continued. "You couldn't be allowed to leave after that."

"What I've seen," said Geraldi, "was with the eyes, and my eyes have nothing to do with my tongue. But, as I said, I just came up to look you over and see how business stands."

Hayman actually smiled again. "You're a cool fellow, Manhattan," he said.

"Yes," Geraldi confirmed, "I'm cool. And I can still cut when I'm red-hot."

"You know yourself?" said Hayman.

"As well," said Geraldi, "as you know yourself."

"And what proposition do you make to me? You see that I'm still willing to talk . . . for a while."

"I'll play second fiddle to you," said Geraldi. "But only to you. I'll have no orders. But I'll take advice. Does that sound all right to you? If not, I'll catch up my horse and leave."

"No," said Doctor Hayman, "it doesn't sound all right, and yet you won't leave!"

Chapter Thirty

FACE TO FACE

Now that the ultimatum had been spoken, Geraldi stood quietly, waiting. There was no ready solution. He might draw and try to kill Doctor Hayman; but for the first time in his life he really doubted his ability to dispose of another man. Or, on the other hand, even supposing that Hayman was dead, how was he to dispose of the expert corps of fighters yonder in the clearing? So he waited, casting his mind not ahead, but straight against the impassive face of Hayman.

"You understand my position, Manhattan . . . if that's your name," said Hayman. "The man who turns me over dead or alive gets something like fifty thousand dollars. The fellow who gives information leading to my death would be able to split the fifty thousand. That's a stake large enough to interest even a man like you, Manhattan. Even you have an interest in fifty thousand cold cash. If I seem a little hard, it's because the government has driven me into a corner. When they offered a thousand, five thousand, ten thousand, even, I hardly cared. But when they offer fifty thousand dollars, you can see that poison is in the air I breathe. It seeps up out of the ground. Now, you're a bold fellow, and a man with a will and with brains. You're material that I'd like to use for our mutual benefit. But, if you work for me, you're as absolutely under my lead as the stupidest brute I possess."

He said these things without any air of extravagance. He spoke with a slow consideration, as one who wishes to express the exact truth, no more and no less.

Geraldi studied him. Suddenly he wondered. Of all the men he ever had encountered, this was the one who seemed most dangerous in mind and craft of hand; but he was housed here in a dingy shack, surrounded by a reckless and brutal crew of young ruffians whose virtue was simply that they obeyed their master. There was no mountaineer or shepherd who lived more crudely than this man lived. Furthermore, he was condemned forever to such a life. He might make some foray into a lowland town, or drop south of the border to enjoy himself and throw money about wildly for a few days. But this was a man of some culture, who must crave in his soul all of the delights of books, of conversation, and every beauty which can meet the eye or the ear. What was a frontier debauch to him, except a disgusting rout?

Likewise, from the great cities he was barred. From the society of decent men he was shut away. The fifty-thousand-dollar reward, as he himself had said, poisoned the air in which he moved, and would make the very walls of a room sweat against him.

What reward was his? Geraldi knew the reward as well. There was the joy of matching small forces against great, and, by swiftness of maneuver, adroitness in tactics, shrewdness of striking, to win battle after battle, like another Napoleon. There was the supreme joy of being first wherever he moved, of mastering the men about him, of defying the law, of living as freely as a hawk in the upper air.

That was why he would not consent to Geraldi's suggestion. He must be first. Those who joined his band were his servants, not his comrades. So, as he thought these things, Geraldi nodded. He understood. He pointed to the table. Upon it lay a large combination lock with a small, bright litter of steel tools around it, as though someone had been taking the thing to pieces.

"You know, as well as I do, Hayman," he said, "that everything has a price."

"True," said the Doctor. "What price will you offer?"

"I'll read the mind of that combination for you."

Hayman started. "Do you know that lock?" he asked.

"I never saw it before."

"How long do you ask for the reading of it, then?"

"Half an hour."

The other bent his brows darkly on Geraldi.

Then he said: "Step outside with the other boys. I'll set the combination. Then I'll ask you inside to solve it and leave you alone with it for a half hour. If you solve the thing . . . then you're worth to me even the independence that you ask for. I'll fit you in a notch above all the rest. But if you fail to solve it. . . ." He made a movement of his hand, as though fanning something into thin air. It was the life of Geraldi that he referred to, and Geraldi knew it well.

So he left the hut, and, as he did so, he heard Hayman say behind him: "Malone, you and the others keep an eye on Manhattan Jimmy, will you? I want him right here in front of the shack."

"Aye, aye, chief," said Malone, and, without haste, without a scowl, he instantly drew a revolver and held it across his knees, pointing toward Geraldi, who was aware that Bud Maker had done the same thing behind his back.

Then the door closed, and Geraldi knew that the Doctor was busily engaged in devising the most complicated set for the combination. He was profoundly worried. He knew locks. He had studied them for many years, with a more passionate interest than ever a scholar had poured out upon hard books. It was a subject in which he had mastered much, but it was also a subject in which no one can master everything. He had spoken not by chance, but because he saw in his proffer the one possible chance of changing the mind of Hayman. And change it he must. To accomplish what he wished to do here with the gang, he must have an authority almost equal to that of the Doctor, and he must have it at once. But he felt that he was walking the slenderest wire stretched over an infinite chasm.

"Sorry," Stew Malone was saying. "But you know how it is with the Doctor. Nobody fails him twice. We gotta watch our step when he gives an order. So, Manhattan, if you'll kindly sit down yonder and keep your hands mighty quiet, there won't be no gun accidents, and everybody'll be mighty obliged to you."

Geraldi did as was suggested willingly. Now, breaking out from the trees at the lower end of the clearing, came a youthful rider on a fine black horse, gray with dust and with foam fleckings. He waved to the group and passed out of sight behind the house.

It was Jack Tucker, and he looked all that the photograph of him had promised — tall, straight, wide-shouldered, lean of belly and haunch, the true type of the Western rider. There was courage in his jaw, danger in his eye. He came back from the corral presently, carrying the heavy saddle lightly over his arm.

"How is it, Jack?" asked Stew Malone.

Jack Tucker, before he answered, turned upon Geraldi the bold, insolent eye of an untamed youngster who never has been put down.

"Who's this?" he asked.

"Manhattan Jimmy," said Stew Malone. "Double Deck Joe brought him in, and the Doctor is cooking up a stew for him, I guess.

What've you seen, Jack?"

"They've got the windward of some news of some sort," said Jack, throwing down his saddle. "They've got on a new watchman. I saw the old one, and he told me that they're beginning to keep an eye on him and doubt him. He says that we ought to wait a while till things quiet down a bit."

"The Doctor doesn't wait very often," observed Stew Malone.

"I hope he won't," said Tucker. "I took a look around that place. You put three or four good shots in the upper windows of the hotel across the street from the bank and they'll keep the streets as clean as the palm of your hand. They don't look like a fighting lot, those *hombres*."

"Sometimes the sleepier they look, the harder they'll fight," said Stew Malone. "I remember a time that we went down and stirred up a little place called Digger Creek in Arizona, and there was only about a man and a half and two dogs in that whole town, the way we looked at it. But when the pinch come, that there town just exploded with a bang and pretty near wrecked all of us. We left three men behind, and we were mighty lucky to get out, the rest of us."

Jack Tucker shrugged his shoulders. "There's more than a man and a half in Alexandria," he said. "But I think that six men that knew their business could rip that bank in Alexandria inside and out and make the crowd like it. That's what I think."

Stew Malone grinned. "You're kind of young, kid," he said.

Jack Tucker bridled instantly. "I'm too old for you to talk down to me, Malone!" he declared.

The smile left the eyes of Stew Malone. "Listen to me, son," he said. "You're too damned bent on havin' trouble. But what you wanna remember is that if you start a fight inside the gang, it's the Doctor that'll do the finishing. I've been tryin' to give you a steer, but you're too wise to need advice. Right from now on, you can go to the devil, as far as I'm concerned."

"What you think about me makes no difference," said Jack Tucker. "I'm here, working for the Doctor, not for the rest of you hobos!" He got up, yawned, stretched himself, and sauntered off to put up his saddle.

Stew Malone looked grimly after him.

"Yeah. He's pretty young," said Geraldi thoughtfully.

"He's old enough to eat lead, though," said Malone angrily, through his teeth. "The young fool! I wouldn't. . . ."

Geraldi did not hear the last of the sentence, for now the door of the cabin opened, and there stood the Doctor himself, his solemn eyes bent upon Geraldi.

"Come right in, Manhattan," he said, "and make yourself at home with this little job, will you? I'll wait outside for you. Don't hurry yourself," he added. "You'll have a half hour!"

Geraldi entered. The door closed behind him,

and he sat down at the table upon which lay the ponderous combination, a glimmering mass of steel. He set it up, first, upon its side. He kneeled upon the floor. He waited until his breathing was an imperceptible sound, until the boards no longer stirred or creaked ever so lightly beneath his weight. Then, gathering all his attention, covering his eyes to shut out every other thought, casting into the tips of his fingers every ounce of nervous feeling, he commenced to turn the disk delicately, carefully listening for the fall of the tumblers — a sound ten times fainter than the click of dice rolled three whole rooms away.

Chapter Thirty-One

THE SUPER FOX

All that Geraldi could hear with those super fox ears of his was the breathing of the wind outside the house, like the breathing of an animal, and the sound of human voices, where the men were talking, and those incredibly small murmurs that are forever running through the frame of a house, whether by night or day, in storm or in quieter hours. He felt a touch of panic. The sweat started on his body. There was only a half hour to work, and he knew that the time was very short, indeed.

He told himself, as he had told himself many a time before, that fear must be far from him, because where fear was working, the mind could not work. Therefore, he must rule and so order himself that his brain had a clear chance to operate. So he ruled fear away. He cast it like a visible enemy out of his mind. After that effort of the will, he found that the sound of the wind, of the voices, and the intimate, deadly creakings and rustlings through the frame of the house were drawn off to a distance, and that he was more keenly and nervously aware of the work that lay under his hand.

So it was, far off and thinner than the hum of a bee carried dimly down the wind, he heard, or felt — he could not say which it was — a slight shock or a slight click within the lock. His heart leaped. His fingers did not turn the numbered disk another thousandth part of an inch, but, quickly raising his head, he looked, and saw that he had reached a number. Seventeen! He jotted that number indelibly down in his mind, and then he returned to his work.

It seemed to him that the light which struck against his closed eyelids gave a rosy glow, even passing through skin and blood to the ball of the eye. So he snatched out a handkerchief and bound it like lightning about his head, stifling his sight more completely. That done, he fell again to the work. Now it was like the passage from dawn to full daylight. What had been dim as figures moving by middle night, now resolved into clear and more clear. They walked, as it were, over the horizon of his mind, and so entered his clearer consciousness. If he had heard voices of the men, and of the wind, and of the house, before, he heard them a thousandfold more keenly now, but they were shut away. As one brings a burning glass to bear upon a definite focus, so that the gathered rays will burn with intense heat upon a small pinhead of space, so he gathered all of his faculties of touch and of hearing to focus upon exactly what was happening inside of the lock, and upon nothing more near, and nothing more far away. Only one thing now existed for him — only one thing troubled him — and that was the occasional thumping of his heart. But even through this he was listening with a might and an intensity of which other humans could have little comprehension. He heard the click again. He read the number — one hundred and fifteen.

Back he went to his work, with the second number read and the bandage readjusted to his eyes. He found a number again — ninety-two. So he played the combination, tearing off the blindfold in triumph, and whirled the disk to the right numbers, and then wrenched at the lock to see it open.

But it did not stir! A wild, cold panic came over him. He felt that he was being cheated, that he had read the mind of the lock correctly, but by some trick he was prevented from winning. Then he went to the rear window of the shack, and, looking out, he saw Jack Tucker and another man seated under a tree, their rifles beside them.

He knew why they were there. So would the house be guarded upon every side. That was the way of Doctor Hayman, he could gather. The proposal which Geraldi had made had been accepted seriously. If he failed within the half hour, the Doctor would work swiftly to encompass his death.

Geraldi gripped his hands hard. It was very difficult, after all. Yonder was the lad whom he had come to save from the mortal dangers of this outlawed life. Yet, with a rifle in his hand, he was prepared to shoot down his rescuer like a beast, if Geraldi should attempt to break loose.

Such thinking brought on savage madness. Geraldi cured the madness by looking at his watch. Twenty minutes had elapsed. He had ten remaining in which to save his life — and give yonder Jack Tucker a chance for a law-abiding existence, also. That second problem was mysterious and difficult enough. Its solution would wait upon the solution of the secret of the lock.

So, Geraldi, an instant later, his eyes once more bandaged, was on his knees beside the table, his ear pressed close to the combination. The surge of his own blood was like the murmur of a distant surf. He could hear nothing! Again he willed that physical weakness away. Then he heard the outside sounds of wind and voices. Finally he banished those grosser noises, also, and was back again at the intimate heart of things, listening to the still, small voice of the combination lock, thinner than ever was the voice of conscience in the worst of rogues.

The tumbler fell. He heard it clearly. This time he knew that he was right. It was not a noise, perhaps. It might have been more than a throb, detected by the oversensitive nerves in the fingertips of his right hand. He looked. Seventeen! Had he erred, then, on the first number? Had he, after all, turned the disk, the extent of one number, past the proper point, or by some reflex action turned it back again? He had done such things before.

Now, rapidly, deftly, he turned again to the two last numbers of the combination as he had heard them, or thought he had heard them — and suddenly the lock worked — the massive bolts slid back — the mystery was his.

He looked again at his watch. There still remained two minutes. He employed them to the full. He dragged out a handkerchief, mopped his forehead, and wiped the back of his dripping neck. He swung his arms rapidly and breathed to the bottom of his lungs. He rubbed his cheeks, which were cold as stone. He opened and blinked his eyes rapidly and made them stare, for he knew in the intensity of his concentration behind closed lids that the pupils had contracted to mere black points.

Someone knocked on the door.

"Why, hello, Hayman. Is that you?" he called cheerfully.

"This is I," said the hard, steady voice of Hayman. "Have you anything in there to show me?"

"Nothing of much importance," said Geraldi. "But you might be interested to see it."

The door pushed suddenly open, and there was Hayman standing before him. He gave one glance to the face of Geraldi. The next look was for the combination. When he saw what had happened, he made a quick half step forward, incredulity on his face.

"By heavens, Manhattan," he said, "you knew the lock beforehand."

"You know how it is," said Geraldi. "Sometimes a fellow can read the mind of such a thing. I'm one of the lucky ones. That's all."

Doctor Hayman blinked. Then, turning a little, he stared straight at Geraldi. It seemed to the latter that Hayman was trying to print his features in his memory, as an artist will do with hungry glance, when he wishes to make a drawing later. Then Hayman nodded. "It was a hard pull, Manhattan, wasn't it?"

Geraldi drew out an honest answer. "I had just two minutes to spare," he said simply. Then he smiled, the cold, quick smile that so many men had seen — and more than one the instant before they died.

Doctor Hayman nodded again. He went to the combination lock, lifted the massive steel thing in his hands, weighed it, and looked downward, as though striving to make out in his heart of hearts just what this achievement was worth. At last he said, still looking down: "Manhattan, what's your real name?"

Geraldi said nothing. He merely shrugged.

"I'm asking you," said Doctor Hayman, "because I know that you're a celebrity of some sort. You have another name than Manhattan. If I heard that other name, I'd recognize it, I'm sure. The fellow who solved this lock has broken the heart of more than one sheriff and marshal. I'll put my trust in that. However, I can't ask you to confess to me. Only, I'm turning over one thing in my mind."

"What thing?" said Geraldi.

"What brought you here?" asked Hayman.

Geraldi wished that he could look straight at him, but still the Doctor was staring down.

"Everybody wants to find easy money," said Geraldi tentatively.

The Doctor merely laughed. "Manhattan," he said, "if you've worked this combination without the key . . . and I see that you have . . . you can walk straight through closed doors. You can pick the strongest locks in the world, and carry away fortunes. The smartest locksmith that ever worked in Sheffield has spent fifteen years of his long life in making this lock. You've worked it in no time at all . . . a mere half hour. Half an hour to read the piled-up secrets of fifteen years . . . yes, of a lifetime of effort. And yet you tell me that you've come up here to make money!" He snapped his fingers.

"Not only the money," said Geraldi. "There's another thing."

"What other thing?"

"There's Doctor Hayman," said Geraldi.

"Ah?"

"That's it," said Geraldi.

"You wanted to read me, if you could, as you've read this lock?" asked Hayman.

"And why not?" Geraldi said calmly.

The other, for the first time in several minutes, turned his head and stared straight at Geraldi.

"Manhattan," he said, "that's a lie." After a pause he went on: "Because you know that I'm not made of steel. I'm made of more intricate and sterner stuff. But in the meantime, we won't shake hands . . . we'll simply wait and try to know one another better. I think that now the books may be worthwhile reading."

Chapter Thirty-Two

OVER A VOLCANO

Men know one another by a peculiar intuition. When people speak of that intuition which instructs some women, they forget that in men, also, there is a similar extra sense, often controlling them to the exclusion of reason and logic. So, when the champion exchanges punches with his challenger in the first round of the fray, a blinding spark may strike through his mind, and he knows that he has met his master before the serious blow is struck. So the runner, well in the lead, knows without looking back that the pounding feet behind him are equipped with wings that will fly past him to the winning mark.

Geraldi, as he met the gaze of Hayman, realized that here at last he had met his equal. His superior? Perhaps. It was a strange feeling. He had had his back against the wall many times, but always there had been several enemies, or some peculiarity of position that put him at a vast disadvantage. Here, for the first time, he saw the individual from whom he shrank. For the first time he had met a man over whom he felt no superiority of mind or of body. It was only a cold comfort that his dexterity had enabled him to open the lock that had baffled Hayman.

The latter, in the meantime, appeared to have lapsed into an easier manner, but Geraldi was not taken off his guard. "I could tell you an odd thing," said the Doctor, after a moment. "Now that we're friends and associates . . . on your own terms, Manhattan . . . I could tell you a thing that would make you laugh."

"Tell me," said Geraldi.

"You'll only laugh."

"Well, I'd like to laugh."

"It's concerning whom I thought you were?"

"Well, Hayman, who did you think I was?"

"Geraldi!"

The word shocked Geraldi. It struck him fairly between the eyes and left the base of his brain numb. He dared not meet the gaze of Hayman then. Instead, he looked down at the floor and shook his head slowly. At length, as though an idea had come to him, he looked up and nodded.

"Geraldi?" he said. "I've heard that name."

"Have you?" asked Hayman ironically.

"You mean," Geraldi said, "the crook who makes his living off the crooks?"

"Yes, I mean that man."

"But," said Geraldi, "he's a bigger man than I am. I've heard him described. Besides. . . ."

"You've heard him described," Hayman said. "So have I. But always by fools. You and I, Manhattan, are able to look men and facts in the face. But most people let their imagination work.

Imagination can put four inches and forty pounds on any man! Take you and let the imagination of a fool work on you, and you'd be the sort of fellow that I've heard Geraldi described to be."

"I?" said Geraldi. "Well, that's amusing. But I understand. He does sleight of hand, opens safes, and reads the minds of combination locks. So do I! Is that it?"

Hayman neither nodded nor shook his head. "You lie well, Manhattan," he said. "I don't accuse you of lying just now. But you have the good poise and the air of a liar. The frank and open way. However, let that go. Not even Geraldi would dare to come up to my camp here."

"Oh, he's an enemy of yours, is he?" Geraldi asked blankly.

"Enemy?" said Hayman, his brow darkening. "Enemy? The cur! The hypocrite! Enemy? If I could put my hands on him, I'd die happy in killing him. If I had Geraldi in my power, I'd boil him inch by inch in oil!"

"So?" said Geraldi. "He's blocked your way, here and there?"

"Blocked my way?" answered Hayman. "Geraldi's the frigate bird who takes what honest thieves have stolen. He finds a superior morality in that. He never steals except from the stealers. He plays the game for the sake of the game, and he thinks that covers him. He never made honest money. But because he never takes

257

from honest men, he feels better about his stealing. I tell you, I've heard sensible men talk about him and even plead the cause of Geraldi, and distinguish him from other thieves, and declare that he never really has done any wrong. But if I could ever meet with him. . . ." He paused. His face was working. His whole complexion had darkened, and that same fire that Geraldi had seen in the eye of the Doctor before was now aflame in it.

"I understand what you mean," said Geraldi. "This Geraldi is a sneak. I've heard something about him. What you say reminds me of other things. They tell me that Marshal Tex Arnold is on his trail now. And I believe that Tex Arnold's quite a man."

"A man?" said Hayman, sneering. "Oh, he's brave, honest, industrious, and willing to die for his cause . . . the fool! But he's not dangerous. As well put a single dog on the trail of a grizzly as to put that marshal on the trail of Geraldi. Geraldi has melted through his hands. He'll do it again. Geraldi will never meet with his match unless. . . ."

He stopped himself short, but the word he had left out was too obvious. It was plain that Doctor Hayman desired nothing more from life than a chance to measure himself against Geraldi, the famous. The latter could hardly keep from smiling grimly to think that, like the boy under the Wishing Gate, the great criminal now had — unknown to him — the thing for which he craved.

At the same time, he realized that the ground he walked upon was liquid fire and nitroglycerin mingled, a volcano. Only one man in the camp, so far as he knew, was acquainted with his true identity. That was Larry Burns. Burns was never famous for an ability to hold his tongue. And besides, others might come in who knew him. Or there might be some chance encounters on the way. Danger would be in the very air around Geraldi so long as he remained near this camp, or in the company of the outlaw and his men.

Doctor Hayman had apparently dismissed the last subject from his mind.

"There's a fellow," Geraldi said, "that I'd like to meet. Because I've heard that he understands locks better than any man. Yes, I'd like to exchange ideas with him."

"Locks?" exclaimed the Doctor. "What are locks to Geraldi? Oh, he's a magician with them. I've heard what he can do. But what good is it to him? The locks he opens are the locks of robbers. Not the locks of banks. If he were to go after banks, he'd be another Rockefeller inside of a month, or less time than that. Oh, I understand what Geraldi could do, but the cur prefers to bury his teeth in his own kind — the bloodsucker!"

It was odd to see the criminal wax furious on behalf of his own kind. Geraldi watched, noted, and was strangely moved.

At this juncture Hayman drew out a package of cigarettes, offered one to Geraldi, and, when the latter motioned that he preferred to make his own, lighted one, and went on with his talk. "Now, Manhattan," he said, "I don't like to speak about Providence and such rot. But you're the man for me, and right out of the sky. You see that lock?"

Geraldi nodded.

"Let me tell you a story," said Doctor Hayman. "There's a little town named Alexandria . . . that name was put upon it by a large-minded fool . . . and in the town of Alexandria there is one important man, named John Ponson. In the life of Ponson there is but one important thing . . . his bank. And in the bank there is the whole soul of Ponson locked up in a safe. The whole soul of Ponson generally amounts to about two or three hundred thousand dollars in cash and in negotiable securities. And that safe is closed by a combination lock which is an exact duplicate of this one. There you are, Manhattan! You see why I say that you've dropped from the sky?"

He leaned forward a little and smiled upon Geraldi, and the latter nodded.

"We ought to take in two or three hundred thousand, then," said Geraldi.

Hayman nodded.

"What share comes to me?" Geraldi asked.

"I could blow that safe," Hayman stated.

"Not without raising the town," Geraldi suggested.

Hayman nodded. "That's it," he said. "I tell

you a truth now that you'd simply learn later on. It might raise the town, and the town might be dangerous."

"I heard a young fellow outside, who's just come in, say that it isn't dangerous."

"He told me the same thing," Hayman confided. "But he's a fool. All youngsters are fools, and he's the youngest I ever have seen. I say that the town may be dangerous. Sleepy townsmen may make the hardest fighters. Manhattan, I think that we'll ride tomorrow. Take today to think it over, and work some more with this lock, if you wish. Because tomorrow we'll make our haul."

"And my share?" persisted Geraldi.

Hayman smiled suddenly. "The fellow Geraldi I was speaking of," he said, "would never have asked that question. No, you're not Geraldi. But the same touch is in the pair of you. At least, for locks. Your share will be a flat sum. Thirty thousand dollars!"

"It's not enough," Geraldi said bluntly.

"It's all you'll get. There are other men to consider."

"Fifty thousand," Geraldi insisted, "or I stay home."

Hayman considered him gravely, impersonally. "I like you better and better, Manhattan," he said. "We'll call it fifty thousand, because a silent job may be worth the extra money. Fifty thousand, then. Does that suit you?"

"Down to the ground," said Geraldi, nodding.

"That's all, then," Hayman said, and he waved his hand toward the door. "Only," he added, "this may be the last time that you ever make a bargain with me on your own terms, Manhattan!"

"Tomorrow can take care of itself," Geraldi responded insolently, and, turning quickly on his heel, he left the cabin.

Immediately outside the door, he passed Larry Burns. The latter sat on a stump, whittling a slim stick with a great knife.

"Well?" said Burns, under his breath.

Geraldi paused, making a cigarette for himself, and very softly he murmured: "If you name me . . . if you even think my name . . . I'll have your heart out, Larry!"

Burns replied, also *sotto voce:* "I've stopped thinkin', Jimmy, since I saw you in this here camp. I'm just too plain scared to think."

Geraldi walked on slowly, indifferently, aiming his steps toward the place where Jack Tucker was rolling dice on a blanket with a couple of the gang.

Chapter Thirty-Three

LOADED DICE

Murphy and Bud Maker were the other pair in this game, and, as Geraldi came up, Jungle was shaking the dice box and winning rapidly — winning from Tucker, that is to say, for Maker did his betting very conservatively and seemed rather willing to make side bets with Tucker against the latter's luck than actually to buck the game of Jungle Murphy.

"I'm flat broke," Tucker said to Geraldi. "I never saw dice run so solid . . . not honest dice."

Jungle glared at him. "Whatcha mean by that?" he asked.

Tucker shrugged his shoulders. "I'll let it stand at that," he said. "I'm not askin' for my money back."

Geraldi stepped into the breach and drew attention to himself. "Let me take Tucker's place," he said. He placed ten dollars.

Jungle, rolling, spun out Little Joe. He passed the box to Geraldi.

"The kid is out here lettin' folks guess that I've crooked the dice on him," he said. "Go ahead, Manhattan. A young fool is the worst fool."

He did not look toward Tucker as he spoke, but his words were within the hearing of Tucker. The latter, however, said nothing. Neither did he leave. With a black face and a contorted brow, he stood by, as though gathering his wrath for an outbreak.

Geraldi shook the dice box. He looked his invitation, and Jungle Murphy threw down a fifty-dollar bill. Fifty-dollar bills seemed about the smallest currency in the Hayman camp. So Geraldi shook the dice again, and, from the free rattling, it seemed certain that they were jouncing together up and down the length of the box. He rolled. Side by side the dice spun over and over, stopped, and a deuce and a five lay glimmering in the light of the sun.

Geraldi let his winnings lie. "Who'll have this, or any part?" he asked.

Two more fifties instantly fluttered down onto the edge of the blanket.

He rolled again. A six and an ace appeared. "My luck looks good to me, boys," he said. "The sky's the limit now."

"I'll take a hundred," Jungle Murphy said, his face blank, but Bud Maker shook his head.

"I'll have a couple of looks first," he said.

Out spun the dice, and a four and a three appeared snugly side by side.

There was a grunt from Jungle Murphy, and Bud Maker said softly: "Three sevens in a row!"

That was not all. Jungle Murphy, with a grim persistence, laid another hundred against the

264

luck of the dice thrower, only to see another six and a one appear. Even then, blinking, his jaw hard set, he continued to bet.

"We'll call it five and two this time," Geraldi said, smiling a little, and he rolled once more. There stood the pair of dice, exactly as he had called them, a five upon the left and a deuce upon the right.

Jungle Murphy and Bud Maker stood back a step and stared both at the gambler and at one another. The crookedness was obvious now. The nonchalant smile of Geraldi completed the picture and made his triumph the more insulting.

Six sevens had been rolled in a row. Chance could hardly perform such a miracle as this. Above all, the last roll had been announced spot for spot.

Geraldi, paying no attention to the money on the blanket, said cheerfully: "I'm tired of this game, boys. It's too monotonous. Excuse me, if I step out of it."

So he dropped the box, turned on his heel, and went up to Tucker. A gesture from him made Tucker follow, and the pair walked on under the trees, leaving Murphy and Maker to stare after them. Tucker, striding with a long stroke at the side of Geraldi, was the first to speak.

"You wanted to show me that they were rolling crooked dice right from the first. Was that it?" he said.

They were now out of earshot and out of sight

of the others, and Geraldi turned on him.

"I wanted to tell you that you've been made a fool," said Geraldi. "You've been snarling and growling around the camp and asking for trouble. But when the trouble comes, it's going to be more than you can swallow. Of course, Jungle Murphy was rolling crooked dice. Didn't you see the way that Maker was laying his bets? If you didn't know, Maker knew. The only reason you didn't know is because you're only about half baked. Less than half baked. I wanted to get your eye and give you some advice on the side. That's why I rolled the dice as I did."

Tucker studied him with a scowl. "Manhattan," he said, "let me tell you something. I've never taken from anybody what I'm taking from you. And I don't know that I'm going to take it from you."

"You'd sooner fight, I suppose," said Geraldi.

"Why not?" asked Tucker. "Except that I'm too big a man to hit a fellow of your size. Besides, I think that you've been trying to do me a good turn."

"A good turn?" Geraldi said with the same sneer as before. "Why, I was simply trying to do the whole camp a good turn by shutting you up. Because even a fool can get sensible men to fighting with one another."

"By God," muttered Jack Tucker. He struck with the flat of his hand for Geraldi's head, but missed. He felt a grip on his elbow, and another at his wrist, burning his flesh to the bone. His arm was jerked over the shoulder of Geraldi, and, as the latter stooped strongly, big Jack Tucker heaved resistlessly from his feet and hurled into the air.

He struck against the trunk of a tree, rebounded from it, and fell flat on his face, breathless. There he lay for a moment, struggling and gasping to get back the wind which had been knocked out of his body. Geraldi stood by with a calmly thoughtful face, considering those struggles.

At last the youngster managed to get to his feet. He was white from the shock, and white with shame, also. For the first time in his life, his hands were chained. For the first time he had been worsted in a physical encounter — and by a much smaller man. If he resumed the contest, he knew that he would be rushing to ruin against the inhuman trickiness and skill of this Manhattan Jimmy. He saw, furthermore, that it was not a time for him to resort to a gun play. So he stood there at a loss, mutely brushing the pine needles and the dust from his clothes, and still breathing somewhat brokenly.

A hand appeared before him. It was the slender hand of Geraldi, and Tucker looked up in bewilderment, for it was extended in a friendly greeting.

He shook his head. "You've made a fool of me, Jimmy," he said. "Do you want me to congratulate you on account of doing that?"

"Why, Jack," said Geraldi, "I've tried to show

you what you're up against in this camp. You think that you'd have a square chance and a fair break if it came to a fight. But you wouldn't. You haven't lived long enough to know what a real crook can do. These fellows are real crooks . . . like me. They're not the soft-boiled variety, like you."

"You took pity on me. You wanted to show me?" asked Jack Tucker. "You're a smart fellow, Manhattan, but you're not the first man in the world who ever learned Japanese wrestling. What do you want to say to me?"

"I want to tell you to keep your ears pulled in, to put it one way," Geraldi explained. "Keep your voice down, and use your eyes and your ears. Don't swagger in this camp, Tucker. You take it for granted that you're tough enough to break a hangman's rope simply because you've been let into the gang of Mister Murderer Hayman. But you're only a fool of a kid."

Tucker glared at him. "I've heard you say that," he answered. "I've heard you say that once too often. What do you get out of this, Manhattan?"

"I get out of it," Geraldi stated, "the hope that you'll open your eyes and see one main fact to begin with."

"What's that?" asked Tucker.

"The hand that I'm offering to you. You need a friend up here, son. Are you going to turn me down?"

The pallor departed from the face of young

Tucker, and in its place came a flood of burning crimson. "You think I'm a fool and a puppy," he said. "You don't want that sort for a friend."

"I'm not wanting you for what you are, but for what you may turn into," said Geraldi. "You're clean bred, or I'm all wrong. Your blood's right. The rest of these fellows are débris . . . rubbish. Hayman's the only man of the lot, because Hayman's the only one who could have been honest, if he hadn't decided to turn crooked. He had a free choice. And you've got a free choice."

Tucker started. "You want to persuade me to chuck this business? Is that it?" he asked.

"You're pretty young, Tucker," said Geraldi. "Do you think that I'm working for the Salvation Army? No, I'm simply trying to gather in a recruit who may be useful to me. Perhaps I'll not be with Hayman's gang forever. Is that a secret big enough to choke you, or can you keep it down?"

Tucker blinked. He did not need to cry out that men who were once in the Hayman gang were never allowed to leave it. There had been a few desertions — but death had followed in every case, inescapable death.

Geraldi smiled at the boy who towered above him. "You're afraid of Hayman," he said. "But let me tell you this . . . Hayman doesn't waste time on his young hands. And I do. I'd make you a crook able to walk through any door in the world. I'd make you great, not a mere wire-cutting, gate-jumping blockhead of a 'puncher gone wrong. Kid, do you take my hand and stand on my side?"

Suddenly the vast grip of Jack Tucker fairly swallowed the hand of Geraldi. "I dunno know why you're doing this," he said. "It's almost as though you wanted to make a fool of me again . . . but somehow I'm trusting you, Manhattan!"

Geraldi tugged his hand free. "You've spoiled my hand for at least twenty-four hours," he said ruefully.

"You don't despise me?" muttered Tucker. "You don't think that I'm crawling like a dog, simply because you've been able to handle me like a child?"

Geraldi sighed. "Tucker," he said, "you go back to camp. And remember that a man who's about to ride through fire doesn't pick out a dog to keep him company."

Chapter Thirty-Four
GERALDI TAKES A CHANCE

Tucker came straight back into the clearing before the camp, while Geraldi took the circuitous route through the trees until he had arrived at the pasture. There he caught up the gray gelding, saddled and bridled it, and rode straight off through the wooded mountainside. Well before this, his three hobo assistants should be in place at the town of Kempton. There he wanted to find them.

He rode on as though he had not the slightest care concerning who found or followed his trail, but, as a matter of fact, he turned more than once and sighted suddenly back along the way he had come. The difficulty with him was that he did not wish to be observed or to be followed. But if he made a trail problem that might shake a possible pursuer off the trail, at the same time the very fact that he had constructed such a problem would prove that he wished to get outside of the ken of the people of Hayman's camp. There was nothing for it, however, save to ride straight down to Kempton on the chance that no one would suspect or follow him.

In fact, who was there in the entire camp who had showed the slightest suspicion concerning him? There was only Hayman himself. But that was enough. The deep brain of that arch-scoundrel was capable of reading hearts and brains fully as subtle as that of Geraldi's. Therefore, the latter went in deep depression of mind.

As well as he could turn the matter back and forth in his mind, there was only one solution that he could find for the riddle he had on hand. He must get to his three men, and he must use them to the full in what lay before him, or else all was ruin for Geraldi, for Tucker, and no one gained saving Mr. Murderer Hayman. The dread of that man rode like a ghost at the side of Geraldi all the way into the little town of Kempton.

He entered that place with little fear, however. It was true that a great price was upon the head of Hayman, and that for the apprehension of any of his men liberal rewards were offered, but the lumbermen who made up the greater part of the population of Kempton had little desire to make trouble for the outlaw.

In the first place, Hayman never bothered them, and none of Hayman's wild fellows ever shot up the town or so much as started a drunken brawl there. There was a standing rule in the band that whatever was done in other places, no one of the crew must dare to take a drink in Kempton, or pull a gun, or so much as double a fist in the little town. There was a well-known story of how one of Hayman's hardiest gun-fighters allowed himself to be crowded into a corner and actually took water, rather than strike back with hand or bullet against a towering hulk of a lumberjack.

Rather than a nuisance, Mr. Hayman's bandits were an actual blessing to the town. For instance, when hard times had struck the camps three years before and two of them had to close down completely, money appeared from an unknown source to comfort and take care of the lumberjacks when they went broke, or to help them on their way to other jobs. The source of that help was unknown, but it was guessed to be Hayman, and the good deed was rightly laid to the Doctor's credit.

When Ben Holloway's fall from a tree broke his neck, Hayman's cash kept the widow going for six months. Two or three crippled lumberjacks were enjoying pensions from the crook.

More than this, the women who raised in their back yards chickens and geese and pigs, and who pastured cows and raised veal in the pasture lands of the mountainside, were sure of a high price for all of their products when they sold to Hayman's agents. The price asked was the price paid. Only shame controlled the market.

For these reasons, when officers of the law penetrated as far as Kempton in the hunt for the outlaw and his men, they found the trail went out at that point. No man, no woman, no child could be found who knew anything of Hayman or his wild tribe. No one could be found who would really believe, also, that Hayman's gang had committed such terrible outrages, such free-handed killings. Of such reports, the inhabitants of the town were apt to say: "Newspaper stuff!" And they refused credence. The good repute of Hayman in the town of Kempton was a tower of strength, and it availed the crook much.

So Geraldi, as he rode into the town toward the end of the day, when the trees along the western ridge stood black as painted cardboard against the crimson of the sky, felt little fear of inquiry or of awkward questions asked in the town.

Other young men mounted on fine horses — youngsters never seen before — happened from time to time in the streets of Kempton, and, although many paused and looked them over carefully, no questions were asked, no voices were raised. Only a head would be shaken, here and there, and a muttered word passed among the villagers.

So Geraldi came down the main street of the town and went past the general merchandise store. There he saw, lounging against one of the wooden pillars of the verandah, red-headed Pete, the hobo. The sight of that red hair, glowing even in the half light of the day's end, cheered the very heart of Geraldi.

One glance he exchanged with Pete, and then waved his hand forward as though brushing a fly from the neck of his mount. After that, he jogged steadily on through the town, and at the verge of the forest he dismounted, took the bit from the mouth of the horse, so that it could graze comfortably on the long grass, and sat down on a knoll to wait.

He made and lighted a cigarette and smoked it to a butt. Still no one came. In the meantime, the day was darkening toward twilight, and the lights began to shimmer behind the windows of the village, and sharp-voiced children drove in the cows from the pasture. Doors slammed. Women came to windows and called in shrill wails for youngsters who were playing too late. Men came out of the forest trails, walking slowly, their heads and shoulders bent forward, the weight of the day's work still depressing them. Their voices were quiet. Rankness of tobacco smoke floated from their pipes and blew back over their shoulders. Teams of mules came out with rattling, lumbering trucks behind them. The mules walked briskly, knowing that hay, grain, and water waited at the end of a few more minutes. The drivers snapped their blacksnakes and whistled to encourage them.

This is the curse of the teamster's life. When the other laborers are through, he has still half an hour or an hour's work to attend to — more than that, if his conscience is a tender one, and there are collars whose padding needs shifting to ease sore shoulders, or galled backs to be dressed.

Geraldi saw this procession at the end of the day with pain in his heart, for his mind went back to his own land, and the swift swirl and gallop of the horses when they came up to the pasture gate at the end of the day, and the tossing of their heads, and the bright, wild flashing of their eyes as they waited for him to let down the bars. Labor had a curse in it, but it had a redeeming blessing, as well. He sighed as he thought of the small house, and the poplars that grew around it, and the flash and the singing of the stream that curved down the hill.

Larry Burns had burst that picture like a bubble for him. No, perhaps it was not Larry Burns. It was simply that a hand had reached for him out of his old life, and so his work was destroyed by a single gesture.

Something stirred in the brush nearby. He started to his feet, with a gun snapping into his hand. He waited, crouched low, glaring like a beast, the pupils of his eyes expanding as he penetrated the dimness of the twilight. Then a breeze fanned his forehead. The upper branches whispered together, and the same rustling sound was heard again in the brush. The wind, after all, he could trust. He sighed once more and was about to sit down again, when he saw a bulky form striding toward him. Two more followed the leader, and presently Pete, Jerry, and Bob, the tramps, the criminals, stood before him. They seemed to be in the highest spirits, but excited.

"Whatcha think?" Pete said as a greeting. "That hound of a Wendell, he's up here in

Kempton, holdin' his ear close to the ground. I gotta mind to sap him over the head! He gettin' kind of a nuisance."

"A good sluggin' would help him out," declared Bob, with his deep, strange voice.

"Wendell is here?" said Geraldi. "You fellows let Wendell be. You're not going to stay long in Kempton."

"Where do we head for, chief?" asked Jerry.

"You ever hear of the town of Alexandria?"

"Nope."

"I have," said Bob. "It's in Egypt."

"Shut up, you fool," said Pete. "I've heard of Alexandria, chief. It's a no-account cow town. What about it?"

"You're going there," said Geraldi.

"What for?"

"You fellows back up and let me be alone here with Pete for a while," Geraldi said.

They drew back.

Geraldi said: "I've got a plan that's complicated. It needs a man of brains to turn the trick for me. Will you be the man, Pete?"

"Sure, if I can. You brought all of us luck, chief. We're with you till we bust . . . or you bust."

"Listen to me, then," said Geraldi, "and keep your ears wide open."

"A whole hoss could walk right through 'em into my brain," said the other cheerfully.

Then, with a deliberate voice, Geraldi began the detailing of his plan, and he saw Pete cock his head uncertainly first to one side, then to the other, and at length shake it violently.

"It'll never work!" Pete argued.

"It will," said Geraldi.

"It'll never work," Pete groaned. "I'll just get myself kicked out onto my face. So'll all the others."

"Do exactly what I tell you to do," Geraldi stated. "Let me do the thinking."

"And I'll collect the kickin'," Pete said ruefully. "Well, then, I'll try. So'll the other boys."

"Then start now," Geraldi said. "And get away from that Wendell. He's a ferret that will be drinking your blood fresh and hot from the throat one of these days. Get out tonight, and make a long march. You'll get to Alexandria while it's still dark. Then do as I told you to do."

Pete was about to answer when Geraldi jerked up a hand and stopped him. Intently Geraldi listened, and it seemed to him that he heard from the brush a thin, rustling sound again, and this time, oddly enough, it appeared to be withdrawing — against the course of the lightly running, tiptoe wind.

Chapter Thirty-Five

THE SNEAK

Geraldi went into the brush headlong, but without a sound. The great bull moose, despite his spreading horns, can fade into and out of the twilight shrubbery without a sound. His lofty front appears suddenly before the hunter, where nothing but close growing trees and bush stood the instant before. The roar of his call from behind makes the ground tremble under the feet of the unsuspecting shooter. So perhaps it was no great miracle — although it appeared one to Pete and his two companions — when Geraldi rushed into the bushes and left no more sound behind him or sign of his going than a bull moose moving silently through the forest despite its great bulk and spreading horns.

There must be eyes in the feet, eyes and extra nerves in the hands, and sensitiveness of the whole body to every touch. Geraldi had these gifts, and he used them now. He had his ear canted. The woods were almost black, so that he could not trust his eyes. Instead, he trusted almost entirely to the sense of touch, which enabled him to progress rapidly and gain upon that

279

subtle rustling sound that preceded him.

The wind came again with a gust and a rush, but, once having located and isolated the first sound, he did not confuse it with those which overlaid it. Very surely he went on until the thing was close before him. Then, stepping more cat-like than ever, he strained his eyes through the murk of the shadows to see what he could.

At that moment the form of a man rose dim as smoke from the ground and stood before him. There was a grunt of surprise and fear, the dull gleam of a gun — and then Geraldi drew and fired. He knew that he had made a center shot through the man's body. But he did not wait for that to end the battle. He sprang in and grappled with that shadowy form. It was as though he had seized upon a stuffed body — a thing without real flesh and bone in it — for the fellow melted through his arms and lay groaning on the ground.

Geraldi whistled three times, not overloud. Then he knelt by the fallen man.

"Have you got it, stranger?" he asked.

"I've got it," said the other. "I'm going out like a light. I'm going fast. . . ." His words choked away with a groan.

"Nobody's out till the count's finished," Geraldi stated. "Here comes company, in the meantime."

Pete, Bob and Jerry came loudly through the underbrush, panting in their haste.

"Strike a light, will you" Geraldi asked.

"I've got a lantern," said Bob proudly. "I'll give you a light."

It was a small, collapsible bull's-eye affair, and, when it was kindled and the face of it thrown open, Geraldi found himself looking down upon the face of Stew Malone.

Malone blinked at the radiance which seemed to make the agony show more clearly in his eyes. There was no soul in that face now. There was only pain.

"Hold the light closer," commanded Geraldi.

With that illumination he opened Malone's coat, bared the strangely small orifice of the wound, then turned him over as the man groaned feebly, and saw the place where the slug had come out.

"A dead center," Malone murmured. "That was good shooting, Manhattan, in the dark." He attempted to laugh — a sound that ended in another bubbling moan.

Geraldi, however, was interested in another thing. It was a small, purple-tinged furrow that ran around the ribs of the man and connected the first aperture with the more gaping wound in the back.

"Malone," he said, "you're not a dead man. That bullet glanced around the rib bones. If it had drilled straight through, you never would have known what had hit you. You're going to live, if you'll give yourself a chance."

"I'm going to live?" gasped Malone, and in his astonishment he tried to sit up.

Geraldi pressed him back. "Lie still," he said. "You're not fit to wriggle around. I say that you've got a chance to live. What brought you down here?"

"Me? Nothing much," said Malone.

"You came to trail me," said Geraldi.

"Trail you?" Malone murmured. "Why should I do that?"

"Trail you?" Pete of the red hair repeated. "Trail Geraldi?"

Geraldi turned on him, with a gritting of his teeth. It was the one thing that he wished to keep a secret from Doctor Hayman and his gang. "You fool!" hissed Geraldi.

Big Pete winced before him. "Didn't he know?" muttered Pete. "I thought the whole world just about knew you, Jimmy."

"Geraldi!" gasped the fallen man. "Geraldi! And only this size!"

"Oh, he's big enough," Bob interjected, rubbing his head thoughtfully. "He's bigger than you think. Sizes in dynamite don't have to be like sizes in men in order to start things moving."

"Geraldi!" Malone exclaimed under his breath again. "If the chief could know. . . ." He stopped himself.

"Now, then," Geraldi began, getting down on one knee near the wounded man, "you're going to have your chance to live, if you'll tell me the truth. Come clean and I'll tie up your wounds and have a doctor for you. But if you lie or won't talk, you can bleed to death here."

"Why shouldn't I talk?" asked Malone. He opened his eyes wide and looked straight up at Geraldi.

"You were eavesdropping a while ago," Geraldi declared.

"Yes," Malone admitted.

"Who sent you to do that?"

"I sent myself," Malone answered. "We've never had another in the camp like you. I wanted to make out what you were, so I took your trail and followed it down here."

"You lie," said Geraldi without heat. "You were sent."

"I'm tellin' you the straight of it," Malone insisted.

"Stew," said Geraldi, "I watched you in the camp. We looked at one another a little. You weren't curious enough about me to come down here and play the sneak on my trail. You were sent."

"Never in my life," said Malone.

"All right, boys," Geraldi said. "We'll just leave him here a while to think it over. I hope he does his thinking before he bleeds to death." He rose and turned.

"Hey! Will you wait a minute?" gasped Malone.

Geraldi turned slowly back. "Do we get the truth?" he asked.

"I'll give you the whole truth," Malone said. "It was the Doctor."

"I thought so," remarked Geraldi. "What did he say to you?"

"He said," Malone replied, "that you were either going to be the best hand in the gang, or else you'd be a blast that was likely to blow us all to pieces. He asked me to trail you . . . my God, he'll have the inside of my heart, for what I'm telling you now."

"He may," said Geraldi, "unless I have his first. He sent you on my trail, then, to find out what you could?"

"Yes."

"What did he tell you to look for?"

"To see whether you met any other men."

"Well," said Geraldi through his teeth, "you saw me meet them. He's a wise fellow, is the Doctor."

"Cut clear of him, Geraldi," Stew Malone advised. "I've been doing a dirty business in trailin' you like this. But I tell you now, man to man, that the best thing you can do is to get clear of him. I know somethin' about you, Geraldi . . . by reputation. I've heard folks talk about you. But I give you the lowdown now . . . you'll never make any headway with the Doctor. Because he ain't a man. He's a devil."

"I've heard what I wanted to hear from you," said Geraldi. "I don't want advice." He turned to Pete. "What'll we do with this one?" he asked.

Bob of the unsavory past put in a hurried word. "Bash his head in for sneaking," he said. "Otherwise, what'd we do with him?"

"Yeah, what'd we do with him?" Pete echoed. "Stay out here and nurse him, maybe?" He laughed, a short, hard, ugly laugh.

"You ain't promised him nothin'," said Jerry, arguing the point. "He come down here and put his head in the lion's mouth. Just close down and give it a crunch. It's all that he's got comin' to him!"

"Geraldi!" Malone gasped. "God knows I've been a sneak. I shouldn't have done the dirty work . . . but up yonder, we gotta do what the Doctor tells us to do. . . ."

"Tush, man," Geraldi said. "I wasn't really asking for advice. I was only thinking. You can see how it is. With you on my hands, my game is about spoiled. I wish to heaven that I'd put that bullet through your heart, Malone. I dare say that you've done enough to deserve a slug in that spot."

Malone closed his eyes. His face whitened dreadfully. He said nothing in response.

"I've given him my word that, if he came clean, he'd have his chance to live," said Geraldi through his teeth. "We've got to take care of him. Jerry!"

"Not me," Jerry said. "I want to be in on the party!"

"Jerry," Geraldi asked, "will you listen to me?"

"Yeah. I'm listenin'."

"You're going to stay here and take care of Malone. If you keep him safely and bring him through . . . mind you, *if* you bring him though . . . you get your cut the same as the others who are down there where bullets are apt to fly. Will you take this job?"

"I get my cut just the same?" Jerry queried anxiously.

"Just the same," affirmed Geraldi.

"Well, I'll take the job, then," Jerry replied. "But I don't like it. I'd rather change with one of the other boys. . . ."

"It's settled," said Geraldi. "Go into town and get some blankets and whatever you need to dress his wounds. He won't bleed to death. That was only talk on my part. But keep him warm and well fed. The rest of us will try to do our work."

Chapter Thirty-Six
THE RETURN

Geraldi left Pete and Bob to make their way toward Alexandria, and Jerry to maintain guard and care for wounded Stew Malone. For his own part, he rode straight back through Kempton, and it was as he passed the hotel that he saw Marshal Tex Arnold again.

The door of the hotel opened as Geraldi went by, and he saw a tall form step out into the light that streamed from within. He saw the lean face, much thinner than before, and eyes sunken in deep shadows. The very back of Tex Arnold seemed to be bowing beneath a weight, and his mouth was pinched, as though a sharp pain were stabbing at his vitals.

Geraldi took note of the man and was glad of the darkness that covered him. There was, first of all, a sense of triumph in that he had beaten the famous marshal so thoroughly. The repute of Arnold was no longer what it had been when first he rode out upon the trail of Geraldi. Men shrugged their shoulders now, when they heard mention of Arnold's name. They laughed. How could they keep from laughing, indeed, when the man had failed so signally and allowed the eel to slip twice through his hands? Yes, Tex Arnold was beaten, baffled, shamed.

The fierce pleasure of Geraldi did not endure very long. It was true that he had kept from the hands of Arnold and tormented the soul of that man-catcher. But, after all, it was not for himself that Arnold chased him. It was for the sake of society. Society might fail with one of her servants, but with another she would succeed. What Arnold could not do, time and many new hands would accomplish, and at length Geraldi must go down, as if under the waves of the sea. He knew it. He accepted the end. But it was a changed and melancholy man who rode on to the camp of the great Doctor Hayman.

There was a fire in the clearing. Three guards kept outpost watch, and one of those stopped Geraldi on the way in, then, recognizing him, allowed him to go on.

He found Hayman by the fire, toasting his hands, smiling at the flame. The brightness of the fire illumined only the hands and the face of the man, like a Dutch portrait, and the blackness of the night swallowed up the rest of Hayman's body, except a shadowy outline. He was smiling at the flames and thinking his own thoughts. Geraldi watched him with an odd mixture of wonder, admiration, detestation, and fear. This was like no other man. This was *not* a man. It was merely a divorced intelligence. If Geraldi had baffled and fooled such a person as Marshal Tex

Arnold, was it a sign that he would be able to baffle Doctor Hayman, also? He doubted it greatly.

"Arnold's in Kempton village," Geraldi announced.

"Oh, you've been there, have you?" asked Hayman, still smiling at the fire, still without shifting his glance from the dance of the flames.

"Yes, I've been in there. I saw Tex Arnold."

"You know him, eh?"

"I know enough of him," Geraldi said.

"There's nothing to fear from him now," said the Doctor. "He can't find our trail. He's blind to it."

"He's a good trailer," Geraldi commented, "and he has plenty of men with him."

"He's blind," said the outlaw, "to everything except to Geraldi. He won't think of anybody else. That's the beauty of such a fellow. Frigate bird, whatever you want to call Geraldi, nevertheless, he strikes such a light that he calls the attention of the sheriffs and the marshals to himself. I'm glad that he's come out of retirement again and that he's working. He takes a good deal of attention from me." He laughed a little and repeated: "No, Arnold won't bother me."

"He's bothered one of your men already, I hear," answered Geraldi.

"What one?"

"I didn't hear the name. It was simply a rumor in the town that Arnold's men had caught one of your gang and that he'd been sent off under escort toward the railroad." He waited.

"You didn't hear the name?"

"I think someone said Malone, but I'm not sure."

"Malone?" cried out Hayman. "They'd never catch Malone. He's not the sort to give up without fighting."

"There may have been a fight," Geraldi said. "I wasn't asking all the questions in the world, as you can imagine."

"Malone!" said Hayman, showing an emotion that surprised Geraldi. "I would rather have lost a dozen men than Malone."

"You liked him, eh?" Geraldi said.

"Yes," Hayman replied. "He was always a delightful problem. There was so much kindness in that fellow that, after he'd robbed or killed a man, or both, he was always tortured with remorse for weeks following. He'd rob a store, and then, out of conscience, he'd fairly throw the money away at the next poker game. He was the greatest fool I ever saw. I've lain awake at night and laughed about him. He was better than a king's jester for my nerves. Yes, that was Malone. I'll have to do something about him, though. I'm surprised. Malone was the sort who'd fight to the death, rather than go into the hands of the hangman."

"Perhaps he was trapped," said Geraldi.

"It's a fast trap that works quicker than the gun hand of Stew Malone," remarked Hayman. "Now, Manhattan, let that drop. We start for Alexandria at once. You and I, and Bud Maker, and two more."

"Do we go by railroad?" asked Geraldi.

Doctor Hayman raised his head. "Railroad?" he repeated.

"Yes. Blind luggage, perhaps. Or in a boxcar?"

Hayman laughed a little, turning the sound gently over his tongue, as it were. "Manhattan," he said, "you're a cool devil. D'you expect me to show my face near a railroad without a mask on it? No, no, Manhattan. I'm too well known for that. It's worth fifty thousand dollars to any man to cause an accident to me."

Geraldi nodded. "Horses, then?" he said.

"Yes. Horses," answered Hayman. "Go out there in the pasture and pick out your nag. That gray of yours has had enough work to do, I take it. If we make time, we'll get to Alexandria at nightfall the day after tomorrow. That means riding all of tonight and laying up part of to-morrow for rest. Can you stand it?"

"Of course," Geraldi assured, and he walked toward the pasture to make his selection.

On the whole, he was more than pleased with himself. He had avoided killing Stew Malone in cold blood, and at the same time he had been able to make a sufficient explanation so that Doctor Hayman would not grow suspicious be-cause Malone did not return to the camp. All seemed well, in the eyes of Geraldi. He could not know what was happening between Malone and Jerry at that moment.

Chapter Thirty-Seven

A WEAK BROTHER

Yonder, in the dark of the woods near to Kempton, Jerry, the tramp and outside man, had obeyed all the orders of Geraldi. He had brought blankets, made down a bed of boughs for the wounded man, and then had cleansed and bandaged his wounds securely. That done, he gave Stew Malone tinned sardines and crackers to eat and coffee to drink — coffee heated in an old tin over the most scrupulously small fire that Jerry could contrive to build.

It was by the light of the remnants of this fire — a dull, red glow that barely touched the faces of the men and showed with a glint in their eyes, now and again — that Stew Malone began to do his first talking. He had kept a resolute silence, for the most part, since Geraldi had left. But now he felt much better. The nausea that had followed the shock and pain from the bullet, the horrible lassitude of despair, which had come with the conviction that he was dying, now gave way, in turn, to a rising strength and greatness of heart. As his spirits rose, he saw before him the problem that he must meet. He even talked it over with Jerry.

A loose tongue was the worst of Jerry's many faults. And Malone had struck on a topic, moreover, which induced an expansive mood in Jerry.

"You been thick with Geraldi for a longish time?" Malone asked, bunching the blanket beneath his head so that it was raised to a higher angle.

"No, not long. Never been fast enough to break into company like Geraldi before," said Jerry. "He just happened to pick up the three of us."

"He picked you up all at once?"

"Yeah," said Jerry. "It was this way. We got fresh with him in a boxcar. How was we to know that it was the great Geraldi? So we piled into him, and he smashed the bunch of us. . . ." He paused, with a wide, gaping grin. He shook his head.

"He slammed all three of you?" echoed Malone. "That little runt?"

"Aw, he ain't no runt," Jerry said loyally. "He's made kind of round . . . he don't stick out in bunches, but he's as solid as lead pipe. He's around a hundred and fifty pounds on anybody's scales. And every pound of him is soup."

"Yeah. I felt the grip of him," Malone said thoughtfully. "Only, the idea of him tackling all three of you . . . and all of you big and looking like fighting men, too!"

"I can handle my dukes a little," admitted Jerry. "But I ain't a professional. Pete was, though. He made one pass at Pete and laid him out. *Jujitsu*, I guess it was."

"I've seen some of them funny tricks," declared Stew Malone. "Handy, for anybody. How's it been with you and Geraldi? Fat?"

"Yeah. He treats us all fine," Jerry confirmed. "He don't snarl. He don't snap over his shoulder. He's pretty clean and straight, I'd say."

"Aw, sure he'd be that way. He's too foxy to be mean to the gents that work for him," said Malone. "Then, when he cuts the big melon, how much do you come in for?"

"Oh, only forty or fifty thousand apiece, I guess," Jerry bragged, with a contented grin.

"Aw, he'll forget about you," the other assured him.

"You think so," said Jerry, unmoved. "But he won't. He's straight. That's what he is."

"He's never straight with crooks like you and me," Malone contradicted. "That's why they call him the frigate bird. He makes the other crooks work for him. He lives on what he takes from 'em. You're being a fool, old son."

"I ain't a fool," insisted Jerry firmly. "I know him. I've seen a time when he could've held his hands and let us rot in jail. But what does he do? He cracks that jail wide open, the smartest and the bravest that I ever seen. He takes us all out, gets us on horses, fills our pocket with coin. Is that letting us down?"

"He's saving you, because he wants to use

you," said Malone. "When the big tumble comes, you'll bust your necks, he'll laugh in your faces, and ride off with the dough. That's the way that he always does."

Jerry started to deny this, but, consulting his own nature, it appeared to him such a human truth, or at least such a strong possibility, he could not make the words of his denial come forth. "You don't know him," he was only able to say.

But Malone was already smelling victory, as it were, afar off, and he continued, without too much haste. "Look at the plan that he's got on hand now. He's right there in the camp of the Doctor. And he's going to try to get away with Hayman's stuff."

"What stuff?" asked Jerry.

"Why," Malone answered, "you'd oughta know . . . most people know . . . that there's a hundred thousand, or a couple of hundred thousand dollars on the Doctor all the time. There's that, and the fifty thousand on his head, dead or alive."

"I see," said Jerry. "I dunno why anybody would carry that much cash, though."

"Not in bills, you saphead," said Malone, easily. "He can carry a quarter of a million condensed so small that it don't make a bulge even in his vest pocket."

"Sparklers, eh?" cried the other, gaping.

"Yeah. Of course."

"What are they? Diamonds?"

"Rubies. All rubies. That's what they are.

That's what he loves, next to blood. Blood's the same color. Yeah, that devil carries the stuff with him all the time."

"You seen 'em?"

"No, but a gent told me that had seen 'em. Spike Wainwright."

"Yeah. I've heard of him. I thought he was dead."

"He is. He's dead because he seen those rubies. I'd be dead, too, if the Doctor knew that I'd heard about 'em."

"You mean that Hayman bumped him off?"

"Yeah, I mean it. With a pretty left-handed shot, just as Spike was pullin' his gun."

"He must be a devil," Jerry said, sighing.

"I'll tell you what he is," said Malone seriously. "He's one that gives you a fair break. Don't make any mistake about that. He pays up. *He* ain't any frigate bird. Not him. He takes where he can, he takes plenty, and he splits it fair and square with the rest of us."

"You'd think that he'd bury the stuff, and not carry that price around with him," suggested Jerry.

"What does he care?" Malone responded. "He'd rather live happy than scared all the time. And he wants the rubies because he enjoys lookin' at 'em. That's the way with the Doctor. He takes his pleasures as he goes along. He's a man, old son."

"Yeah," said Jerry. "I reckon that he's a man, all right."

"Whatcha think? Would he be afraid of the whole gang?" Malone asked. "No, but the whole gang would be afraid of him. Only . . . he's gotta know what he's up against. If he knew that it was Geraldi, he'd beat Geraldi, too. . . ."

"I doubt that," Jerry contradicted. "You ain't seen Geraldi move. But I've seen him move. The snap of a whiplash is mighty slow compared to the way he flicks a gun in and out of sight. I don't even know where he packs his six-guns. And I've seen him use 'em plenty, too."

He took a long breath of despairing admiration, and Malone watched him curiously from under the shadow of his brows.

"You'll never see what he does with the stuff that he lifts off of the Doctor, either," said Malone. "He'll make that disappear under your eyes. Look the way that he's always done. He crooks the crooks, like you and me. Everybody knows that."

"I never heard it before," said Jerry.

"That he lives on crooks?"

"Yeah. But I mean, I never heard that he crooks his partners!"

"What kind of partners are you three?" demanded the other. "You jump him, and he slugs you, and then he lets you work for him. He gives you day's wages. That'll make his conscience pretty free, won't it? You ask yourself what you'd do in that case."

"If I thought . . . ," Jerry said passionately. He stopped himself.

"Aw, you know that I'm right," said Malone. "You're just tryin' to kid yourself a little bit, ain't you?"

"I feel kind of sick," said Jerry. "Suppose that they cut and run, when they pull the trick there in Alexandria, and leave me out in the cold . . . ?"

"In Alexandria?" Malone said. "What's that?"

"I mean, the bank deal," Jerry responded absently.

Malone grunted with surprise. "What d'you know about that?" he asked.

"Why, just what Geraldi told me. That's all. The boys are to beat it down to Alexandria, then try to get into the bank and bust up the game of Hayman. . . ."

"The devil!" Malone exclaimed.

"They'll do it, I guess," said Jerry. "He's told 'em how to work it. He's got a brain on him, Geraldi has."

"Bust up the game . . . oh, damn him! Damn that Geraldi!" groaned Malone. Then he said, fierce with his eagerness: "I'll tell you what, Jerry. Geraldi offered you forty or fifty thousand that you'll never see. How'd you like fifty thousand *real?*"

"Like it?" said Jerry. "Hell, man, I'd *love* it!"

"Then get me back to the camp. It ain't far. I could walk, now. I could ride, too. Get me onto a hoss and take me back to camp, and then I'll get word to the Doctor, and we'll trap Geraldi. You think that the Doctor won't pay? He'll pay you so high that your head'll swim!"

"What makes you think so?" said Jerry.

"You fool, there's three or four hundred thousand all laid out on the Alexandria deal. Does the Doctor want to lose that and get his gang all shot up, besides? No, he doesn't! Besides, he hates Geraldi. Always *has* hated him. Just the same way that Geraldi hates crooks like us and Hayman. Hayman plays square. He's an out and out crook. But Geraldi, he plays in betwixt and between. That's the way he is. A skunk. The Doctor wants his blood, and someday he'll have it . . . only, now he ain't got a fair break. He don't know that it's Geraldi who's joined him. He don't even suspect it."

"Fifty thousand," murmured Jerry.

"I'll swear that Hayman will pay you that much," Malone said. "He'll pay the price of his own head for a crack at Geraldi."

"Wait a minute," said Jerry. "Are you sure that you could ride?"

"Of course, I could ride," said Malone. "On a job like this, I could ride to the end of the world, even with six slugs in me. I feel fine."

Eagerly they talked as, having mounted, they rode through the woods. The horses that Jerry had hired made good time, even at the walking pace to which the hurt of Malone had limited them. As they went along, Jerry unburdened himself of Geraldi's plan. The excellence of it made Malone exclaim and curse repeatedly.

A moon was riding high in the night sky, and

so bright was it as it shone through the thin, pure mountain air that they could hardly see the glimmer of the campfire until they were very close to it. A voice challenged them sharply.

"Who's there?"

"Hello, Double Deck," said Malone. "Speak very soft and easy. Don't yell. I'm Malone."

"The devil you are," Double Deck Joe said. "Malone was caught by Marshal Tex Arnold's men and is on his way to the railroad."

"Who told you that?" asked Malone.

"Manhattan Jimmy . . . that new man. Who's with you?"

"The fellow who gave me the lowdown on Manhattan Jimmy. Where's the chief? Get to him, and bring him out here. Not a word to anybody else. I've got news that'll blow things sky high. There's gonna be some action around here."

"Get to the chief?" Double Deck said. "How can I? He's left for Alexandria, and Manhattan Jimmy with him!"

Chapter Thirty-Eight

THE BLIZZARD

"Come in by the fire. I gotta see to talk!" exclaimed Malone, when the importance of the last statement came to him. He pushed his horse ahead, with Double Deck Joe puffing and trotting at his side. When they reached the fire, Malone slipped to the ground. Double Deck caught at him and steadied his companion.

"What's happened to you, Stew?" he demanded, alarmed. "You've been hurt. You're all over blood. . . ."

"Manhattan Jimmy plugged me," said Stew Malone with great calm. He was thinking ahead. His own present condition appeared to trouble him not in the least.

"Manhattan Jimmy!" Double Deck Joe exclaimed.

"Yeah. Jimmy Geraldi . . . Manhattan Jimmy."

"My God . . . Geraldi!" gasped Double Deck. "What you sayin' to me, Stew? Geraldi? The devil!"

"He's about that," declared Stew Malone. "But he's away with the chief, is he?"

"Aye. His right-hand man."

"He'll smash the whole game," Malone said with the same calm, the same forward look in his eyes. "Who's left in camp here with you?"

"Nobody. I'm alone, Stew."

"You've gotta get a pair of hosses and tail out after the chief. You've gotta pass the word along to him," Malone said.

"Catch the wind, you mean!" said Double Deck Joe, looking down with a shake of his head at the size of his stomach. "Me catch up with the chief? You know the way the Doctor rides."

"Don't talk. Don't argue," Malone said impatiently. "I'm tellin' you the only way out. Otherwise, it's all a bust. Geraldi has got the Doctor framed . . . just the way the Doctor would frame Geraldi, if he got the chance. But Geraldi is on the inside. He has the know, and the Doctor ain't. Listen to me!"

"I'm listenin'. My God, how I'm listenin', son!"

"Geraldi's got the deal all cooked. He'll get into the bank. . . ."

"How?" gasped Double Deck. "Have they got that all framed?"

"Through the door, you fat-faced fool!" answered Malone angrily. "Do locks mean anything to Jim Geraldi? Don't you know what he can do?"

"Yeah. I know," muttered Joe. "I'd forgot that. He can walk through anything, pretty near."

"When he's inside, he'll take a look around. While he's lookin', he'll unlock the back entrance to the building. He's got two gunmen stacked up ready to come inside on the sneak, and they'll work with Geraldi against the rest of the boys. They'll take 'em by surprise. Who's with the Doctor?"

"Dick Kennedy, Larry Burns, Manhattan . . . I mean, Geraldi . . . Bud Maker, Jungle Murphy, and Angel Ray."

"That's the Doctor and five tough ones, ag'in' Geraldi and two that ain't half so tough," said Malone. "But Geraldi and the other pair will have the jump. Geraldi, they say, can make a split second hold the work of any other man's hour. Double Deck, you get the two best hosses out of the corral, and you light out for the Doctor's trail. You ride your heart out. If you don't get there in time, Hayman and all the rest of the boys will be tapped on the head, and then that's the end of our good times. Savvy?"

Double Deck gave one wild look around him, and then, without a word, only with a grunt of effort as he started, he rushed toward the corral.

This left Stew Malone alone with Jerry, and the latter said, bewildered: "It looks to me like I'm gonna put in a little time collectin' that fifty thousand, partner."

Malone greeted him with a scowl. "How could I tell that the Doctor would be on the trail already?" he declared. "That wasn't in the books. Wait until he comes back, and he'll fix things right."

"Suppose that he don't come back?" said Jerry, the awful possibility beginning to dawn more clearly on his crooked brain. "Then what?"

"Then you're out fifty thousand. That's all," Malone snapped.

"Out fifty thousand," muttered Jerry. "Hell . . . Geraldi will be out for my scalp."

"Geraldi won't be out for your scalp," Malone said contemptuously. "When he catches fish your size . . . he just throws 'em back in the river!"

The insult did not scar the mind of Jerry.

"What's the matter with Geraldi?" he moaned. "What started him after the crooks? Ain't he a crook himself? Ain't the law after him?"

"I've wondered the same thing," said Malone, "but, now that I've seen his face and the eyes in it, I understand pretty good. The fact is that he likes to play ag'in' the whole rest of the world. Otherwise, he wouldn't be able to keep his hands full. Man, I've heard of wild ones before, and brave ones, but I never heard or seen one like Geraldi before. If Double Deck gets to the Doctor in time . . . it's the last of Mister James Geraldi . . . and you can lay your money on that!"

Jerry said nothing at all. He merely stared at the fire as Double Deck rounded the corner of the house at a gallop. His low-built, powerful pinto was under the saddle. A tall bay with mighty quarters strode behind on the lead rope.

He pulled up for an instant beside the fire.

"I forgot the new kid . . . Jack Tucker. He's along with the Doctor," he said. "That makes 'em six to three. They can't be beat, no matter what Geraldi tries. There's no use me riding in!"

"You fool!" shouted Malone. "You fool! I tell you, Geraldi is poison . . . and he's used the poison on *me*. Now, will you travel, or stay here and shoot off your stupid face some more? It's up to you to save the Doctor, or the Doctor will never save any of the rest of us again. Ride! Ride like hell. Because it's going to be hell, and a lonely hell, for the rest of us, if you don't beat 'em into Alexandria!"

Double Deck Joe was at last convinced. It took him a considerable time to make up his mind, but, once an idea was lodged in it, it held him strongly. So now he leaned in the saddle, gave the pinto the spurs, and dashed across the clearing and away through the trees. He went like a madman for the first mile or so. Then, realizing the length of the journey and the perishable nature of horseflesh, he slackened his gait and let the pinto go on at the long, rolling lope of a Western range horse. The big bay followed freely on the lead rope, and the miles began to slide away behind Double Deck.

He was traveling light. He had not even taken his Winchester in the long holster beneath his right leg. For food, he had some parched corn and jerked beef. He had a canteen filled with water. As for weapons, he depended upon a single Colt revolver, an old and tried friend. He knew that every pound he cut off his traveling equipment would save him hours in the end of the long run, so he had whittled things down to the bone. He did not even carry a slicker, although he knew very well that the short cut along which he was riding would take him over a high mountain pass.

So he rode doggedly on. Every two hours he shifted from one horse to the other, but he made no real halt until the gray of the next morning. He was halfway through the pass, by this time, and a blinding blizzard struck him out of the north, whipping and cutting his face and stopping the horses as though with a white, solid wall.

He pulled in behind a high rock and dismounted, but there was no wood for the building of a fire, and the cold whipped about his body and chilled him to the bone. Inaction was much worse than any sort of plugging. So he mounted again, and spurred the tired pinto into the teeth of the gale. By this time the snow lay sheeted across the rocks. Here and there, the wind had wiped it clean, but only to pile up deeper drifts through which they floundered.

The horses were already very tired, and the cold completed their exhaustion at a stroke. Yet Double Deck Joe gallantly forced them on. He gave over spurring. He actually feared that he might injure them with the brutally cutting rowels of the spurs. Instead, he pulled out his quirt and slashed them heavily with it. "I'll warm 'em!" said Double Deck Joe, through his blue lips. Then he pushed on again.

It seemed to him that he existed for an eternity in the whiteness of this hell in which he now found himself. It seemed to him that he had been a child ever to complain of hot summer days. He would never curse the broad, fierce face of the sun again, not even during a dusty ride across the August desert. Was there really a warm sun, anywhere? And what a fool he had been not to take with him the slicker to turn the teeth of the wind that now bit him to the core of his soul. Hours that misery endured.

Once the big bay, when he was riding it, slipped and fell to its knees, then rolled upon its side and refused to get up. He got down and jerked and strained at the head of the fallen animal. It would not budge. At last, he managed to light a match, during a lull of the wind, and this he held to the hip of the horse. The fur hissed, sizzled, and then began to burn with a thin smudge of smoke. That was enough. The bay endured the pain for only one more instant, and then sprang to its feet, made young again. Double Deck Joe tried to smile, but felt as though his face would crack. But, in half an hour more, he was conscious that he had crossed the summit, and that the trail was now pitching steadily downward.

He could see nothing. All was a white mist before him, filled with dancing specks. Then this cleared a little. The sky above him was milk white with the thickness of the storm, but where he was riding was a thinner mist, and the wind blew against him with far less violence.

He went on. The air cleared still more. Presently, straight ahead of him, near the horizon, he saw a spot of blue. The storm mist gradually withdrew. It gathered high above and behind him, a gigantic wall of white and shadow. Double Deck Joe was riding now in a pleasant, green valley, and the unbelievable sun was pouring down upon him, and there were actually birds singing along the verge of the water course. So Double Deck Joe spread his elbows at the board, as it were, felt himself gradually thawing, and rubbed the ache from his eyes.

His work was not finished, but, having completed that first hard hurdle, he felt that there was some chance, now, of success. God would not let him do so much and then give him failure at the end.

If only he could help to overthrow Geraldi — he, the man upon whom the slender stranger had first of all imposed. It seemed to him that he could look back now clearly to the moment when he first encountered that fellow, a man both young and old, with the strangest eyes that ever had looked into the face of Double Deck Joe. He should have known then that he was meeting such a man as had not his fellow in the world. And he, Double Deck Joe, had brought in the destroyer and let him loose in the Hayman camp.

It was an old story. All men knew of the manner in which Geraldi had smashed other gangs of criminals long before this time. He had met them when they were as numerous and well nigh as powerful as the Hayman organization. He had not, perhaps, confronted a criminal intelligence quite on a par with that of the Doctor. But many a time he had overthrown complete bands with a devilish boldness and cunning.

Was this to be another triumph for him? Double Deck Joe, groaning with weariness and with an aching heart, was sustained in his strength by the wildfire of hatred that ran burningly along his veins. All that day it sustained him.

Twice he made halts, not so much on his own account as because the horses were so terribly beaten by their work. When he was still twenty miles from Alexandria and the sun was low in the west behind him, the bay gave out completely, stumbled, fell, and could not rise without a vast effort and the help of the rider.

Then Double Deck cast the bay adrift with its bloody sides and its welted skin. He had the stout pinto still left to him, badly worn down, but still with something of power in its heart if not in its weary body. With the pinto alone, Double Deck started on the last march that was to decide whether Geraldi or Doctor Hayman should conquer that night.

Chapter Thirty-Nine
PIGEON'S-BLOOD RUBIES

Under a shadowy arcade in front of the general merchandise store, Geraldi and Doctor Hayman stood side by side. To their left, the big gasoline lamp of the hotel verandah was flaming, throwing a powerful light that, from time to time, gave a strong pulsation. Those sudden flutters made even the strongest nerves tremble.

Across from them was the front of the bank. Like the face of an ignoramus, it was low and wide, but the windows were of plate glass, and it was possible to look through them — even from across the street — as far as the gleaming bars which fenced in the cashier's cages.

Geraldi and Doctor Hayman, having come within view of the quarry, held back and did not close in upon it at once. They made cigarettes and smoked quietly. The other men were coming up, one by one, and taking certain stations near the bank.

The Doctor seemed happy, and he was speaking in his deep voice, that was low-pitched without the usual roughness of such a key. Only now and then, when he was stirred, a vibrant thunder rolled from his throat. Tonight, he was talking gently, as if to a girl. He seemed to be smiling in the darkness and wooing Geraldi's best possible opinion. Geraldi replied hardly a word. He leaned against a pillar and looked fixedly toward the face of the bank, although that was not what he was seeing.

"What are you thinking about, partner?" said Doctor Hayman.

"About Geraldi," replied the other.

"Ugh!" grunted Hayman. "I'd rather have a gun jolt me in the ribs than that name in my ears. What the devil brought up Geraldi to your mind?"

"I've been wondering why you hate him so badly."

"He hates me, that's the reason," said the Doctor.

"Do you want me to believe that?" Geraldi asked. "He's never even seen you!"

"I'll tell you a story," said Hayman. "One of the best men that I ever had was a fellow by name of Ramón Stevens, half Mexican and half American. Ramón was a beauty. He was all gold and a yard wide. If I wanted someone bumped off, I whispered a word to Ramón, and he went off on the trail. He was more than ambidextrous. He could hit his mark with a heavy knife at ten or fifteen yards. He shot very well. And he knew twenty ways of letting poison do the work for him.

"Now, this Ramón Stevens goes on the trail of

311

a thug who had tried to double-cross me, Oscar Paul, the cur. He'd almost been the cause of the entire gang being shot up. I sent Ramón after him. He deserved to die. Nobody ever deserved death more. I told Ramón to make it a slow trail. I wanted Paul to have the taste of death a good while in his throat before he actually died. And once he sighted Ramón behind him, he would know what was coming to him.

"That was what happened. Ramón let Oscar Paul have a good look at him, and then he started for him. He trailed him for a month. Oscar Paul went nearly mad . . . and I don't wonder. He was afraid to walk three steps without turning to look over his shoulder. He was always feeling the thud of Ramón's knife in the small of his back. He was afraid to eat, for fear that Ramón had managed, somehow, to sift a little poison into the food.

"He was worn to a shadow, that fellow Paul. He tried to get police protection, but Ramón sifted right through the police and called on Paul in his room at a hotel in San Antone. Paul was so frightened that he jumped right out the window and would have broken his neck, except that he landed on a load of hay. Paul started running and riding again, and finally he was a wreck, and Ramón was about to push him off, when he ran into Geraldi!"

His voice changed. The thunder came rolling and trembling into it. Geraldi did not smile with satisfaction in the dark of the night. He felt a chill of apprehension as Doctor Hayman went on: "That Geraldi, like a ghost, went straight down the trail and began to hound Ramón Stevens. They fought. He shot the gun out of Stevens's hand. But he wouldn't finish him. He simply drove Stevens in circles through the hills. For three days and nights, Stevens never stopped moving and never paused to eat. He killed his horse. He kept stumbling on by foot.

"At last Ramón was picked up by Tom Foster. Tom didn't recognize him. Ramón was a ghost. Tom brought Ramón back to his camp, and I saw that the soul was dead in Ramón. I fattened him up and sent him south across the border. He hadn't the nerve of a ten-year-old girl. A few months later, a nigger beat him to death . . . and Ramón hadn't the courage to pull a gun! That's what Geraldi had done to him."

Geraldi, in honest horror, bowed his head. "That's the worst thing I ever heard," he said.

But he was thinking not of Ramón Stevens, murderer by profession, but of Oscar Paul, that poor, deluded, romantic young fool who had been harried to the verge of death by Hayman's manhunter. He thought of Paul's face. He remembered how the big Swede had sat by his fire, weeping, covering his face with his hands because there was still a trace of manly shame in him. Geraldi still recalled vividly the cold, white anger that had moved in him when he rode down the trail to wreak upon the manhunter all possible retribution. Only one thing he regretted —

that he had allowed that broken man — murderer though he was — to live and die a more lingering, a more brutal death.

"I've never forgotten Ramón's face, when he was brought into camp," went on Doctor Hayman. "All he could do was to chant a single word, night and day . . . Geraldi. He screamed it, sobbed it, groaned and moaned it in his broken sleep. He drove the boys mad. I had to isolate him. I took care of him myself, but I couldn't patch him up. His hand was smashed. But that wasn't his hurt. His soul and pride were torn to bits. I couldn't heal hurts that were as deep as that. And that's only one reason I hate Geraldi, Manhattan."

His voice had not been raised. Only the vibration of it had become greater and made a tremor through the entire body of Geraldi. The Doctor was so worked up that he began to finger impatiently something in his pocket. He even raised it a little above the lip of the pocket, and the hawklike eye of Geraldi saw a single ray of light strike dimly upon something as red as blood between the thumb and forefinger of Hayman. It was red, and there was an odd sparkle to it, as though the light had not impinged upon it from the outside but was glowing from within.

A pigeon's-blood ruby? Geraldi said calmly to himself.

"Now who do you want with you, Manhattan?" said the Doctor. "You'll want somebody inside the bank with you, I suppose?"

"I could use a good man . . . the right man," said Geraldi casually.

"Of course, you could," said the Doctor. "And every one of the fellows I've brought in tonight is of the right metal. All except Tucker. He's new. I've brought him along on this job simply to give him experience. That's all. Take any one of the others."

"I'll take Tucker," Geraldi declared.

"What?" exclaimed Hayman. "Did you hear what I said? He's wild. He's new to the game. He needs experience before he becomes a useful man."

"You know, Hayman," said Geraldi, "that I don't need his experience to open the safe. What I need is a fellow who can stand behind me and keep my mind at rest. The others . . . well, some of them I wouldn't want to have in there, standing behind me, when I'm concentrating on that combination. Give Tucker a dark lantern. He's the one I'd rather take in with me."

Hayman hesitated. Then he said: "Well, you know your business, Manhattan. I think you're a fool to select him, however. You're apt to find him all thumbs, when it comes to this job. You understand? All thumbs! You ought to take Angel Ray. That boy is all the purest steel. I called him in the other day especially for this work. But if you don't want him, there's Larry Burns. He's an old hand."

"He looks like prison shakes to me," said Geraldi in his quiet, decisive way. "And Ray would be as good as a leveled gun behind my back. I don't like that lad. No, I'll be contented with Tucker. He only needs brains enough to work the dark lantern. That's all! Confound the moon! We could do this a lot better in the dark."

"I like the moon, myself," Hayman stated. "By moonlight people think that they're seeing clearly. But they see everything a little wrong. It's a hard job to shoot straight by moonlight, for instance. Well, you pitch on Tucker, do you?"

"Yes."

"I'll have him here in a moment," Hayman said.

He went off down the walk, but, as he turned, the movement caused the lapel of his coat to swing open, and the slim, incredibly rapid hand of Geraldi slid inside of the flap and dipped into the vest pocket of Hayman. Out it came again, and, as Hayman stepped down the walk, Geraldi flashed the distant light from the gasoline lamp upon what he held in the shallow palm of his hand.

He smiled, his teeth gleaming in a white streak. It seemed to Geraldi like a little stroke of fate, for there were four red stones, almost of an equal size — one for himself, one each for Bob, Jerry, and red-headed Pete. If he were any judge of jewels, then each of these red, shining beauties would bring in even more than he had already promised to the three tramps. He smiled again, and made the rubies disappear in one of his pockets.

In the meantime, he knew that he had trebled or quadrupled the danger in which he walked, for it might be that Hayman would fumble again in his vest pocket for the sake of thumbing over the rubies. It was, perhaps, an unconscious gesture. In the moment of greatest excitement, Hayman had actually lifted one of the stones above the pocket's edge.

And now what would happen? He could only hope that the hands and the wits of Hayman would be too occupied by the adventure immediately before him, but, if the Doctor discovered his loss, he would certainly remember how close he had stood to the slim fingers of Manhattan Jimmy, the latest addition to his band.

But Geraldi, when he had summed up the chances, snapped his fingers and shrugged his shoulders. Without danger, there was no living. Without danger, at least there was no spice in life.

Hayman came back with big Jack Tucker. The glare in the latter's eyes was distinctly noticeable even in the shadow beneath the arcade. He stared fixedly at Geraldi's face.

"Here's your man," said Hayman. "Now take him along. It's time to move, Jimmy. Everybody's in place. Wait till the watchman goes by on his next round. Then go."

Chapter Forty

INSIDE THE BANK

Geraldi began to rub and knead the fingers of his right hand with the left, and a chill went through him when he thought how much depended upon his skill with those delicate fingers upon this night.

It was not a matter of money. That he had already, and he had taken it from Doctor Hayman, thief and scoundrel *par excellence*. The thought of it was more than wine to the soul of Geraldi. It was not money that he was after. But he intended to pick the lock of Jack Tucker's mind and take from him all desire for the wild freedom of a lawless life.

He intended to take Jack Tucker back with him to his father's ranch. When he did that, what would be the look upon the face of the old rancher? What would be the look on the face of Mary? Geraldi caught his breath. His nerves leaped so violently that he had to control himself with a great effort of his will.

Then the watchman came around the eastern corner of the bank and sauntered across the face of it until he was near the door. There he paused.

He took out a pipe and filled it. He lighted it, and, when he stepped out of the shadow of the doorway and walked on, the light from the gasoline lamp showed white streamers of tobacco smoke floating behind the big shoulders of the watchman.

He was a big fellow, with an honest, powerful look to the set of his shoulders. The moment he had turned out of sight around the western corner of the bank, Geraldi touched the arm of Tucker and led the way across the street. They kept to the shadow cast by the high shoulder of the general merchandise store that had a lofty false front. Reaching the opposite sidewalk, Geraldi turned west, and then stepped to the side into the deep shadows of the doorway of the bank.

Tucker was just behind him. He heard the straining effort of Tucker's irregular breathing. The boy was frightened. But he was game. Vaguely Geraldi noted this and the significance of it, while he worked with the picklock at the door. It gave quickly. He opened the door and stepped inside with Tucker beside him.

A shadow bobbed on the dimly illumined floor of the bank — illumined at all merely because the powerful rays of the gasoline lamp glimmered upon the metal work and the mirrors inside, and was reflected, also, from the white walls.

Geraldi pulled Tucker down and flung himself upon the floor. Outside, the watchman sauntered casually past the front of the bank. At the door, he paused and stood for a time with his hands behind his back, teetering to and fro like a reversed pendulum. He began to whistle, and Geraldi remembered the words of it well. He had heard it more than once upon the cattle range, when 'punchers foregather.

I love not Colorado
Where the faro table grows,
And down the desperado
The rippling bourbon flows;

Nor seek I fair Montana
Of Bowie-lunging fame;
The pistol ring of fair Wyoming
I leave to nobler game.

Sweet, poker-haunted Kansas
In vain allures the eye;
The Nevada rough has charms enough
Yet his blandishments I fly.

Shall Arizona woo me
Where the meek Apache bides?
Or New Mexico where natives grow
With arrow-proof insides?

Nay, 'tis where the grizzlies wander
And the lonely diggers roam,
And the grim Chinese from the squatter
flees

That I'll make my humble home.

I'll chase the wild tarantula
And the fierce coyote I'll dare,
And the locust grim, I'll battle him
In his native, wildwood lair.

And I'll seek the gulch deserted
And dream of the wild redman,
And I'll build a cot on the corner lot
And get rich as soon as I can!

The watchman, having sung, hummed, or whistled his way through an entire ballad of "Westward Ho!" now put back his hand, as though mechanically, and tried the knob of the front door.

There was a stir in young Jack Tucker that moment. A Colt came into his hand. His arm extended stiffly with it, as he drew his bead upon the back of the man outside the glass of the bank's front door.

Geraldi caught that arm and jerked it rudely down. Such a fury blazed up in him that he hardly knew the few blasphemous syllables that he breathed into the ear of his companion on the floor, but Jack Tucker, as though stunned, made no struggle to free his gun hand.

And the watchman — was it not as though he realized there was danger behind him — suddenly left the door without fully turning the knob, and went with what seemed a hastier step down the front of the building.

"He's seen us," breathed Jack Tucker.

"Not unless he has as many eyes as a fly," Geraldi assured the kid. "Now come on with me."

He got up and led the way to the tall, spike-crowned fence of steel, gilded at the top, behind which glimmered the wide forehead of the safe. At the door, Geraldi paused only a moment, then it opened under the magic of his touch.

"How do you do it?" murmured Tucker.

"It's a simple trick," Geraldi answered. "Go in there and spot the combination for me. Light your lantern."

"It's lighted already," said the other.

"'Good," Geraldi said. "I want to look over the lay of the land, and I'll be back in a minute."

He found his way back through the long room. It was treacherous going, with chairs here and there more lost in the dull mottling of shadow, moonshine, and the distant glow of the gasoline lamp than if thick night had crowded the entire place. But Geraldi touched against nothing.

He came to the back door of the building, kneeled in front of it, and in a moment the picklock moved the bolt in the well-oiled wards. He tried the door. It opened freely. He closed it again, and now there was open an avenue through which his helpers could come to him. There was also open a door through which more exterior dangers might move in upon him. But he was accustomed to chances. He knew that danger was likely to show him the full, dazzling brightness of her face, this night, but his nerves did not flinch from the appointed work.

He returned to the safe room, and there he found young Tucker, erect as a statue and as motionless in a corner of the room.

"Kind of thought you might not come back . . . ," began Tucker.

For answer, there was a distant, almost human moan. The wind was up. The strong hand of the gust rattled a door at the back of the building and shook the window beside them. There was nothing old-fashioned about the place. It was full of windows.

Geraldi waited until the noise of the wind had died down. Then he bowed before the combination, pressed his ear against it, and waited for the tremor of his nerves and the pounding of his heart to cease. It was the old trick, over again, but its fascination did not fade out of the blood of Geraldi. The years had not dimmed the exquisite enjoyment of his own skill.

First of all, there was the iron-handed exercise of his will, banning all impulses, all thoughts, all desires, except the one desire to read the steel heart of this mystery. When that was accomplished, and his whole being was as still as the open ear of midnight, he began to move the combination delicately, delicately. He could feel his own pulsations in the balls of his fingertips, but even that faint thing must be banished from his consciousness. There must be nothing of physical consciousness except those nerves hypersensitive to feel, rather than hear, the shadowy fall of the tumblers inside the lock.

So he worked on. In his bowed position, his back and his legs began to ache. He had to put away all though of physical discomfort. Like one frozen stiff in a clumsy position, so was Geraldi frozen upon his feet, while he strained toward the solution of the mystery.

Now and then he paused and raised one finger, and, when he did so, Jack Tucker loosed from the dark lantern a single ray that struck the ruled margin of the disk of steel with a faint, faint glimmer and showed Geraldi the number.

He found one, he was sure. He found a second. He was working fast, and never more sure of himself. A glow of confidence filled him, as it fills the mathematician when the solution of a problem is sensed long before it is reduced to figures upon a paper. Then — a quick turning of the disk this way, and that. And the door lunged open slowly, silently. It stood wide, held open by its own weight, and the square fronts of the safe boxes stood before them.

"Great thunder," Jack Tucker said, "do you have to open *those* besides?"

"We could rip 'em wide," said Geraldi. "But that would make noise and take still more time. Here's one open for you. Take a look through it, will you? Here's another . . . and another. These things are not locks. They're only putty imitations. They're the easiest that I ever saw. Are you finding anything? Throw the good stuff on that tarpaulin. Chuck the rest back into the box, every time. You know the look of securities when you see 'em?"

He talked softly, as he worked on. But Jack Tucker seemed to be stirring slowly at his appointed task. Suddenly there was a click.

"What's the matter?" Geraldi asked. "Why did you shove that box back in? Don't you know that the spring will lock it again?"

"Let it be locked and be damned," Jack Tucker declared. "We don't want that money."

"Not want it?" exclaimed Geraldi, angrily in appearance, although his heart was leaping with pleasure. "Why don't we want it?"

"Why, it's a widow, Jimmy, that's left her stuff to a sick fellow with one leg . . . there's a picture of him, here. And there's the mention of him in her will. It's the first thing that my eye dropped on."

"How much cash?" Geraldi asked. "How much in securities, I mean?"

"I dunno," Tucker said sourly. "We don't want that kind of money. Hold on . . . listen to that!"

There was a creak, a sudden jar of a door shuddering against its bolt.

"The wind," Geraldi said, but he was not as confident as he sounded. The devil was up tonight. He could feel it all through his bones.

Chapter Forty-One
THE CHIEF COMES

He went on opening the safe boxes, and Tucker rummaged through them behind him. Presently Geraldi heard him cursing very softly. Another box was thrust back in place with a click. Yonder on the tarpaulin was only a small heap of cash, of jewels, and of securities.

"We'll never get on at this rate," growled Geraldi to the young fellow. "What's the matter with you?"

"I'm sick of the business," Jack Tucker replied. "That's another batch that we don't want."

"We don't? You're playing the fool!" said Geraldi, straightening and whirling in pretended rage upon the young man. "Why don't we want it?"

"We don't, that's all," said Tucker. "It's only five or six hundred bucks, anyway."

"If five or six hundred is not worth a grab of your hand," said Geraldi, "you must be the emperor of China. Wait till I get that stuff."

He reached out for the box. Jack Tucker caught him and threw him back.

"Five hundred bucks . . . no, there's more than two thousand, if you want the straight of it. More than two thousand, and it's to go to prison welfare. Hell, Manhattan, here we are, a pair of birds ready for the jail, and we find a poor fool ready to waste honest cash on the like of us?" He snorted with indignation.

"What do you want?" Geraldi argued. "Where d'you think that you're going to get your easy money, then, if you don't take it out of the mouth of somebody else?"

"There's plenty that are rich and crooked and mean," said young Tucker. "We'll take their stuff . . . and let the others go. I can't stand it, Manhattan, and I won't stand it."

"Open that box," said Geraldi, "or pull your gun right here."

"I won't open the box," Tucker announced. "I know that I've got no chance against you, Manhattan. But I'll sooner fight than let you take that money. I'd be sick at the stomach all the rest of my life, if I took that cash."

"What do you want?" Geraldi asked. "We take the chances and we collect the coin . . . or else a flock of lead slugs. So why shouldn't we take the money? Nobody'll know that we did it."

"*I'll* know what I did," replied the young fellow. "I didn't realize that it would be this way. I thought that a bank. . . ."

"Was just a place where money was dumped, eh?" said Geraldi. "But it's not. Every box there is a human being, Jack. The welfare of a whole family, perhaps, is in every one of 'em. There's the education of children and the food of old people. There's the money that poor devils have worked a whole lifetime to collect, so that they'll have a little when they're laid up in their old age. But why not take it? That's the money that makes Hayman fat. That's the money that keeps his gang going. That's the money that's been feeding you these last weeks. That's the money that bought the horse you rode into Alexandria. Don't you complain, now, about your dirty hands. They're dirty already. They were dirty the minute that you got the idea of Hayman into your mind! Now you want to back out . . . because you're yellow!"

The word gave no offense to Jack Tucker. He merely said: "I've been a fool. I've got my hands dirty. But this sort of dirt will wash off them. I'm through with you. I'm through with Hayman! I'll go and tell him so. I didn't know that it would be this way. I sort of thought. . . ."

"Why, you fool," Geraldi snapped, "don't you know that Hayman will never allow a man to leave his gang?"

"I'll take my chance," said the young fellow doggedly. "I'd a lot rather be bumped off than to sneak by with such a crowd. You can tell Hayman so. I'll take my medicine. I've made my bed, and now I'll lie in it. But I'll tell you this, Manhattan. . . ."

Geraldi stretched out a hand to him. The boy looked stupidly from that hand to the thin, handsome face of the cracksman.

"What do you mean, Manhattan?"

"Call me by my right name," Geraldi said. "I'm James Geraldi."

The jaw of the young fellow sagged as though he had been struck heavily. "You're not," he began, and then stopped. "By thunder, I half think that you are. I *know* you are. No other man in the world could have opened those locks so quickly. Geraldi, you're not a friend of Hayman's. What in the devil brought you up here? Hayman would rather have your blood than anything in the world!"

"I came for you, Tucker," Geraldi began. "That's why I brought you in here with me. I wanted you to see what the inside of a safe box may hold. You've seen some papers and a couple of human hearts inside of 'em, Jack. The whole business is that way. It's too rotten for you. I wanted you to see it before you'd taken part in any real crime. I knew it would revolt you. Now, Jack, we'll close this up and break away."

"Hayman's gang is keeping watch all around the bank," said Tucker. "Geraldi, will you tell me, for God's sake, what made you decide to pull me out of this mess?"

"That doesn't matter," said Geraldi, "if you're going to go straight."

"Go straight, or die straight," said Jack Tucker. "I'll go straight from now on, Geraldi. I won't thank you, not in words. Only, someday I'll have a chance to try to show you."

"Never mind that," said Geraldi, "the first thing. . . ."

Tucker grasped the arm of Geraldi. "Did you hear?" he breathed.

Geraldi nodded. There was a whistling of wind through the bank, a rattling of papers, a vibration of windows and doors — and then all of this ceased as suddenly as it had begun.

"Someone's come in through a back door," said Tucker.

"Wait here," Geraldi answered, and faded like a ghost through the door and into the larger section of the room.

He saw them at once — two bulky shadows that moved dimly against the outer wall of the room, ducking low under the windows. He admired the steady slowness of their progress. Any eye less keen than his might have remained an hour in the room and never have marked those blotchy, awkward shadows. Lightly, daintily, he made a swift circuit and came up quietly behind them.

"Well, boys?" he said in his quiet voice.

They leaped to their feet; he heard the whistling intake of their breath. Each of them had a gun in his hand.

"My God, Geraldi," red-headed Pete declared, "it's better than a million dollars to have you with us again. We've been up against it!"

"How?" Geraldi asked.

"That hound of a Tex Arnold got wind of us."

"The devil he did!" said Geraldi. "You mean

330

he's on your trail again?"

"He ain't no other place but on our trail," said Bob. "He must've quit Kempton and gone to watch the railroad. He must've thought that you'd be working the rattlers."

"He followed you down the railroad?"

"He followed us? He had his claws into us, pretty near," Bob said.

"Did he pick up your trail again from the railroad line in this direction?"

"I dunno," answered Pete. "We done our best to build up a little trail problem that would keep him busy for a while readin' it. But he's got a nose on a man-trail. He's hard to shake."

In spite of himself, the next words of Geraldi were almost a groan. "I'd rather that you'd stayed away than come up here trailing Arnold behind you. You think he may be on your heels?"

"I'm telling you the straight, chief," Pete stated. "I dunno just where he is now, but we headed for you as fast as we could. Bein' out in the open with Arnold behind us, and no Geraldi along, it was a pretty chilly business, I'm telling you."

"Come back here," said Geraldi. "Get over there by the rear door. I've got another man to pick up in here."

"One that's with us?"

"Yes, one that's with us."

"Have you got the stuff?" asked Pete eagerly.

"I've got the stuff for you," said Geraldi. "As

much as I promised you and then a little left over. Go back there and wait, will you?"

"We'll wait," Bob said. "But make it fast. I'm getting the jumps and jerks. This here business is hard on a fellow's nerves. Waitin' is a pile worse than shootin'."

There was more than a little truth to this, Geraldi felt. He hurried back to the safe room, and there he found Tucker close to the door.

"Quick, Jack!" Geraldi hissed. "It's time to make our break. . . ."

"Look," Tucker said, his whisper tremulous.

He pointed, and Geraldi saw two men standing at the front door, dim, black silhouettes behind the glass. He recognized the broad shoulders and the large Napoleonic head of one. It was Doctor Hayman in person!

Chapter Forty-Two
THE FIGHT IN DARKNESS

But even the coming of the Doctor would not have meant so much to Geraldi, even at that moment. It was the outline of the head and shoulders beside him which meant still more. For he who stood beside Hayman was none other than Double Deck Joe.

Geraldi could not, of course, guess at the whole meaning, but he could surmise that Double Deck, who had been left behind as the sole camp guard, would not have come this distance except for some most urgent reason. Geraldi could not, of course, understand how Double Deck had left his dying horse on the edge of Alexandria and staggered on foot the rest of the way, how he had found his chief, and how his entire message had burst out in the single word: "Geraldi!" Then Doctor Hayman, instinctively fumbling in his vest pocket in that moment of shock and astonishment, had discovered that he had been robbed.

No details like this were present to the mind of Geraldi. He merely guessed that something was decidedly wrong. Then, leading Tucker with him, he hurried out into the larger room and toward the back door.

Red-headed Pete and Bob were there, waiting. When they saw that Geraldi was close behind, they pushed the door open. Out they stepped into the face of a rifle volley!

Bob, staggering back, fell and rolled heavily upon the floor. Red-headed Pete bowed over and grasped at the first support. That being the knob of the door, he in turn pitched backward. He staggered back, toppled over, and the door slammed mightily, with the weight of the wind behind it.

The suddenness of this stunned Jack Tucker. Two men had been puffed out like candles. They might not be dead, but, at the least, they were knocked out of commission for the fight. Then Tucker turned and saw that the other two were no longer at the front door of the bank. No, they were inside, doubtless, and shifting forward among the shadows.

What he next saw was the form of the watchman, running frantically at full speed around the corner of the building, with a riot gun grasped in both hands. A pair of shadows leaped out at him — down went the watchman head over heels, and the shotgun sent out its deep, hoarse blast of thunder.

How long would Alexandria be in rousing, now that this crazy tumult had begun? Tucker thought of this, but, chiefly, he thought of the cold, insane rage of the Doctor, as he hunted for his hated enemy, Geraldi.

The rear door burst in again, and there was Angel Ray, that poisonous little destroyer, glimpsed one instant as he stood against the dull glow of outside light, then lost as he dodged away into the comparative blackness inside the room. After him came a larger man, the great hulk of Larry Burns. Still Tucker, following the movements of the intruders with his leveled revolver, could not fire. With all his might he strove to, and he was deterred. He would not have minded, if their guns had been fixed straight at him. But he could not take any advantage; he could not do what seemed to him cold-blooded murder.

In that moment he sensed the vast distance that really lay between him and such ruffians. Advantages were the very things that they looked for, and a safe fight was to them far better than an honest chance taken. Geraldi had seen it. Through Geraldi his own eyes had been opened. He had looked inside of the safe and had seen . . . his true self.

The wildness went out of young Jack Tucker, then. In its place came a great desire to strike at the side of his new friend. The next moment, he heard the voice of Geraldi crying out: "Hayman! This way, Hayman! Turn your guns this way. Here's Geraldi, waiting for you, you murderer . . . Mister Murderer Hayman!"

In answer came a roar like the roar of a lion, and he knew that it was the voice of the infuriated Doctor.

Then guns barked inside the room, and Tucker saw the long, spitting of fire from the muzzles of revolvers and watched the gleam of the steel barrels, kicking upward after the explosions — kicking upward just a trifle, as though recoiling from their own dangerous work. A devil was inside the room, and it was a roaring devil. Just behind him, he felt, rather than saw, something moving, something holding its breath. He turned. A form rose out of the floor, and a gun exploded under his very nose. He had side-stepped just in time, but the bullet had clipped the rim of his ear, and by the dazzling light of the explosion he got a glimpse of Double Deck Joe.

Even then, Jack Tucker did not fire. But he gripped his own weapon by the barrel and drove the heavy butt of it fairly into the fat face of Double Deck. With a heavy groan, the bulky form of Double Deck doubled up and disappeared in the shadows on the floor.

Other guns were exploding in the back of the room. Tucker heard Hayman shouting: "This way, boys! This way. Geraldi's up here. It's the last night that he ever shoots men in the back . . . the dog! Geraldi's here, and no better than a dead man."

Other men had come in through the back door. Every man in the gang was focusing upon the place where Geraldi fought his lone fight against odds.

Jack Tucker lurched forward. As he ran, something rose from the dark. He collided with an-other man. They rolled head over heels.

"Geraldi!" gasped Jack Tucker. "Is it you, partner?"

Great arms had clutched him, but at the sound of the words the arms relaxed their hold.

"Tucker, is it you?" gasped someone at the ear of young Jack. "If you're for Geraldi, come on with me. I'm Larry Burns. I owe him my life, and he can have it, if he needs it tonight. Come on with me. . . ."

They rose together. Together they lurched on into the dimness, toward the sound of the uproar.

"This way! The wildcat's got around to this side," shouted the thundering bass of the Doctor. "This way, fellows!"

Now it was that Tucker and big Larry Burns had sight of a strange spectacle. It was no more than a glimpse, but it was enough to show them Doctor Hayman, half hidden behind a massive desk, revolver ready, peering about a corner of it as around the edge of a rock — when, across the top of the desk, a shadowy form flung through the air with a slithering speed that seemed like the spring of a beast of prey. Hayman, struck un-awares, disappeared with a shout of rage and as-tonishment and dismay.

The blood of Tucker froze in his veins. He doubted not that Geraldi would win that hand-to-hand battle, but, when that fight was ended, there was the rest of the gang to deal with, and he could distinguish the impatient voice of Angel Ray, clamoring for a light. Grant the Angel the least glimmer, and he would soon be putting out lives like candles. Tucker turned, then, and floundered blindly forward toward Geraldi. At the same time, he heard outside of the bank the rush of many men, the exploding of guns, and a loud voice of command, directing men to guard different posts.

Larry Burns loomed beside Tucker. "Tex Arnold's here," he said. "Tex Arnold, and damnation for me and the whole Hayman outfit."

Tucker hardly heard. He only knew that just before him, in the dull gleam of a shaft of pale light that struck through a window, there lay two men, one huddled upon the other. The upper figure was the larger. He dragged it away, turned it upward, and saw that it was Hayman, with a streak of blood across his ghastly face, his eyes half open, and every aspect of death in his countenance, except that the blood was still welling from a horrible wound in his head. Blood did not flow, after death, Tucker had heard somewhere.

Big Larry Burns was now raising the smaller form, the man underneath. It was Geraldi. Not dead, indeed!

He gave himself one shake and stood near them, panting a little. "That was near!" he said. "Hayman was a man. . . ."

"He's still alive," said Burns, "but here's the final finish of him. . . ."

Geraldi knocked down the leveled revolver.

338

"Not that way!" he said. "Out there for ourselves! Fast, my lads! Where's Tucker? Here, thank God. Now start moving." He led the way toward the back of the bank building at a run.

The gangsters were still there. Tucker heard the barking voice of little Angel Ray, still true to his gang leader, calling the name of Hayman. Others were stamping here and there, and so Geraldi and the other two gained the place where Bob and Pete lay.

Bob was dragging himself to his knees; Pete was rolling back and forth, groaning. They were badly hurt, apparently, but there was still some life in them. Help must come to them now from other hands. Geraldi leaped through the rear door of the bank, with a revolver in either hand.

The open air of the night was, like that inside the bank, stained with the foul odor of burned gunpowder. Voices were shouting here and there. The sleepy town of Alexandria was wakening. Marshal Tex Arnold was there at the forefront, ready to lead in the fight.

They headed straight down the little alley behind the bank, and, as they swarmed about the first turn, crashed fully into two members of the posse, appointed to block that exit.

They had dismounted. Several led horses were following on a long rope, so that the hands of the two would be freer for fighting in case of an emergency. But they were unprepared for this blind rush, like the charge of football players. Like linesmen in that game, they were bowled

339

over, and Geraldi stood covering them with his guns while Burns and big Jack Tucker selected horses and held one for Geraldi. Still covering the amazed pair, he mounted in turn, and off they sped.

But guns were still roaring behind them, and every booming note was to Jack Tucker's ear the sound of another death knell to the gang of Hayman, the admirable Doctor.

Someone was singing nearby. Tucker turned his dazed attention that way and saw Geraldi, sitting erect in the saddle, only canted forward a little against the speed of the gallop, his eyes half closed, laughing and singing out of sheer excess of joy!

Chapter Forty-Three

REUNION

Good news does not command great space in journals, as a rule, but when there is a stroke of good and bad news at the same time, the headlines are spacious enough.

Now, when Mr. Tucker sat at the head of his table and read from the newspaper the account of the great attempted bank robbery at Alexandria, although he read slowly, tracing out the words with his blunt, callous forefinger, every one of his cowpunchers listened agape, grinning, nodding, their eyes flashing with excitement.

They did not notice that the expert cook and waitress, who had been attending them, was no longer scurrying back and forth from the kitchen to the dining room and back again. She sat on a chair on the kitchen side of the door, her head leaning against the wall, her eyes closed, her face very white, but a ghost of joy smiling upon her lips.

"Look-it!" broke in one of the older 'punchers. "Something had oughta be done for Geraldi. That's what I say!"

"I say so, too," said another. "He's only a

crook when he's crowded to it. He's done more good than any ten sheriffs."

"Hold on a minute," said Tucker. "Here's something more . . . wait . . . it says that the Hayman gang is all bust. There's one young feller that they call Angel Ray. He's the only one got loose. Hayman is laying stretched out in the jail, with a doctor watchin' him night and day."

"They're gonna save him, so's they can hang him," said one of the 'punchers.

"I'll tell you," said the oldest waddie of all. "If they save him and cure him and make him sound, he'll just about melt right out through the walls of the prison. The rope ain't made that'll hang the Doctor, by my way of thinking. It takes Geraldi to handle him!"

"He ain't gonna get any too well," said another.

"Geraldi put five wounds in him. Any one of 'em's enough to kill most men, it says here," commented Tucker. He raised his head. His face was gray, with the color coming slowly up into it.

"There ain't no mention of my boy, Jack, in this here list of the Hayman gang." Then he added, with an expression of sudden pain: "Maybe his name is tucked away under some of them here nicknames."

"No," broke in the elderly 'puncher. "Jack Tucker'd be known. He ain't among 'em, chief. He's away. Thank God."

A murmur that reinforced that expression came from the rest of the table. In the kitchen, an incredulous word of joy from the girl.

"Here's something more," said Tucker, from the head of the table, stirring the sugar into his coffee and scowling at the small print. "It says that . . . whatcha think about this? . . . it says that they've sent up a deputation from Alexandria. Every dog-gone soul in town had his savings in that bank. And they're appealing for a pardon for Geraldi."

"It ain't any wonder," said the elderly waddie. "He's saved their socks for 'em. That's what he's saved."

"Hey! That beats me, though. Who d'you think's at the head of the Alexandria folks to get that pardon?" exclaimed Tucker. "It's federal Marshal Tex Arnold, dog-gone my eyes! Yes, sir, it's Arnold himself!"

There was a general murmur of appreciation from around the board. And, with one voice, they voted Tex Arnold a white man, too.

"Well, Arnold has scooped up enough glory by taking in the whole blooming Hayman outfit," said one. He voiced the general opinion.

"There was a couple of fellows that worked with Geraldi," said Tucker, reading farther down the copious account. "They're both laid up in the Alexandria hospital. The town's raisin' a purse for 'em. Alexandria sure oughta treat 'em fine."

"Alexandria *will*," said one of the 'punchers. "I know that town. Sleepy, but it's got a heart, all right!"

There was much talk all the rest of that day at

the Tucker ranch. That night, when they came in for dinner, they found that their steak was burned, the fried potatoes more than half raw, the coffee hardly worthy of the name, while the sour-milk biscuits had failed to rise in the oven.

But there were no complaints. Complaints could not very well be lodged against a face so gentle and pretty as that of their cook. Besides, she had treated them royally up to this moment. She went about this evening with a dreaming look, as though strange news had come to her.

"She's got a headache," said one of the men. "Keep your face shut and try to swaller this coffee. It's the first mistake that she's made out there in the kitchen, I reckon."

So no more was said about the cookery. It was toward the very end of the meal that the back door of the dining room was opened from the verandah, and through the opening came striding the tall form of Jack Tucker.

One or two of the men jerked around so that the feet of their chairs screeched against the floor. Tucker himself stood up, slowly, and looked at his son with a gray face. No one spoke for a moment, until Jack stepped farther into the lamplight.

"Father," he said, "I reckon that I was all wrong. I've been showed the right way. I've come ridin' in to see if you want me back. I've come along to say that your way is the right way for me, too, if you want me."

It was an elaborate apology; it was such a speech as comes with difficulty out of the proud young heart of a Westerner. But no man present made any mistake about it. It was not that the spirit of Jack Tucker had been broken. It was because he had become a man, and had returned to face the music. They got up hastily, one after another, and slipped out, while the father took his son by both hands and gripped them hard, unable to speak. Such things passed between their eyes at that moment that words were unnecessary. And Jack, stepping hastily toward the kitchen, closed the door with a slam.

He turned to confront his father again, and found that the room was empty, now, except for the older man. All the 'punchers had vanished with as much speed as possible.

"Now, Jack," said the elder Tucker, "what happened? What changed your mind?"

"I didn't change my mind," Jack said. "My mind was changed for me. I'd be a bank robber and a thief, right now, if it hadn't been that my mind was changed for me."

"By whom?" asked his father.

"By Jim Geraldi!" said Jack.

"Geraldi?" cried Tucker. "Geraldi, did you say?"

"Aye," answered Jack. "By that same fire-eater, that fire-handler, Geraldi. The most wonderful man in the world, Dad."

"You talk soft, Jack," said the father. "As if he could hear you praisin' him."

Jack quickly hooked his thumb over his shoulder, and his smile was very broad.

"He *can* hear me," he said. "He's yonder in the kitchen!"

"What?" exclaimed old Tucker. "Why'd you let him into the kitchen? Ain't he safe and welcome to sit at my table? Would I let a soul in the world lift a hand ag'in' him?" He started to rush toward the kitchen door, but Jack stopped him with a raised hand.

"There ain't enough hands on this ranch," he declared, "to make Geraldi back up. I've seen him in action, and I know. It ain't for eating that he went out into the kitchen."

"What in thunder *is* he after, then?" asked the father.

"The best thing that's in it," answered Jack.

"Hello!" breathed the rancher. "Is that what you mean?"

"That's what I mean," replied Jack.

"I'd rather lose five thousand dollars than that cook, pretty near," said the rancher.

"You just try to keep her," replied Jack, grinning. "Even you try to keep her in a bank safe . . . that wouldn't be any good, with Geraldi on the trail."

The elder Tucker took a long breath. "Let's ask Mary if she'll put on another cup of coffee for us, all around," he suggested.

"Hush," said Jack. "Listen to that, will you?"

A soft and steadily running pulse of sound reached them from the kitchen. "She's sobbin' her heart out, Dad," said young Jack. "What' the trouble?"

"It might not be trouble," said the elder Tucker. "Womenfolk mostly take joy and sorrow from the same kind of a face. There a tolerable lot of baby in most girls, Jack." He nodded triumphantly. "Listen to that, now, will you?" he exclaimed.

For the pulse of the sobbing had ended, and in its place ran a bright thread of girl's laughter that made both of the listeners smile very broadly.

"I guess that's all right," said Jack.

"Knock on the door," said the father. "My tongue's hangin' out for some more of that coffee."

There was no response, and, therefore, Jack opened it. But he found that the kitchen was empty. Neither by the stove nor by the sink was Mary. But just outside the kitchen window, coming through the blackness of the night, they heard laughter once more, a musical blending of the soprano of a woman and the deeper note of a man.

"Listen!" said Jack. "That sounds pretty good to me. That sounds like Geraldi has her again. God bless him, I hope that he finds all the happiness that there is in this here world!"

"God bless him," said old Tucker with a grunt. "But I wish that he could find his dog-gone happiness somewheres outside of my kitchen. Jack, you slam a pot of coffee onto the fire, will you."

"All right," said Jack. "Hold on. The fire's plumb out!"

"Clean out?" said the rancher.

"Yep. Clean out. I'll build another."

"Let the coffee go, then," said Tucker. "We'll have a smoke, instead. But dog-gone Geraldi's heart, he's gonna have some trouble with that girl, what with bad coffee and no fire in the stove."

Jack Tucker shook his head solemnly. "It ain't Jimmy that'll have the trouble. It's poor Mary. It's the girl!"

"How come?" said the rancher.

"Listen!" said Jack.

Out of the distance came the faraway howl of a wolf. "It's one of them loafer wolves come down the draw," commented the rancher.

"Aye," said Jack Tucker. "I hope that time never comes heavy on Geraldi's hands, and he never hears one of them brutes singing in the dark. Because that's what he is, Dad. Wild! And meant to live alone."

About the Author

Max Brand is the best-known pen name of Frederick Faust, creator of Dr. Kildare, Destry, and many other fictional characters popular with readers and viewers worldwide. Faust wrote for a variety of audiences in many genres. His enormous output, totaling approximately thirty million words or the equivalent of 530 ordinary books, covered nearly every field: crime, fantasy, historical romance, espionage, Westerns, science fiction, adventure, animal stories, love, war, and fashionable society, big business and big medicine. Eighty motion pictures have been based on his work along with many radio and television programs. For good measure he also published four volumes of poetry. Perhaps no other author has reached more people in more different ways.

Born in Seattle in 1892, orphaned early, Faust grew up in the rural San Joaquin Valley of California. At Berkeley he became a student rebel and one-man literary movement, contributing prodigiously to all campus publications. Denied a degree because of unconventional conduct, he embarked on a series of adventures culminating in New York City where, after a period of near starvation, he received simultaneous recognition as a serious poet and successful author of fiction. Later, he traveled widely, making his home in New York, then in Florence, and finally in Los Angeles.

Once the United States entered the Second World War, Faust abandoned his lucrative writing career and his work as a screenwriter to serve as a war correspondent with the infantry in Italy, despite his fifty-one years and a bad heart. He was killed during a night attack on a hilltop village held by the German army. New books based on magazine serials or unpublished manuscripts or restored versions continue to appear so that, alive or dead, he has averaged a new book every four months for seventy-five years. Beyond this, some work by him is newly reprinted every week of every year in one or another format somewhere in the world. A great deal more about this author and his work can be found in THE MAX BRAND COMPANION (Greenwood Press, 1997) edited by Jon Tuska and Vicki Piekarski.